blood

Book two of the 360 series

By Cheryl Twaddle

Chapter 1

I stood at the edge of the forest squinting my eyes so I could see into the trees. Nothing. I took a step closer and felt Cocoa pull back her head, tightening the rein I held in my hand. I looked back at the tall, brown horse and shook my head. It was hard to believe that not too long ago the thought of riding Cocoa or any other horse terrified me. Now, I rode alone every day, even letting the horse run, not feeling a twinge of fear. Horseback riding was becoming natural to me, another testament as to how different it was here. I never would have touched a horse from my old life. No way, a car was my mode of transportation, that or the bus. Cocoa pulled back again.

"But I thought I saw something!" I pleaded with her. She let out a low neighing sound and shook her head so that her mane flew from her neck. I looked back to the trees and tried to focus on the tiny movement I thought I had just seen. Barker had to be in there, somewhere, I knew it. It had been well over four months since the out-of-towners' camp burned down and still no sign of the shepherd cross. I came here almost everyday looking for him. I missed the comfort of having him beside me wherever I went.

It was getting colder now but, luckily, no snow yet. Thank goodness! I wasn't sure how I'd be able to cross the fields once they were filled with a couple of feet of snow. And with the cold came even more worries about Barker. How would he be able to keep warm? His fur was so short and wouldn't provide a lot of warmth. I started towards the trees again. Cocoa stomped her hooves into the dirt and pulled back more tightly on the lead, almost knocking me off my feet.

"What?" She was starting to annoy me. "I can barely see anything from way back here."

I knew why she didn't want me to go into the forest; it was the same reason the rest of them didn't want me out here. Ryan. My old classmate had not been seen since the fire and everyone believed he was still out here, plotting his revenge. I knew Ryan, he had only been a couple of years ahead of me in school when he disappeared down to this world, and I knew that if he truly wanted revenge, he would have done it by now. At the very least he would have made his presence known. No, I think he saw Robert kill Sarah and wanted no part of his revenge and got the hell out of here.

It didn't matter to me whether he was in the woods or in China, I needed to find Barker and I was tired of everyone coddling me. I could handle myself. Didn't I prove that by killing Butcher and setting fire to the camp? Of course, I did. Besides, it was hypocritical of them to worry about me when their lives were becoming so complicated.

Emma Lee had tried hard to fight off Cornelius' advances, but the lanky, good looking Brit was persistent. All his wooing coupled with the time they spent together up the mountain when the dam blew, and Pig was shot had brought them closer together. Now, despite the southern belle's love and loyalty to her recently deceased husband, the two were inseparable. I even caught them holding hands and laughed at how red Emma Lee's face got. She was feeling guilty for being happy with someone else.

"Hey, it's not a lot of fun down here," I told her. "You either live forever or you die and it's way harder if you have to do either one alone. We're very social creatures you know; we actually need to be with other people. It's in our nature." She smiled and walked away and the next time I saw her and Cornelius together they were holding hands without any fear of anyone seeing them.

Robert was a different story. As if losing Madge at the hands of Sarah wasn't enough, he returned to his home only to find more heartbreak. The chickens, whom his wife had loved

3

so much, were all dead. Madge had gathered them up before we headed out to the out-of-towners' camp and put them back underground for safety. She gave them enough food and water for a couple of days, but we were gone for much longer than that. They were hungry and desperate and fought each other for food, eventually killing one another with their constant pecking or dying of thirst and hunger. It was awful and, for Robert, it was like losing Madge all over again. We knew he could no longer live there and convinced him to come live with the rest of us at Marshal's.

It was a generous offer, and everyone really wanted to help Robert, but it made Marshal's small house very crowded. We had to make it bigger; make something that could fit all of us and still be easy to put up and take down when the winds came. This was a problem. We had no wood and all the lumber stores had blown away with the winds. The only solution was to tear down Robert's house and move all the materials to Marshal's. This required Cocoa; the beautiful brown horse was strong enough to pull wagon loads of wood and furniture across the fields to Marshal's.

This made my treks to the forest to look for Barker those first few days limited. I didn't have a lot of choices as to when I could go. I did walk every once in a while, but it took so long to go back and forth plus all the time searching for him. It was so much easier just to ride Cocoa. So, I got up early every morning and went out in search of Barker. I started to like the early morning ritual, so, when we were finished building, I kept to it.

Then there was the gardening. We planted so many vegetables after the winds and they all required daily tending. My hands had blisters over blisters from using shovels and rakes and hoes. My fingernails were broken and caked with dirt from pulling out weeds. But it was worth it. Everything we planted prospered greatly. It was weird how time stood still within all of us and, yet, the plants grew and produced food so heartily.

Harvest almost killed me and there were a few days I had no energy to make my trips to look for Barker. I felt guilty but I was just too exhausted to go anywhere but bed after picking, peeling, cutting and canning all day. It's funny, if you'd have asked me anything about gardening and canning before I fell down here, I would have nothing to say. I was clueless when it came to food preservation. My closest thing to vegetables were the peppers and tomatoes in the salsa I dipped my nachos in. Now, I knew how to pickle carrots and cucumbers and can tomatoes and green beans. I even dug up rows and rows of potatoes, cleaned them and put them into sacks to store underground. I was proud of myself and had a new appreciation for farmers. Now, the harvesting had been completed for about two weeks and I could come out here whenever I wanted.

Marshal worked hard throughout the summer, but I could tell that he wasn't right. The time in the out-of-towners' camp and the loss of Sarah had affected him. He was still a little goofy and spoke in sets of three, but I could see the sadness in his eyes. I knew he really cared for the pretty schoolteacher and I cursed her for being such a bitch. I tried once to talk to him about it, but he laughed and said I was just imagining things and walked off. I felt bad for him and hoped he would be okay.

I thought about our little group and how different everyone was, not just because we were all different ages but because we all fell down here in different years, different times. Even Billy and Kitten, the little girl from the out-of-towners' camp, had their differences. Ten-year-old Billy fell down here in the fifties and Kitten, also ten, fell in 1901. I was amazed that someone so small and frail had lasted so long down here. I guess being a slave to the out-of-towners had its advantages. She had to work like a dog but, in return, they kept her safe. Our group now consisted of myself, Marshal, Robert, Emma Lee, Cornelius, Billy, Kitten and sometimes Max.

I thought about Max with his Scottish accent and pirate boots and felt the butterflies take flight in my stomach. I cursed myself. I didn't want to have feelings for Max. Ever since that day we put out the fire and he brushed his hand across my cheek I've been in constant debate with myself over him. I see how he looks at me and I feel my body tingle when he does. I'll admit I find him attractive and I could probably melt into his arms if I let myself, but I won't. I'm still not sure about him. I mean who is he really? I can't trust him one hundred percent and it scares me. I know he wasn't really part of Pig's camp; he was working undercover but it's scary how easily he fit in. That has to mean something, doesn't it? Who can do that so easily? Especially since I know that he had already walked on the wrong side of the law when he was a pirate. I just don't want to take any chances of getting hurt. I saw how devastated Marshal was over Sarah and I didn't want that to be me.

He said he has 'feelings' for me but Cornelius hinted that he's had 'feelings' for many other women as well. In fact, Cornelius warned me after we got back to Marshal's to be careful. Max had broken a lot of hearts down here and Cornelius didn't want to see me get hurt. We had become good friends and he was looking out for me. So, I didn't know if Max was being genuine with me when he said he wanted us to get closer or if he just saw me as another conquest. I couldn't figure it out, so I kept my distance from him, and I could tell it was making him angry. I guess he wasn't used to not getting his own way.

Just the other day he asked if he could come with me to look for Barker. I said no; that this was something I liked doing by myself, which was true, but it didn't sit well with Max. I can still see the angry disappointment in his eyes as he shook his head and stomped away, cursing under his breath. That was two weeks ago. He hadn't spoken to me since. In fact, he had gone out of his way to avoid me and, although this was what I wanted, the vain little girl inside of me was a little disappointed. Oh, I was so confused about my feelings for Max and it frustrated me.

Cocoa nudged my back with her nose, snorting out air that felt warm through my jacket. That was it. I was sick of standing way out here trying to see through the dark trees to find my dog. I turned around and looked the horse squarely in the eyes.

"I'm going in there," I said firmly, "and you're not going to stop me. I can't see anything from way out here and I really want to find Barker. You can stay here if you like but I'm going." I dropped the lead, turned on my heel and started walking towards the trees. Cocoa reared up and neighed loudly. I turned to see here flailing her front legs in midair like a boxer. I rolled my eyes and shook my head. "Drama queen."

I estimated it to be about seven in the morning. The sun was up, and the day looked like it was going to be sunny and clear with no hint of snow. The only thing that resembled November weather was an icy crispness that hung in the air, making my breath visible with every exhale. Despite the blue sky, however, stepping into the trees was like stepping into night. It was dark in here. The trees were tall and seemed to reach out to each other creating a sort of piney canopy, not allowing any sunlight through. I paused for a moment, waiting for my eyes to adjust and that's when I heard it.

A snap, like someone had stepped on a twig and broke it. I turned towards the sound and saw something dark duck behind a tree. It was too tall to be Barker and suddenly I felt the stupidity of my actions. Maybe the others were right. Maybe Ryan was here, in the forest, waiting for someone to come alone. My heart started to beat faster and I could feel tiny drops of cold sweat starting to form on my forehead.

"Ryan?" I called out, fully realizing that whoever it was obviously knew I was there. "Are you there?"

No answer but another snap echoed in my ears. I walked closer to the tree that I saw the shadow duck behind. This time *I* stepped on a twig, creating the same snapping sound. It startled me. I looked up at the tree; I was almost there. The shadow, except it wasn't a shadow anymore, it was a man dressed in what looked like camouflaged army clothes and he was running away.

"Wait!" I called out. "Wait! Please, I want to ask you if...." The man ran fast, and I knew that I better run fast too if I wanted to keep up. The chase was on!

The man darted in and out of the trees but, surprisingly, I didn't lose any ground. I didn't gain any, but I didn't lose any either. We jumped over logs, scurried up hills and splashed through small streams that had branched off the river. We must have run for at least ten minutes before the man just disappeared. I didn't get it. One minute he was there and then, poof, gone. I stopped, put my hands on my hips and looked around, trying to catch my breath. I was standing on top of a small hill covered with wild strawberries and pine needles. There was a huge rock wall to my left that was covered in moss. Water dripped down from above forming a crooked path and colouring the rock orange. He couldn't have jumped up the wall; it was over twenty feet high easily. All I could see to my right were more trees and plants and fallen branches; same as what was behind me. In front of me was a thick clump of bushes. Is that where he went?

I stared at the bushes, contemplating whether or not I should investigate. Could it be Ryan, waiting to capture me? Has he seen me come looking for Barker everyday; standing on the edge of the forest, not brave enough to enter, waiting for my patience to wear thin and cross the line into the trees? I didn't think so. If he really wanted me, he could have grabbed me on the edge. I was just as alone there as I am here. Besides, if it was Ryan, I could fight him. I refused to be scared of that idiot. I made up my mind and cautiously started toward the bushes. Then it happened; it was quiet and short, but I still heard it. A bark. A dog's bark.

"Barker?" My voice wavered as I spoke his name. I missed him so much. I ran to the bushes, no longer caring who the man was. My dog was in there and I had to save him.

I pushed my way through the thick bush, snagging my shirt and scratching my arms on the thorns that grew on the branches. I could hear the man's voice quietly urging Barker to keep quiet. It didn't sound like Ryan and it didn't sound mean. It confused me. Who, besides the remnants of Pig's men, could be hiding in there? I pulled the last branch from my hair and stared at the sight before me, unable to decide whether I should be happy or scared.

Barker was there all right, standing with his ears lying flat on his head and his tail wagging so hard his entire bottom half was swaying back and forth out of control. He was so excited and would have run straight to me if it had not been for the man holding his collar and pulling him back away from me.

"Who the hell are you and why do you have my dog?" I asked, not caring if I offended him.

11

"The girl speaks! I thought that speech was beyond one so young and out of touch! She says you are hers and I say she lies, but we will not tell her that." He gave Barker a pat on the shoulder and laughed as if he believed I couldn't hear him. I looked at him and narrowed my eyes. Was he for real? I knew he saw me. I tried to remember if he was one of Pig's men, but he didn't look familiar. He seemed to be about fifty and was dressed in army fatigues; pants, green t-shirt, army shirt over top and a cap sat on top of his greying black hair. He wore army boots that looked well worn and everything about him seemed polished and routine. I looked at his face and decided he was handsome and must have been very good looking when he was younger. He was not one of Pig's men, that was for sure. But who was he and how long has he been here?

"You know I can hear you, right?" I asked, trying not to anger him.

"She speaks again! All this time, alone in the woods and, finally, a creature talks to me!" He smiled and shook his head as if this was a feat never before accomplished. "Young Private what shall we do about this intrusion into our lives?" He knelt in front of Barker and held his head so the dog could look him in the eye.

"I'm right here and I can still hear you." I waved my hand and took a tentative step closer.

"Exactly!!" I jumped back as the man sprang to his feet. Barker didn't move, as if expecting the man to do this. "We were just talking about this very thing yesterday! How clever you are young Private. I will have to give you extra rations at supper tonight."

"Barker?" I looked at my dog and saw his eyes shift to me then quickly back to the man. He knew I was there, and I felt a small air of relief wash over me. I let my eyes slide back to the man and was surprised to see him staring at me. It was the first time he actually acknowledged that I was there.

"Greetings, miss...."

"Nicky. You can call me Nicky." I told him.

"Very well. Greetings miss, uh, Nicky," he put out his hand for me to shake. I looked at it hesitantly, noticing how clean it was, then reached out mine. His handshake was brief, very businesslike and very strong. "Colonel Albert Young United States army."

"Ok," I said, "army guy, cool. You live out here somewhere?"

"Somewhere, yes I do and you?" he asked.

"No, I don't live here in the forest," I explained. "I live more out towards the flatter land with some friends. How about you? Do you have any friends that live here with you?"

"No. I am alone, and I will stay alone," he stated, lifting his chin and puffing out his chest. I guess this was something he was proud of. "Your friends, are they the group who burned down the tented village?" I looked at him in disbelief. How did he know about the out-of-towners' camp? Had he been spying on them?

"They are," there was no sense lying about it, "but those people in the tents had it coming. They..."

"...were a group of low life bastards who killed, robbed and raped whoever got in their path?" He smiled at the stunned look on my face. "Yes, your group was right to do what they did even if it meant losing the chicken lady."

"Wait a minute," I looked him straight in the eye. He must live close by because he obviously knew what went on around here. "How did you know about Madge and that she liked chickens?"

"I have eyes, my dear," he lifted his hat and slicked back his hair and replaced the hat. "For instance, I know about the red-haired boy who pines after the schoolteacher. Too bad the pompous know-it-all from the east made short work of her but he had to find vengeance for his beloved chicken lady. I know that the irritating child has rescued a damsel in distress from the southern States but has lost her to the star gazing Englishman. It's okay, though, because he has found the little angel." I was speechless. He knew so much, but how? He saw my look of astonishment and it pleased him, so he continued. "I also know that the Scottish pirate has worked both sides but

14

has become smitten with the newcomer. That would be you, my dear. How do you feel about having an admirer that you can't trust?"

"I-I can trust him." My eyes turned to the ground, darting back and forth, trying to hide the blushing red that covered my face. How could he possibly know about my frustration with Max?

"Is that a question?" he smiled and crouched down, trying to see my eyes again. I ignored him and replaced my embarrassment with anger. Who did this guy think he was, spying on us and analyzing our movements?

"If you know all of this, then you must live somewhere close," I said. "Why do you keep yourself hidden?"

"Because I have no time for humans right now," he checked his pockets and turned, obviously searching for something. "I am working on something extremely important."

"What?" I asked, still trying to figure him out.

"Ha! As if I'd tell you," he shook his head and continued searching. "It's classified."

"Fine. Carry on, then. Just let me take my dog and I'll be on my way," I looked at Barker and patted my leg. "Come on, Barker, let's go bud."

"Wait!" He put up his hand to block me. "This 'dog' is my Private and can not abandon his post. He has to come with me.

I've already discussed it with him, and he completely understands his duty."

"I really don't care what you've discussed," I said, playing along with his delusion of talking with Barker, "I'm taking the dog with me."

"I can not allow that." Barker let out a small whimper and looked at the man. "I know but she insists on taking you. I don't think there's any way of getting around it. Yes, but I think we can trust her as long as no one else from her group shows up. Well, why don't you tell her? Ok, ok I'll tell her, but you need to support me this time."

"Uh..." What could I say? He seemed to be carrying on an entire conversation with my dog. This guy had a few screws loose. Who knew if he would have a meltdown and hurt me if I tried to take Barker away? Maybe, this time, I would let the man talk before running my mouth.

"It's been decided then," he smiled and stood with his hands behind his back. "You will follow me and the Private to my barracks where I will explain the mission."

"And what mission is that?" I asked, hoping that he didn't live far and that no one at Marshal's would miss me.

"The one to get out of this place of course." He started off with Barker right behind him.

"You know how to leave? To get back home?" He was already too far ahead to hear me. If he knew how to get out of this dimension, I wanted to know. I ran to catch up, forgetting that Cocoa was out on the edge of the forest waiting for me.

Chapter 2

"I've been working on this mission for quite a long time, years to be exact. It's not easy, you see, I keep having to wait for materials," Colonel Albert Young explained to me as we hiked through the trees. He was taking me to his home which, he explained, doubled as a workshop. He told me it wasn't too far and was well hidden from the 'enemy'. I had no idea who his 'enemy' could be, but I assumed it was probably Pig.

It took us about fifteen minutes, and only because Colonel Al walked so fast, to arrive to what he called home. I saw nothing but I knew better than to assume he was lying about having a home hiding somewhere. After all, I didn't believe Marshal when he first told me his house was right in front of me. I thought he had jumped on the crazy train when he reached down and pulled a cord revealing a trapdoor that led to his underground fortress. I knew not to question anything down here.

"Well?" he asked, trying not to sound too proud. "Can you find it?"

"You mean it's here? You must have done a good job hiding it because I don't see anything resembling a house around here," I said trying to look impressed and not irritated. I really didn't have time for games right now. Not only had I been gone longer than usual; I had left Cocoa out on the edge. Who knew if she went home without me and caused panic among my friends?

"That's it?" He sounded so disappointed. "You're not even going to try? Well, Private, I must say everything you've told me about this one is not true, not true at all. I think you should re-evaluate how you judge people."

"And just what has the *'Private'* told you about me?" This ought to be good, I smiled to myself.

"Oh, about how intelligent and brave you are," he said. "He said you didn't even blink when you shot that horrible man in the head. Just pulled out the gun, pointed and shot without thinking. That's how you got the horse isn't it?"

"What the...?" How the hell did he know about Butcher? Who was this guy? Where did he come from? Who did he know? I wanted to turn and run but my curiosity overcame my fear and I stared at Colonel Albert Young and asked the only question that came to my head. "Who the hell are you?"

"I told you Colonel Albert Young, United States Army." he smiled at me and I wanted to smack him across the face.

"No, no, no," I said, putting one hand on my hip and waving a finger at him with the other, "you don't get off that easy. Who are you? Where are you from? When did you fall?"

"Fall?" he looked at me, confused by this question.

"Yeah, when did you fall?" I asked again. "What year was it when you entered this hell hole dimension?"

"I don't know what you're talking about. I didn't 'fall' anywhere," he laughed. "I was sent here young lady. Sent here to complete this mission."

"What are you talking about? What mission?" Was he really sent here? It sounded impossible but he seemed to believe it.

"The mission to get us all home of course," he turned and walked towards a pile of branches and started pulling them down. I went over to him and grabbed his shoulder, trying to turn him to face me.

"What do you mean you were sent here? Who sent you?" I sounded desperate but I wanted to know if he was telling the truth. Did the people in the other world, the real world, the world I came from really know this place existed? I thought of the American government having a secret department where they knew all about this place. They could have my family right now. I imagined my mom and dad sitting in some secret office somewhere waiting for me to be rescued. I needed to know if it was possible. I needed Colonel Al to explain it all to me right now. Then Barker growled and it brought me back to my senses. I looked at my dog, confused, and let go of the Colonel's shoulder and backed up.

"I'm sorry," I couldn't believe Barker growled at me. Why would he defend this guy? Maybe he actually *liked* being with Colonel Al.

"Your apology is unnecessary," he said and then continued talking as if my little meltdown didn't happen. "I've been here a long time and haven't gotten anything done. Oh, I've patched up some of the circuit boards and recreated the simulator, but I haven't been able to get any of it to work. It doesn't seem to matter what I do; I can't create the power needed to run anything. I wanted to give up, but my training doesn't allow it and, since my mission is top secret, I couldn't tell anyone so, I couldn't illicit any help."

"But you're telling *me,* aren't you?" I asked, wanting to believe everything he said was true and that, somehow, there was a chance I could go home.

"Yes, I am, and I wouldn't have if it hadn't been for the Private," he looked down at Barker and smiled. "He's told me all about you and it was only under his advice that I even considered showing myself. I've been trained well in the art of camouflage and have gone unnoticed all this time. No one knows I'm here. You're the first and the Private has convinced me that you will be the one to help me." He turned and continued pulling the branches away from what looked like the entrance to an old coal mine.

"You mean you haven't talked to anyone down here?" I asked.

"Haven't talked to nor have I been seen by anyone, not one soul, since my mission began." He cleared the rest of the branches away and waited for me to follow him.

"Really? No one?" I found it hard to believe this. *I* ran into Marshal the very first day I fell down here. I guess it *was* in the city but still. Even Ryan, who fell while he was camping and ended up in the woods, found Pig and his camp and Max had fallen into the middle of the ocean of all places and was found by Cornelius. So, how could this guy not run into anyone? "When did you fall?"

"I told you, I did *not* fall. I was sent here to do a mission!" He looked irritated that I wasn't comprehending this.

"Ok," I guess I had to take a different approach, "what year was it when your mission began?"

"What year?" He looked at me as if this was a strange question for me to ask, but he also wanted to gain my trust. "1967."

"1967?" I was shocked by the date. That was over forty years ago. Had he really been on a mission for that long?

"Yes, is there anything wrong with that?" he asked sarcastically. "1967 is a good year."

"There's nothing wrong with that year except..."

"Except what?" he asked.

"Except it was over forty years ago," I explained, hoping he would understand how crazy this all was. "That's a long time to be committed to a mission."

"Well, well, well," he shook his head and laughed at me.

"What?" His laughter angered me.

"I see it has you fooled too," he said. "It had me fooled for a while as well, but I caught on; figured it all out."

"Figured what out?" I asked. "What had you fooled?"

"The time!" he laughed. "You think there's time here; that days, months and even years pass."

"Well don't they?" I asked.

"Of course not!" he looked at me and read the confusion in my eyes. "Don't you see? Here, in this place, there is no time. There is only one, long day. The dimension of time does not exist here. That's why it's so hard to get back."

"What do you mean?" I asked.

"We can't get back because we've lost the dimension of time," he tried to explain but I wasn't getting it. "How can we travel from here to there unless here and there are the same? We need all parts of there down here so we can transverse between here and there. You see?"

"What?" I was lost.

"We can't travel from here to there..." he started to explain again.

"No, but we do have time down here," I said. "The sun rises and sets; the moon comes up at night and I can see stars everywhere. That means we have days and nights. If we have days and nights, we have time."

"Foolish girl," he laughed at me again and, again, it angered me. "Those are not days. Those are physics. We come in and out of the sun because of where we sit in the solar system and because we get shadows and reflections from there, that's all. There is no time here."

"But there has to be," I said trying to convince myself more than him. "You said the year was 1967 when you started your mission and when I came it was 2012. See? Years, time, went by."

"There, maybe, but not here," he said. "There I was fifty when I left for my mission and here, I am still fifty. See no time has passed here. I am still the same."

"But..." I didn't know what to say. Maybe he was right. Maybe time didn't exist down here. It was strange how everyone still looked the same as when they fell. Even Billy hadn't aged beyond ten and he'd been here since the fifties. Could this Colonel Albert Young really know what he was talking about?

"This is why I need you. You have to help me get time here. If I can achieve that, we can go home." He turned to the mine, reached just inside the doorway and pulled out a lantern. "It's dark in there, we'll need light." He struck a match and lit the lantern and then he turned and headed inside the mine assuming I would follow. I hesitated, thinking that it probably wasn't a good idea to follow some strange man I had just met into the bowels of an abandoned mine. It seemed too much like a cheap horror movie and, yet, I couldn't resist. I had to learn more about Colonel Albert Young's plan to get us out of this dimension and back to my home. Barker, who had been right beside the colonel, now stood at the mine entrance and let out a short bark urging me forward.

"Do you really trust him?" I asked my dog. He wagged his tail and whined, reaching out his paw to me. I took this as a yes. "Okay, I'm going to trust you on this." I entered the mine and focused on the light of the lantern a few feet away.

Colonel Al led me through a maze of tunnels, each one lined with wooden frames and braces. I became totally lost and knew that I would never be able to find my way back out on my own. I didn't realize that a mine could be this big. We seemed to be on a constant downward slope, and I wondered how far below the earth's surface we had gone. We never spoke the whole trek and I started to feel uncomfortable and just a little unsafe. I wondered how much oxygen was down here despite the air vents I saw at various intervals. Would we run out if we stayed down here too long? I didn't feel suffocated. I could still breathe deeply, and I noted that the lantern was still lit. If the oxygen ran out, the flame in the lantern would go out too, wouldn't it? Of course, it would. My science teachers would be proud.

"Here we are," Colonel Al said as he entered a huge room that branched off the tunnel. I looked around as I crouched to go through the arched doorway. The walls were what one would expect inside a mine; gray stone with patches of black and rusty brown. They looked like they had been chipped and hammered at over the years, maybe by miners from above or by the colonel himself. I guessed that coal was probably the reason for this mine and wondered if they ever found any. I noticed an old minor's hat in the corner with a light strapped to the front and there was a pickaxe leaning against the wall. Could this be the only tool that Colonel Al used to build his base?

The room had been overtaken by Colonel Al and the instruments for his mission. The first thing I noticed were all the clocks. Clocks of every kind and size were connected to each other with wires like some kind of warped building blocks. There must have been over a hundred of them and they took up three quarters of the room and ran from floor to ceiling. None of them appeared to be working, their hands all stopped in mid tic toc, all pointing to different numbers; different times. I figured they must have stopped the second they fell from the real world. Colonel Al had a generator, the kind that campers had in their rvs, hooked up with wires and cables to the clocks. As I got closer to it, I could smell a faint trace of gasoline. Near the generator was a row of watches strung together with even more wire and attached to a car battery. In the corner was a huge pile of batteries of every kind; Cs, Ds, triple AAAs, another car battery and a couple of batteries I had never seen before. They had been thrown aside like garbage.

"This is the 'clock room'," he said. "As you can see, I've been trying everything to start the clocks, but nothing has worked. I just can't seem to get any power here; no one can."

"But these are wind up clocks," I pointed out. "Why would you need power to start them?"

"Ha, I knew you would say that," he smiled and pat Barker who was sitting by his side. "I've tried winding them. In fact, I tried winding them for the first, what I calculated to be if we had years down here, five years. After that, I gave up and went the power route; batteries, steam, generators, anything I could get my hands on. The watch thing never came to my attention until about ten years ago. It hasn't been any more helpful. And now the watches that come down here, at least I think they're watches, are useless, blank, no hands, no numbers, nothing."

"That's because they're smart," I offered looking more closely at the clocks.

"Smart? What's that supposed to mean? I'm smart. I've lasted this long, haven't I?" He was angry, thinking that I had insulted him. I laughed.

"No, the watch is smart," I tried to think of the best way to explain it to him. "You see; watches are like tiny little computers. You can download all sorts of information on them. But if their battery is dead, they don't turn on and their screen is blank."

"What do you mean by download?" he asked.

"Well, you know, there's all sorts of information out there and if you want to, you can take it and put it on your computer, or phone, or watch or any other device you might have."

"Information? What kind of information and where does one find it?" He lifted his hat and scratched his head.

"Oh boy," what had I gotten myself into. I didn't want to explain the entire computer age to Colonel Al; it would take forever. "You know it's just a little too complicated right now. How about we talk about it later. What else do you have to show me?"

He took me to a room that was just a little smaller than the clock room. It had been chiseled out similar to the first room and I wondered if these rooms existed when the colonel got here or if he had done all the work himself. By the way it was so expertly braced with wood, I figured the colonel found them this way.

He explained that this was the room that had the simulator and circuit boards he said he worked on. I was a little disappointed when I saw it though. He had circuit boards, all right, but they were totally useless. He had ripped them out of computers and tried to hook them up to, what looked like, old radios and walkie talkies. His 'simulator' that he tried to recreate looked interesting though. He had a panel of buttons and switches mounted on a table that must have covered at least three feet. Each button and switch were wired to some sort of instrument that kind of looked like a receiver under the table. There was a chair pulled up to the table that I guessed was for the colonel.

"What's all this for?" I asked.

"I've been trying to achieve communication with my superiors," he explained. "So far, nothing."

"No?" This didn't surprise me.

"Same problem as everything else," he said. "No power."

He headed back to the main tunnel and I followed. The next room he showed me was smaller than the first two and a little darker. In here there were shelves of flasks and beakers, each one filled with different coloured liquids and every one of them labeled and corked or covered with tin foil. He had jars of different plants and rocks; some floating in liquid and some just sitting in the jar. There was a long table in the center of the room set up with test tubes and tubing connected with clamps, forming a maze of tubes that liquid could run through. At the end was a flask half full of purple liquid and suspended in the air by a clamp. Underneath was a small pot with holes punched in the side. Al had placed some small pieces of wood in the pot. He must have had a small fire going earlier because some of the wood was charred and I could still smell a faint hint of the fire.

'Great,' I thought. 'A chem lab. If he wants my help with any of this, he'll be disappointed. I know nothing about chemistry.'

"This is my lab," he said as if reading my mind. "I've been running experiments, trying to simulate power by using different chemicals and minerals I've discovered down here. Did you know that the breakdown of minerals works very differently down here?"

"No," I said, trying to sound excited by this news and trying to actually care about it.

"Yes, well I can see this news has jolted you," he said sarcastically and then turned to Barker and spoke as if I wasn't there. "This girl is not very intelligent at all young Private. I suggest that when you return to the city this time, you befriend a more capable specimen." He turned back to me. "Shall we continue?"

"Return to the city?" I looked at Barker and felt a nudge of betrayal forming in my stomach. "Just how long has this dog been helping you?"

"The Private?" he answered. "This particular Private has spent a few tours with me. He goes to the city every time it reappears, looking for my helper. He's been promising me that the perfect one was coming but I was beginning to doubt his word. Then he found you and now, here you are. I have to say, though, I'm not really encouraged. "

"I-I think I have to go now." I wasn't really listening to what the colonel was saying. I felt used. I thought Barker was mine; that we had both fallen to this world together. From the first time I saw him, I was sure we had a connection. I thought we were both experiencing this crazy place together for the first time. Now, I find out it was all a lie? Barker had been down here for longer than I thought; years probably. I thought he was mine. I searched for him every day for months; needing to have him back. Someone, even if he was a dog, who came from my world, my time. Someone who felt like a part of me. I had to go, get out of this cave. The walls seemed to be closing in on me and the air felt heavy and it was hard to breathe. "I need to get back to Marshal. I need to go. Thank you for showing me your base Mr. Colonel Al but I can't help you with any of this. I must be leaving now. Goodbye."

I turned and ran from the room, ran down the tunnel trying to find my way out. Which way had we come? Which tunnel should I take? I turned one corner and the light was gone. Without Colonel Al's lamp I was in darkness. I hadn't thought of this. I would have to feel my way out. Could I do it? I tried and ran into a wall, banging my head on the low ceiling. It hurt and just added to my frustration. This was impossible and I sat down with my back against the wall and waited to be found. It only took five minutes before I felt the wet tongue of Barker licking my face. I felt my anger melt away and all I could feel was relief that my friend was okay. I reached my hands up and buried my fingers in his fur.

"You stupid, silly dog," I nudged my face into his neck. "I've been so worried about you and you've been hiding with this crazy army guy the whole time. And he tells me that you've been his for a long time. How could you? I want you to be mine. I thought you were from my time, my city. How can you possibly be someone else's?" I leaned my forehead into his neck and closed my eyes. He felt so calm and relaxed and then he let out a small whine and licked my face again. Oh, how could I stay mad at him? He was just a dog after all. "You're so lucky you're cute because I'm really considering walking out and leaving you here, you know." Barker let out a small whimper then nudged me with his nose, wanting me to get up and go back to the colonel. "I know you trust him, but I really don't think he knows what he's doing and, if he does, I don't think I can help him." He barked so quietly, like a whisper bark and I knew I had to go back.

"Okay, I'll try," I said as I got to my feet and went back to the room with all the beakers and test tubes. Colonel Al was studying something under a microscope that I hadn't noticed before.

"Have you calmed down?" he asked, continuing to look through the microscope.

"Yes," was all I said.

"Good," he finally looked up and stared at me. "Right then, I think you should leave."

"What?" I did not expect this. "Why?"

"You've seen everything that's important," he said. "You've been briefed on my mission. Now your job is to go back to your friends and ask them if they have any idea on how to make power."

"I'm pretty sure they don't," I said. I knew that they didn't know how to make power. If they did, they would be using it for lights and cooking and so much more. "But I'll tell them about your mission and maybe they can come and look at what you've done. Maybe they'll become inspired and you guys can figure it out together."

"Oh, no, you don't," he laughed and looked back down through the microscope.

"What? Oh no I don't what?"

"Tell anyone about me," he spoke, not lifting his eyes.

"But how else am I supposed to explain to them about..."

"About power?" he looked up, meeting my eyes one more time. I nodded my head. "I would think that power is something they would be looking for anyway."

"But..." I assumed he wasn't going to change his mind on this.

"Goodbye," he said.

"Okay, then," I started to turn for the door, "but I'm taking the Private with me. He knows his way out of here and I don't. So, no questions, he's coming with me." Colonel Al took his eyes away from the microscope but kept them on the table in front of him.

"Very well," he said. "Private escort this girl back to her camp. I will see you later." He returned to the microscope and I patted Barker, congratulating myself on this small victory.

Barker led me out of the old mine slowly, making sure I always had a hold of his tail. It was pitch black, but the shepherd cross knew exactly where he was going, confirming my suspicions that he must have been with this Colonel Al for a while. It frustrated me that this dog who I loved so much, was someone else's pet. It made me wonder just how long he'd been down here and how long he'd been living with this crazy army guy. Maybe he wasn't really happy here. Maybe he was just as happy to find me as I was to find him.

"Oh, Barker," I said as we made our way through the entrance and out into the fresh air. "I wish you could talk; I have so many questions to ask you." The dog sat down and looked at me, cocking his head to one side, waiting for me to say what I had to say before we hiked back to Marshal's. "But you can't talk, and my questions will never be answered, so, we might as well just get on with it and go back." Barker came and licked my hand and turned to head back through the trees.

As we walked, I talked out loud, voicing my thoughts on Colonel Al and his mission. Could he be for real? "You know, Barker, it isn't too unreasonable to think that someone up there knows that this place exists," I said. "I mean, it's possible that it's been kept top secret, away from the general public. Could you just imagine the panic if people knew that, at any time, they could disappear from that world and come to this one and that there was no hope in getting them back? I think people would either freak out or line-up to get down here. That's the way people are, you know, jumping into things without thinking about the consequences." We climbed over a fallen tree and I looked around, not remembering any of this when I ran through here earlier, chasing the colonel. Boy, I had really come far, hadn't I?

"On the other hand, though, it seems pretty unusual for the American government to send someone down here without having a way to get them back or even communicate with them, doesn't it?" I asked. "I just don't know what to think of Colonel Al. Is he crazy? And, if he was really sent down here, why is he up here in Canada, hiding in the woods? Shouldn't he be somewhere in the States? That would make much more sense, wouldn't it? I think he's a little disturbed but..." Barker seemed to sense my doubt and let out a small bark. "...but I think what he's doing makes sense I suppose. If we can get time back maybe, we can merge the two worlds back together. Maybe that's what we are, a fragment of the world that got caught in some sort of time warp and once we get back time, we'll go back." I was so desperate to go home, back to my old life with my mom and dad and even my little brother. Back where I could text my friends and spend hours on my computer, not caring about how I was going to survive the winter. I leaned down and called Barker to me. I wanted to pet him and let him know how happy I was that I had found him. He licked my face and wagged his tail. "I did miss you so much."

We had made it, without realizing it, we had made our way back to the edge of the woods where I had left Cocoa. I stood and looked at the sky. It had been so clear and blue when I stepped into the trees and now it was white; a snow sky. I must have been at the colonel's longer than I thought. There was a shadow approaching and I stood and waited.

"The lady appears!" It was Max. He was riding Cocoa. I wondered how long they had been there waiting for me. He slid off the horse and walked towards me. I felt my stomach flutter and cursed myself for it. "Imagine how surprised we all were when your trusted steed returned without her precious passenger."

"I was fine," I replied like a scolded child. I looked at Cocoa and glared teasingly at her. "Traitor." She huffed through her nose and pawed the ground with her hoof. Then Barker stepped out from behind me and Cocoa whinnied her approval that the dog was back.

"Well, well, well, the mighty Barker has been found!" exclaimed Max and I smiled despite myself. "Where'd you find him?" He stepped forward and started patting Barker, not caring that the dog was licking his face and getting dog drool all over him. This was the Max that I was attracted to.

"Interesting story, I suppose," I wondered if I should tell him about Colonel Al. Barker turned and barked at me. The dog was just too smart to be any ordinary canine. "But it can wait for now." It was all I was willing to give the colonel. I knew that I would probably tell everyone about his mission just to see if they believed it or if they thought it was total nonsense.

"I hope it doesn't wait too long," said Max as he stood and looked at me, all signs of the joy of seeing Barker gone.

"Why?" I asked.

"I'm leaving," he stated, and I was taken aback. Had I really driven him away with my reluctance to let my heart fall into his hands.

"Leaving?" I asked, crossing my arms in front of me.

"Yes, Nicky, despite your joy of sharing my company and the fact that you crave my undying attention, I will be taking leave in the morning." He smiled but I could see the hurt in his eyes behind the sarcasm. I hadn't shown him any joy and I definitely did not seek his attention.

"I'm sorry that I haven't been swept off my feet by you," my face was burning red, "but it's so, so different down here. I'm different and I just have to figure out what's going on inside my head. It takes time. I've told you that. I'm sorry but it's all I can give you for now. I've only had two boyfriends in my life, both in junior high, and you're so..."

"Charming," another sarcastic remark and it made me angry.

"No, you're so..." I searched for the right word, "...worldly."

"Hah! Now that's an insufferable word!"

"Well, you are," I said. "You've been a lot of places and you've seen a lot of things, a lot of women..."

"Ah, the real truth," he shook his head and rolled his eyes. "You're still thinking about what dear Cornelius said about my past encounters and you're worried that I'll treat you the same."

"That's not it!" It was a part of it though; a big part of it.

"I told you, I'm different now," he tried to explain. "You're different from all those other women. You've..."

"What? Changed you? Made you an honest man?" I laughed.

"Yes," he said quietly, knowing it had no effect on me.

"You don't understand." How could I tell him that these were qualities he should have had before he ever met me?

"You're right, I don't," he said.

"I'm only seventeen. I need time to figure it out," I said.

"Nicky, you've had four months to figure it out!" I could feel his frustration and looked down at the ground, not wanting to look at him. He went on, sounding defeated. "Whatever. You'll have lots of time to think things over now; think about me, maybe even miss me. If I'm gone, maybe you'll realize that you actually do have feelings for me."

"'Absence makes the heart grow fonder'. Is that what you're counting on? Is that why you're leaving, to make me miss you?" This kind of angered me, yet, flattered me at the same time.

"That is a thought, isn't it? But, alas, no," he said, "that is not the reason why I'm leaving. I'm leaving because of the Blood Demons. Emma Lee's persistence that they are on their way here has become increasingly hard to ignore. There's been discussion that someone should go and scout them out, see if she's right."

"Discussion? What discussion?" I was surprised at this. "Why haven't I been included in this discussion?"

"Because, my dear," he sighed, "you have been engulfed in your search for the ever-elusive Barker, which, I am happy to see, has paid off. You were right; he is not dead, and he looks perfectly healthy. The woods seem to have agreed with our friendly furry friend. It's almost as if someone took him in and looked after him."

"It seems that way, doesn't it," I tried to change the subject. "Shall we go back to Marshal's. I'd like to find out more about these discussions I've been missing. Besides, it's getting chilly. I can feel a north wind closing in on us."

"I can feel it too," he said. "Would you like to ride or walk?"

"I'll walk," I answered quickly. I knew what sharing a horse ride could lead to. "I don't mind, and I want to keep close to Barker anyway."

"Very well, I shall walk also." He grabbed Cocoa's reins and we headed out. I felt something wet touch my nose, a snowflake. I was right; the north wind was closing in. By the time we got back to Marshal's, the snow was coming down heavier. The flakes were getting bigger and it was starting to lie on the ground, no longer melting into the earth. That meant the temperature had dropped and it was only going to get colder.

Chapter 3

Marshal's house had changed over the last four months; it got bigger. We had taken the materials from Robert's and Madge's house and built an addition onto Marshal's house with them. It wasn't perfect but it was big enough for all of us. We even cut through Marshal's wall and the wall of the new addition to make a sort of doorway between the two. We sealed the gap between them with mud and grass. It worked pretty good and now, in theory, we could share the heat from the old stove if we kept it well fueled. Now, with the snow, we could test that theory out. We had enough wood left over to build a small shelter for Cocoa and we planted enough hay to last her all winter. The snow was starting to blanket the fields and as Cornelius and Billy came in the door with their arms loaded with chopped wood, I could feel the cold wind swoop in and try to take hold.

"Woo, it's cold out there, people," said Cornelius as he stomped his boots to try to knock off whatever snow was stuck on them. "I say we have a real snowstorm on its way. Marshal? There's enough wood out there for about four days if we use it sparingly but we should stockpile as much as we can before the snow starts to really pile up. Even with the horse, it's going to be tough to haul wood through the snow especially if it starts to drift. Billy and I covered what we had with tarps, but I think we should put what we can underground so it stays dry."

"See?" I said. "The snow is piling up and the wind is getting stronger, it makes no sense for Max to leave now."

"I'm flattered for your concern, Nicole, but I'll be fine," Max smiled sarcastically at me and I looked away angry. I may not want a romantic relationship with him, but I did care about his safety. "In fact, I shouldn't wait for tomorrow morning. If I leave now, I might just miss the worst of this storm."

"You think?" I said. "For all we know it could be worse down south. The winds that come through the Crowsnest Pass are strong and could make the snow drifts twice as high down there as opposed to up here."

"She's right, right, right," Marshal said, agreeing with me. "It could be far worse, worse, worse in southern Alberta than here."

"I'll be fine!" Max repeated. He was getting angry with us for our lack of faith in his abilities.

"Are we still on about this?" asked Cornelius. "I thought we had this settled when the lad and I went for wood?"

"Ask Nicky," said Max, looking frustrated. "She seems to think I can't cut it out in the cold."

"I never said that," I argued. "I just merely suggested you don't rush out into a blizzard for something that might not even be happening!"

Everyone had been happy to see Barker when we returned. They were full of questions about where I found him, was he okay, did I think anyone was keeping him and lots more. I successfully answered most of their questions without revealing the existence of Colonel Al, although it would have been easier to explain that Barker had been with someone who looked after him for the past four months. After all the talk about Barker died down, I quickly directed the conversation to Max's decision to leave. We gathered in what had become the 'stove room' to discuss the Blood Demons. The room was really Marshal's kitchen/living room/bedroom, but it was where the cast iron stove was located so it was just easier to call it the 'stove room'.

I wanted to know why Emma Lee was so insistent that they were on their way here. I know she believed they wanted to live in a world that was low on population and high in resources but that could be a lot of places down here, couldn't it? I even suggested that, maybe, they would head south before they were to ever head north. After all, it was much warmer towards the equator and would be a lot easier to survive. Emma Lee said that may be so, but she was sure she had heard the men talking about the mountains to the northwest. She had also heard rumours on her way here and every one of them centred around the Blood Demons coming this way. She was scared for all of us and wanted us to be prepared.

"I'm afraid Nicole is correct; the trek will be dangerous in this weather young man," added Robert.

"I've been on worse adventures, believe me," Max avoided my eyes as he said this, knowing how much I didn't want to hear about his past escapades. "I know what I'm doing."

"Oh, I believe you do," said Robert. "After all you are a pirate."

"That has nothing to do with it," Max was angry at Robert. He wanted everyone to forget that he was once a pirate.

"But it has everything to do with it," Robert smiled at him. "I imagine the life of a pirate is dangerous, with its own penalties and rewards."

"So?" he asked.

"I was just…" started Robert.

"Just what? Do you think I'm too evil? That I can't be trusted to collect information properly? Do you think that I might join them?"

"On the contrary," said Robert, throwing up his arms in defence. "I believe you to be the perfect man for this job. I was just letting you know that it's going to be cold so bring warm clothing and warm shoes. I think you should be prepared to be gone for a long while. If this is the start of winter, you may be stuck somewhere with no way to get back here. It's important that you take the right supplies with you."

"Yeah," he was surprised that Robert was on his side and was actually encouraging him to go. "Maybe you can help me with that."

"But Robert, don't you think he should stay?" I, too, was surprised at Robert but for very different reasons.

"Nicky, he's a grown man. If he wants to go, there isn't a damn thing any of us can do to stop him." Max turned to me and smiled a cheeky smile that I wanted to smack off his face. Robert was right, though, not one of us could stop Max from doing anything. I let out a sigh and sat back on the couch, Barker curled up at my feet.

"Well I, for one, am glad that someone is going to scout out the Blood Demons," said Emma Lee who, until now, had been quiet. "Thank you, Mr. Maxwell, for doing this. I think we are all thankful for your bravery."

"Yes, Max," Cornelius had finished stacking the wood by the stove and was now standing next to Emma Lee. "We all bow to your braveness."

"If I were you, I'd keep my mouth closed," Max seemed irritated with his old friend. "Or I'll be requesting a certain Englishman who knows how to chart the skies accompany me on my trek."

"I told you mate," laughed Cornelius, "anytime you want my company just let me know."

"I don't think Mr. Max meant that he wanted..." Emma Lee had no problem sending Max out to scout the Blood Demons but felt differently if it involved her new boyfriend leaving. That angered me even more. I guess I couldn't blame her, though, she had already lost one man to these men. It would be unfair for her to lose another. Besides, Max was unattached. Even if he showed an interest in me, I was trying really hard not to reciprocate.

"Don't worry lass, I have no intention of bringing Cornelius with me," laughed Max. "He's not built for danger. He's built more for stargazing and moonlit walks."

"That would sting if it weren't true," Cornelius said. "I have not an adventurous bone in my body. I do wish you luck however, friend."

"Thank you, but I don't need luck," said Max. "Either I find the Demons, or I don't. Luck, fate or whatever you want to call it, has nothing to do with it." He reached out and shook Cornelius' hand, letting him know that it was all right if the Englishman didn't want to come with him. "Now, I should pack my supplies and change my clothes and be on my way before the snow gets any heavier."

"Let me help," said Robert and the two of them left the room, listing off items that he definitely needed for the winter weather.

I watched them leave and felt something sink to the bottom of my stomach. I guess that was it, Max was leaving and I didn't know if I was sad, or angry, or relieved that I wouldn't have to face any of the emotions that stirred inside of me every time he so much as looked at me. Barker must have sensed my uncertainness because he started to lick my hands and I pat him behind the ears to assure him that I was okay and was reminded of Colonel Al and his plans to leave this dimension. Should I say something now or wait until after Max left? I decided it would be better to wait. If Max knew there was a man out in the woods, hiding in an old mine, concocting potions he would probably go out there and cause trouble of some kind. So, I kept my secret for the time being.

Within an hour Max had everything he needed and was ready to go. Everyone gathered in Marshal's living room to say goodbye. Billy and Kitten said goodbye quickly because they wanted to get back to the game of jacks they had been playing in Robert's newly built house. It didn't matter how long they'd been down here; their minds had stopped at ten and this was where their attention span was. They had no concern for Max and what dangers he could be facing, not when they were in the middle of a cutthroat game of jacks. I envied them and wished I could be ten forever.

Marshal, who never showed any emotion except happy obliviousness, smiled and shook Max's hand, wishing him luck, luck, luck. Emma Lee and Cornelius took a little longer, Emma Lee explaining again how careful he should be if he did happen to run into the evil group of men that had killed all the people she loved and cared about. Max brushed her warnings off, saying he could handle himself. When it came time for Cornelius to say goodbye, Max pulled him over to the corner and spoke quietly to him. I could see Max look into Cornelius' eyes with a somber expression on his face. Cornelius nodded and glanced over at me then back at Max and nodded again. I knew they were talking about me and it made me feel uncomfortable. Then they gave each other a quick hug, pat each other on the back and shook hands.

"I guess that leaves me," I said, feeling a flash of heat rush to my face. I stepped towards him with my hands in the back pockets of my jeans.

"I guess so," he said. "Would you mind walking with me outside for a bit?"

"Ok, just let me get..."

"Your coat?" He held up my coat which he had somehow retrieved without me knowing. He helped me into it and opened the door for me to go outside. I noticed immediately that the temperature had dropped significantly, and the wind had gotten stronger. I pulled up the collar of my coat and tucked my chin inside.

"Wow, it's getting really cold. Are you sure you want to do this?" I noticed the sky was still white. That meant the snow was far from over.

"I'm sure," he answered. "I'll be okay. I have food and water, warm clothes, a sleeping roll that can withstand cold temperatures, matches, cooking utensils, water and a tent that I'm told is good to -40 degrees Celsius, which, I assume, is damned cold."

"Yeah, pretty cold," I laughed. "It's a good thing Marshal likes to collect things. Who knew that a hiker's backpack would come in handy?"

"Yes, it is quite efficient at carrying all of my gear."

"Well, that is what it's made for," I didn't know what else to say. We were walking south, in the direction of where the Blood Demons were supposed to be but, still many, many miles away. I felt awkward and at a loss on how to say goodbye.

"Nicky, I'm glad you have your dog again. I know how much his absence saddened you," he said, stopping and turning to face me.

"Thank you," I said, sniffing as my nose started to run in the cold air. "I *am* happy to have him again and I'm sorry I was so obsessed with finding him. I guess I haven't been thinking too straight over the past few months."

"It's okay, I understand," he smiled, and I felt the butterflies dance around my stomach again. "I know you believe that I'm leaving to be away from you, and I can't lie, that *is* part of the reason. I think we both need to be apart to figure out where our feelings for each other stand. I, for one, can't stand to be in the same room with you and see you turn away from me." I looked down guiltily at the ground. "But that's not the only reason I want to go."

"No?" I gulped down air as I felt my heart start to race.

"I'm also leaving because I believe that there is a real threat that these men will come here and continue their killing," he said and I could see how serious he was, "and there is no way that I will ever let anyone come here and harm you. I know that you have questions in your mind that are clouding your heart, but I also know that, when I kissed you that very first time, it was your heart that responded. You kissed me back. I know what your true feelings are even if you don't. Soon, you will too and, when you do, I'll be waiting, and you'll realize how much time you've wasted denying what's meant to be." He stroked his thumb across my cheek and tilted my chin up to his face. I felt his breath, a rush of warmth in the cold that surrounded me, as he softly kissed my lips and a tingling sensation ran through my body. "Goodbye."

"Max...?" Should I explain to him where Barker had been these past four months? Should I tell him about Colonel Al? No, I couldn't. What if Emma Lee was right? What if the Blood Demons were really on their way here? They could be marching towards us right now. If so, there was no better person to scout them out than Max. Wasn't that the reason I didn't trust him? He had the ability to fit in with the worst down here and I didn't like it.

"Yes?" he asked, looking expectantly at me.

"Be careful," I said, and he smiled and tilted his head to the side.

"Always am, love." Then he turned and walked into the falling snow, his backpack strapped across his back, winter boots replacing his fancy leather ones. I pulled my coat tighter around me and tucked my face deeper into my collar. I stayed like that until he disappeared in the snow. As my hair filled with the soft, white flakes and, as I stared at the falling snow, a thought came to me.

"Colonel Albert Young is wrong, we do have time," I said out loud and then ran in the house. Tomorrow, no matter how cold it was, I had to go visit Colonel Al. I had something very important to tell him.

Chapter 4

I got up early the next day so I could get out of the house and off to the abandoned mine before anyone else got up. The room was dark, but I didn't dare light the kerosene lantern. I'd gotten up in this room every day now for the past four months, so I knew exactly where everything was. I put my clothes at the bottom of my bed last night so, now, I could reach them easily and get dressed. Barker, who had slept curled up on my bed, was up too. He sat patiently waiting for me to get ready.

This room was the second room in Marshal's house and was dubbed the 'girl's room' because this is where I, Emma Lee and Kitten slept. It's a good thing there were only three of us, too, because we needed all the room we could get. The guys slept in two groups now that we had added on an addition to the house. Marshal still slept in the 'stove room', along with Billy and sometimes Max. Robert and Cornelius slept in the new addition. The two had become good friends.

Cornelius had not always liked Madge and was often sarcastic and rude to her, but he liked Robert and felt that he needed to be there for him after his loss. Robert never spoke of Madge or their life together, not once. I was afraid he was keeping it bottled up inside of him and knew that one day that bottle's cap would fly off and all that pain would spill out and probably not in a good way.

It only took me a few minutes to get ready and I slowly tiptoed out of the room, making sure not to bump into anything. I got to the 'stove room' and grabbed my coat and boots. Right now, it was pitch black and very quiet. Marshal and Billy were quiet sleepers, neither one snored. I figured they were probably wrapped up tightly in their blankets sound asleep. I put my coat on and laced up my boots. I had no idea how much snow had fallen through the night and hoped it wasn't too much. As long as the wind had died down, I would be okay. I placed a note I had written last night onto the table for someone to find when they woke up. It said that I had gotten up and taken Barker for a walk and went in search of firewood. I tied a scarf around my face and pulled a toque down over my ears. I got up, put on a thick pair of mittens, and headed for the door. Hopefully I could sneak out without letting in too much cold air.

"You're up early." I jumped. I didn't think anyone else was up.

"Marshal?" I asked. "What are doing up?"

"I couldn't sleep," he said. He sounded sad which was unusual for him. I knew he liked Sarah and her betrayal came as a shock and he was *completely* devastated when Robert killed her, but he was good at hiding his feelings. Nobody else noticed how it had affected him, but I did. I also knew that he wasn't over it yet.

"Are you okay?" I asked.

"I'm fine, Nicky," he sounded irritated. "Where are you going so early?"

"I'm taking Barker for a walk," I explained, hoping he wouldn't hear the lie behind my words. "It's all in the note. I'm walking Barker and looking for firewood."

"Firewood?" I could hear the doubt in his voice. "I thought the others were taking Cocoa and getting wood later."

"They are..." I tried to think quickly. "...but I thought I would go out to the trees, see if the snow covered the forest floor yet. Maybe it's still dry in there and we can get some dry firewood."

"I think they can do that with Cocoa, Nicky," he said.

"Yes, but I could scout it out first and be back before they even get out of bed."

"I see," he said, and I could sense the doubt in his voice.

"Okay? Just let me get the lantern and I'll be on my way," I tried to get out before he asked me any more questions. "Barker probably has to pee really bad."

"That's mighty good, good, good of you Nicky. Now, tell me where you're really going." Now he sounded angry. I let out a sigh and rolled my eyes. What was I going to do? Marshal was not going to let me go without some kind of explanation and I wasn't ready to tell anybody about Colonel Al. I turned towards his voice again; I had to tell him something.

"All right, I'm going to the woods because I found something really important yesterday."

"Really?" His curiosity was starting to overtake his anger. Barker started to growl, and I put my hand on his head, patting him to keep him quiet.

"I know, Barker." I reassured him quietly and then addressed Marshal. "I can't tell you what it is right now, but it has something to do with Barker and where he's been all this time. You have to trust me, Marshal. I know what I'm doing, and I promise you'll be the first one I tell everything to when I can."

"Nicky, Nicky, Nicky, how can I know that you'll be okay?" he asked, and I realized he wasn't really angry with me; he was concerned. It made me feel good, knowing he cared so much but, at the same time, I felt guilty not telling him everything. "That boy, Ryan, could be..."

"What? Out hiding behind a rock. Ready to jump out and kill me?" I laughed. "Marshal if Ryan wanted to, he would have done it by now. I seriously think he's gone; I don't know where, but he's not around here anymore. He lost everything he was working for," I was careful not to mention Sarah's name, "and I think he just took off."

"I think you're right, right, right Nicky," he said. "I've thought that for a long time, but the others are so insistent, and I didn't want to argue with anyone."

"Marshal, are you okay?" I asked. There was a long pause before he answered.

"Yes." It was only one word and I knew he meant it. Maybe his grief for Sarah was fading after all.

"I'm glad," I reached out to him, but the darkness wouldn't allow me to find him. "I'm here if you ever want to talk, okay?"

"Thank you, Nicky," he said. "Now, let's get you gone, gone, gone. I don't think you should be gone too long, though. I may be able to wait for your secrets, but the others aren't so patient. Here, I have the lantern. It's all fueled and ready to go." I could smell the scent of sulphur as he struck a match and lit the lantern. I reached for it and saw him sitting at the table. He was dressed in his ever-present green clothing and I wondered if he slept fully clothed. "It shouldn't take long to slip a bridle on Cocoa."

"You knew I was leaving?" I asked.

"I had an idea," he smiled, probably the first genuine smile in a long time.

"You're smart, Marshal," I laughed. "It's one of the things I like about you."

"Yes, yes, yes Nicky I'm very smart," he laughed sarcastically and waved me out the door. "Now, hurry before anyone else wakes up."

"Okay, I'll sneak out quickly, so the cold air doesn't wake up Billy." I pulled my hat down over my ears and pulled my mitts on.

"No worries, Nicky," he said. "Billy's not here."

"Where is he?" I asked, surprised that he wasn't in the room.

"He's at Robert's," he explained. "They played poker last night and he fell asleep while they were counting their winnings."

"He lost eh?" I figured he got bored with everyone else winning and dozed off.

"No, no, no, Nicky," he laughed. "Billy won. Actually, he won quite a bit, but he doesn't care. No, no, no, he just got tired and went to sleep."

"Cool, so I guess they'll all be sleeping in a bit today?" Marshal shrugged his shoulders. "Well, it would be nice if they did; gives me more time to do what I have to do. I'll see you later Marshal." I heard a short 'bye' as I opened the door and walked out into the cold, Barker by my side, lantern in my hand.

It didn't take as long as I thought to get to the old abandoned mine. Having Barker lead the way made the trek way easier. The snow had stopped but not before covering the fields with about three centimeters of cold, white flakes. I didn't care; it wasn't enough to even make my feet cold. I was wearing so many warm clothes that I was actually sweating by the time we reached the forest. I was right though, the denseness of the trees had let very little snow in.

When we got to the mine, Barker let out a few sharp barks before we entered. It was probably a good idea to warn Colonel Al that we were coming. Who knew what he had to protect himself from intruders? I tethered Cocoa to a tree and entered the maze of tunnels. The first thing that struck me as we got deeper into the tunnels was the smell of coffee and I closed my eyes and breathed it in. No one had coffee down here. I hadn't had a coffee for so long that I had forgotten about it until now. The smell brought a craving to me and I really wanted a cup. I hoped the colonel made a big pot. Barker barked again.

"Is that you, Private?" Colonel Al called out from further ahead. "Why are you back so soon? Did the girl push you out into the snow?" His voice was coming from a room that I didn't see the day before. When we entered, I knew why; it was his private living quarters. There was a small fire pit in the corner with a kettle sitting atop some kind of grill made out of coat hangars. A small, open cupboard with a few dishes stacked in it sat against the back wall. Next to it was some kind of trunk with the lid closed. On the right was a small cot pushed up against the wall, sheets neatly tucked in and a blanket folded on top, very military. To the left was a small table with one chair and sitting on the chair was Colonel Al sipping coffee and looking extremely smug.

"Miss Nicky!" he said sarcastically but with enthusiasm. "What brings you here so early in the morning and risking the cooling temperatures."

"I had a revelation last night and I wanted to tell you about it," I explained, not able to take my eyes off the cup the colonel held in his hand. "Do you think I could have a cup of coffee?"

"Why, yes, you probably could." He smiled and I felt an if coming.

"Thank you, it smelled so good coming in here and I haven't had a…"

"I will be happy to make you a cup of coffee after you tell me of your revelation." He said, again, with a sarcastic grin on his face.

"Seriously?" Of course, he was serious. "Whatever. Ok, last night, while I watched Max leave through the snow…"

"Leave?" he looked confused. "Where has the young pirate gone now?"

"He went to scout the Blood Demons," I explained.

"The who demons?" Was he kidding? How could he not know about the Blood Demons? Humph, I guess he didn't know everything after all.

"You know? The Blood Demons," I said. "They're the group that Emma Lee escaped from."

"The lady from the south?" he asked.

"Wow, something you don't know. Go figure. Let me explain." I started telling him about the group of evil men who had totally destroyed Emma Lee's old community, killing everybody. I also explained that she was convinced they were on their way up here and feared for our lives. "…and that's why Max left-to find out where they are and if they're really on their way here."

"Do you think he'll find them?" he asked.

"I don't know," I answered. "I never really thought about it. I just assumed he would. Max seems very good at finding

62

groups of people up to no good. Can I have a cup of coffee now? I think I've told you enough to deserve one."

"You know, just because a man has done wrong in his life does not mean he will always do wrong. It just means at one particular time, somewhere in his past, he made a bad decision. He shouldn't have to pay for it for the rest of his life. The young pirate means well and has tried very hard to do what is right for you people." He sounded angry with me for questioning Max's integrity and it irked me. I was allowed to have doubts about Max. It was my life after all. "I still haven't heard what your revelation was so, no, there will be no coffee poured into a cup for you yet, my dear. Private, bring me your cup." Barker walked over to the cupboard and grabbed a tin cup from the top shelf and brought it over to the colonel. I watched in disbelief as Colonel Al reached for the kettle and filled the cup with hot coffee and then placed it on the floor in front of Barker. I watched in disbelief as the dog sniffed at the hot liquid and started licking it up. "Careful Private! It's hot! Don't want to burn your tongue and ruin the taste of everything else today."

"Oh, that's nice. Well, as long as the dog gets coffee," I muttered under my breath, not believing, yet, somehow, not surprised that Barker got coffee before I did. I shook my head. "Okay then, the reason I'm here. Last night as I watched Max leave through the snow, I realized something."

"Yes?"

"It's winter!" I looked at him as if this would enlighten him as well.

"And...?"

"And..." I tried to urge him forward, to where my mind was but he wasn't budging. "Don't you see?" Still no acknowledgement. "It's winter and before that it was fall and before that it was summer and..."

"...before that it was spring." He looked annoyed at me. "Yes, child I know that; it happens all the time. Honestly, Private, I'm really thinking of asking for your discharge papers. This girl is hopeless. Young Nicky, this is all part of life; spring, summer, fall, winter repeat. It happens all the time."

"Yes, but not if you live in a place with no time," I smiled. "Yesterday you told me that time doesn't exist down here and that we're stuck here because of it, right?"

"Yes, that is my belief," he said.

"Then why do we have seasons?" I asked.

"I explained that to you..." he started.

"Yeah, I know; physics. That's what you said yesterday," I said. "But I don't buy it."

"There is no buying physics, Nicky," he laughed, but I detected a hint of doubt. "You either abide by its laws or you simply do not exist."

"But, don't you see? This is all about physics." How could I explain this to him when I didn't even understand all the science behind it myself? "The changing seasons is time, having night and day is time, everything we do and say is time!"

"Nicky, I…" He stopped, looking confused. That's good! That meant he was considering what I was saying.

"You see, time is not just any old dimension like 2D or 3D, it's a measurement," I tried hard to explain this to him. "It's a measurement that we can not exist without."

"What do you mean?" He had risen from his chair and nervously stood with his hands crossed in front of him, his foot tapping rigorously on the floor.

"Well, like, like," I searched my mind for something to explain it. "Like me coming here! It took time, see? Or me even telling you this; it takes time. Everything we do or say is measured by how long it takes: time. It exists here; it has to. I think it exists everywhere, otherwise we would be frozen in the millisecond we came here."

Colonel Al sat back down, a bewildered look on his face. He didn't blink or make any sound. It almost looked like he wasn't even breathing. I didn't know if I should say anything or if I should go and shake him. After a few minutes he turned his eyes to Barker who was now sitting in front of him. He rubbed his eyes and shook his head.

"Colonel?" I asked not wanting to upset him.

"Finally, Private!" He spoke but not to me. Instead, he addressed Barker! Ooh! This man was so frustrating. "The girl proves her worth!"

"What?" Did he already think of this? Was his proclamation to me yesterday about there being no time only a test to see how much I knew about this stuff?

"Nicky, you are so right!" He got up from the chair and came towards me holding out his hand. I didn't know if I should take it or turn and run.

"I am?" I knew I was, but I just didn't think he would acknowledge it.

"Yes!" He shook my hand and then turned to the cupboard and grabbed a cup. "Of course, there is time! I don't know why I didn't think of it! All this time, no pun intended of course, and I never even considered it! Time exists! How can it not? I thought if I could get those blasted clocks to work…but that would be stupid, wouldn't it? The clocks have nothing to do with it. She's right, too. We do have seasons; winter has started hasn't it? It has to be something else. There has to be some other reason we're trapped down here. Oh, what a test the government has put on me, but I'll figure it out. Yes, I will. That's why I'm here, too. To figure it out. It has to be."

"Colonel?" He was talking so fast and I wasn't sure if he remembered that I was still here.

"Yes, Nicky!" He poured a cup of coffee and handed it to me. "You can sit at the table and I will sit here on the bed." We took our seats and I blew on the hot liquid in my cup, feeling the aroma of coffee fill my nostrils. "Tell me, Nicky, is quantum physics taught in every school now?"

"Quantum, what? No, it's not," I said. "I didn't even take regular physics. I mean, that's like math to the nth degree isn't it? No, I don't understand any of that stuff."

"Then how did you know about time?" he asked, and I looked at him, trying to decide if he was serious or not.

"Its common sense isn't it?" I said, with no intent of offense.

"Sure, be flippant with me, you've earned that right," he said with a smile on his face. "We must now figure out what's wrong with this dimension because I still believe that there's something that's keeping us from our former homes."

"I don't know, I've only been here for a short time," I took a sip of coffee and smiled at the taste. "I just know that we don't age; whatever age we were when we fell down here, that's the age we stay at."

"Yes, there is that," he said. We both sat quietly for a few minutes thinking about other possibilities.

"Hey, didn't you say that things break down differently here?" I asked.

"Break down?" he asked.

"Yeah, when you were in that potion room?" I prodded him.

"You mean the laboratory?" he asked, obviously not liking my name for it.

"Yeah, you were looking through the microscope and said that things break down differently here." He nodded. "Maybe that has something to do with it."

"Maybe, but what?"

"I don't know," I was getting frustrated. "You should let me tell the others. Maybe they can think of things we can't."

"What? That group of wayward souls?" He laughed at the thought.

"Yeah! What's wrong with us?" I was angered by the lack of respect he had for us. "We're not stupid, you know."

"I never said you were," he put up his hands in defence. "I just don't see anyone in your group understanding any of this. They're from different eras, different centuries. How could they possibly know about the advancements of science? I don't even know everything."

"You think I do?" I asked.

"You know about the latest gadgets and changes in technology." He said, trying to justify his remarks.

"Big deal! So, I know how to work a cell phone; lot of good that does me down here. That doesn't mean I know anything about science or physics!" I told him. "Robert's smart and has a huge collection of books. I bet you he has science books in there too. And Cornelius; Cornelius built himself a boat and used the stars to navigate himself here all the way from England. Could you have done that? In fact, he knows quite a bit about astronomy and would probably be a really good help."

"Do you think?" Could the soldier be wavering? I hoped so. I hated keeping secrets from everyone.

"It couldn't hurt," I said. "I mean, now that you know time actually exists, you really have been working at this for over forty years. Maybe some help from other people will make a difference."

"Yes," he whispered. I was forcing him to face the possibility that all his work was in vain and I could see it physically deflating him. I felt sorry for him. All this time believing one thing and finding out you were wrong. "I think you should leave now, Miss Nicky."

"Leave?" I could tell he wanted to be alone, but I wasn't so sure that was a good idea. "But maybe you should come, too. I could introduce you to everyone."

"No, I have work to do." He got up and urged me to do the same so he could escort me to the door. "I have to figure out what this all means; having time and everything."

"Yeah, but wouldn't you like some help with that?" I asked seeing that he seemed to be in some sort of dazed state. "Like I said, my friends would be willing to do whatever they could to help."

"Yes, that is what you said," he turned to me and put his hand on my shoulder. "Miss Nicky, I must not allow you to take the Private with you. He has to stay and help me with all these changes. Can you make it back on your own?"

"Through the tunnels?" I wasn't so sure I could. "I guess, but I'd much rather take the Private with me."

"No, he will be staying here," he left the room and started heading down the tunnel towards the room with the clocks and the room with the potions, Barker right behind him. "Goodbye Miss Nicky. I will see you later."

"Whatever." I turned and held my lantern out in front of me. I just hoped I could find my way out without getting lost.

Chapter 5

I made it back to Marshal's in one piece, surprisingly.
Actually, I only made two wrong turns in the tunnels and I
recognized my mistakes right away and correctly corrected
them. I rode Cocoa slowly through the fields, not wanting to
tire her out. I knew that Robert and Cornelius were going out
later to gather firewood. Now that the snow was here, we had
to be prepared for anything, even if that meant being snowed
in at Marshal's for days at a time. We certainly had enough
food and we could always melt snow for water. We just
needed to be able to keep ourselves warm.

I also thought about how I was going to explain Colonel
Al to them. Would they believe he was sent down here from
the American government or would they think he was some
kind of crazy wack job. I still didn't know what to believe.
One thing I still couldn't figure out was how he knew almost
everything about us and secret things too! Like me killing

Butcher! He knew how I did it; even how I felt when I did it. I also didn't like how Barker seemed to feel right at home with him. I couldn't handle thinking of him belonging to the colonel before I came here. I still thought of him as my dog.

I took Cocoa to her shelter and took her bridal off. I covered her back with a blanket to keep her warm and filled her trough with fresh hay and left half a bucket of oats for her. Her water had formed a thin layer of ice on top that I broke up and swirled around so she could get a proper drink. I gave her a quick pat on the neck and headed for the house.

It was quiet when I opened the door. I didn't hear anything; no voices or rustling of people moving around and getting up. Despite the fact that the sun was up, and the morning was well on its way, it was still dark in here. There being no windows meant that natural light couldn't make its way through. Instead we used candles and lanterns but only when we really had too. Most of the time we spent our days outside working or playing. I didn't see any light from anywhere and decided this meant that everyone was still asleep.

"Marshal?" I whispered softly, not wanting to wake him if, by chance, he had finally been able to sleep.

"Yes, yes, yes, Nicky?" he answered almost immediately.

"Oh, Marshal, did you get any sleep at all?" I asked, making my way to the table so I could sit with my friend.

72

Marshal took a match and lit the lantern so we could see each other.

"I get enough," he answered, sitting back and blowing out the match.

"I hope you're right," I said. "You know lack of sleep can do weird things to your brain. I read about it once online."

"Online?"

"Yeah, on the computer, you know, the internet…" I stopped, realizing my mistake. "…and you have no idea what I'm talking about do you?"

"Not a clue, clue, clue, Nicky but that's okay. I like when you talk about things from your life," he said. "It makes me happy to know that the world is still there."

"Yeah, it is, I guess," I said. "Is everyone still sleeping?"

"I think so," he answered. "At least I haven't heard anybody, not even the kids." That's how he referred to Billy and Kitten, 'the kids'.

"That's good," I said, relieved that I could tell Marshal about the colonel before telling anyone else. He was smarter than the others when it came to assess what was right down here and what could potentially lead to disaster. I wanted to know his opinion about Colonel Al's mission. "I'm glad I got back here before the others got up. I really wanted to talk to you about something before I tell anyone else, okay?"

"Nicky?" He was leaning forward, searching for something. "Where's Barker?"

"I left him," I answered.

"Left him?" he looked at me, confused. "I don't understand."

"Marshal, there's something I need to talk to you about," I started. "It's really important."

"Go ahead, Nicky, but can't you tell me where Barker is?" he asked again. Evidently, he had grown fond of Barker, too.

"That's part of what I want to tell you," I explained. "Marshal, you know about almost everyone who lives around here and beyond the woods, right?"

"Not almost, Nicky," he said proudly. "I know, know, know definitely about everyone."

"Okay." It was the answer I wanted to hear because if Marshal didn't know about the colonel than I knew for sure that no one else did. "Have you ever heard of or seen any soldiers out there, you know, around where the out-of-towners' camp was?"

"Soldiers? What kind of soldiers?" He seemed panicked. "Nicky, are they the Blood Demons?"

"No, no Marshal," I assured him. "There's only one soldier and he's no Blood Demon. He's actually with the United States army."

74

"Who is Nicky?" he asked, sitting forward and waiting for me to continue.

"This guy I met. His name is Colonel Albert Young and he says he's with the United States army and has been sent down here to bring us all back." I waited for his reaction.

"Bring us back where?"

"To the world we came from--home." I said. Marshal sat back and crossed his legs. He was silent for a few minutes, tapping his fingers on the table and staring straight ahead. "Marshal?"

"Nicky, Nicky, Nicky," he finally spoke, "my home does not exist anymore."

"What? Sure, it does," I said. "It's still there, Marshal. You just said you liked hearing about it."

"Oh, I believe it's there," he smiled. "But *my* home is gone."

"I don't get it."

"Nicky, I came here in 1909," he explained, and I was starting to understand what he was saying. "1909 doesn't exist anymore."

"Well, yeah, but the world is still there," I said. I hadn't thought about how time had passed and, if Marshal, or anyone else, went back nothing would be the same for them. I guess they would feel almost as scared as when they came down here in the first place. "I know it won't be the same, but it will be the real world and you'll fit in no problem."

"But I fit in here no problem," he said. "Going back now would be weird."

"Really?" I was surprised by his reaction. "But we have things up there that we'll never have down here. There's electricity and warm showers and lots and lots of food."

"Let's just forget about going back for now," he said, not willing to argue with me about it. "Who is the soldier boy? Where did he come from?"

"So, you've never seen any army guy before?" I asked. "He's about five-ten, five-eleven, slender, black hair with a little grey. He's maybe forty, forty-five. You've never seen him before?"

"No, no, no, never," he stated, confirming what Colonel Al had told me; he kept well hidden. "Did he just fall with the last 360?"

"No," I explained. "apparently he's been here since 1967."

"That long? Where's he been? I've never even heard of any soldier boy out in the woods!"

"Are you sure, Marshal?" I asked. "No one's *ever* mentioned him before? Or *seen* him before?"

"I'm sure, sure, sure, Nicky," he sounded very positive that this was the first time he had ever heard of the colonel. "Is that where Barker is? With this soldier boy?"

"Yeah, that's where he is now and that's where he was when he was missing for over four months," I told him, "and, apparently, that's where he was before I found him my first day here. It seems my Barker, or Private as the colonel calls him, has been living, out there, with the colonel for a long, long time."

"But I thought he fell at the same time you did. You found him in the city, didn't you?" I nodded. "So, you're telling me that he walked all the way from the woods to the city, found you and decided to live with you for awhile before going back to this colonel?"

"I guess," I said.

"That makes no sense, Nicky!"

"Yeah, I know, but there are a lot of things down here that don't make any sense." Now, it was my turn to sit back and pause. Marshal was pointing out things that I had never thought of. Colonel Al did mention that Barker went to the city every 360 waiting for someone like me to fall but, how did he know that I would even find him? He didn't exactly come looking for me. As I recall, he stood in the middle of the street barking until someone, me, finally found him and calmed him down. Did he know that I wouldn't be able to ignore a barking dog?

"Nicky?" I didn't realize Marshal was talking to me.

"Yeah?" I looked at my friend and wondered if Colonel Al could be some kind of a threat to us. I thought him harmless before but now I wasn't so sure.

"I asked you where this soldier boy lived," he said. "If he's in the woods, then maybe he's part of Pig's old camp?"

"I don't think so," I told him. "He said he knew about Pig's camp and he knew that we destroyed it, but *I* never saw him there and he most definitely doesn't *look* like one of Pig's men."

"Okay, so why don't I know about him?" he asked. "Where does he live?"

"He lives in an old abandoned mine," I said. "It's past Pig's, up the river and built into the side of a kind of hill. He camouflages it with branches; I had a hard time seeing it when I first went there."

"An abandoned mine?" he looked surprised. "I never saw any mine out there before. Weird, weird, weird."

"What's weird?" It was Billy. The boy must have gotten up while we were talking.

"You are," I laughed and messed his hair up. He reminded me so much of my brother.

"Aw, come on, Nicky. Tell me what's weird," he was making a face as he said this, and I tried hard not to laugh at him. "I heard you guys talking. It sounded real serious."

"It is serious, Billy," I said, "but I'd rather tell everyone together, so I don't have to repeat myself."

"Do you want me to wake everybody up?" He looked excited at the prospect. "I can if you want."

"Yes, yes, yes Billy," said Marshal. "I'm sure you can but maybe let's just wait a bit. Do you want something to eat?"

"Okay!" It was so easy to deflect his train of thought. "Do you got any puffs?" Puffs was what Billy called apple turnovers. We had baked some the other day and it was all we could do to keep Billy from eating them all.

"I think there's a couple left," said Marshal. "Enough for you and Kitten to have one for breakfast. Do you want some tea with it as well?" Robert brought his stash of tea with him when he moved his stuff over, and we all enjoyed a cup here and there. It wasn't as good as the coffee I had with Colonel Al this morning, but it was nice and hot on a cold day like today.

"Yeah, that would be nice," Billy was licking his lips in anticipation. "Can I at least go get Kitten? I won't wake up anyone else, I promise. Please! She'll be real mad if I eat a puff without her."

"I don't see why not," I said. "I'm sure she'd appreciate it." He took off to get the little girl, leaving me and Marshal alone once again. "I didn't finish telling you everything about Colonel Al."

"I figured," he said as he proceeded to get out two plates, two cups and put the water on to boil. "You'll say more when you tell everyone else, though, right?"

"Right," I sat back and waited for everyone to get up.

Half an hour later the house was buzzing with activity. Billy, it turned out, was not very quiet when he woke up Kitten and with the two of them giggling and running back and forth; it didn't take long before the others were yawning and stretching their way to the 'stove room'.

They were surprised to learn that I had already been out with Cocoa and asked where we went. They wanted to know where Barker was too, but I tried to put their questions off. I wanted to wait for everyone to get up and gather so I could tell them all at once. Like I told Billy, I only wanted to explain Colonel Al once so, I sat back and watched as each person got up, made tea and took a seat somewhere in the room. After everyone was there, Robert spoke up.

"Okay, Nicole," he said as he relaxed on the couch with his cup of tea. "We're all here and waiting for an explanation for Barker's recurring disappearance."

"Right," I stood in the middle of the room to address them all. "As you all know; Barker was gone from our lives for over four months. He took off before Pig's camp burned down and no one saw him once; not even a trace. He just seemed to have vanished and I was starting to give up hope of ever seeing him again; until yesterday. That's when I actually hiked into the forest to find him."

"Oh, Nicky," said Emma Lee. "You shouldn't have done that. Who knows what could be waiting for you out there?"

"Well, it's not Ryan," I said, a little frustrated that they thought my ex-classmate was still out there, lurking.

"That's not the only worry," said Cornelius, trying to back up Emma Lee. "There're still members of Pig's group that could be out there and I don't imagine they would be very friendly, especially towards you. After all, you were the one who started the fire."

"Do you really think they hung around?" I asked sarcastically. "I mean everything they know is gone; no camp, no home, no leader. They're probably long gone. No one's seen them, unless you count the guy Max shot at Betty's. She said he was on his way north to live with the northerners when he stopped to rob her. She also said that the guy told her that the other out-of-towners were going that way too."

"Yes, but who knows if they're telling the truth," Cornelius said. "Nigel and Betty are afraid of their own shadows. They could have been coaxed into telling us one thing and, meanwhile, the out-of-towners could very well be somewhere planning our takeover."

"Ya think?" I didn't think any of Pig's men were smart enough to plan a takeover. They needed a leader and the only way they would get that was if they went up north. Either that or they'd be killed. From what I'd heard of the northerners, they aren't much better than the out-of-towners. "I doubt it."

"Regardless of where Pig's men went, I don't think it has any bearing on what Nicole is telling us," Robert said, sounding just as irritated. He was tired of listening to this same argument day after day.

"Right, mate," Cornelius said, focusing back on my story, "carry on."

"Okay," I gathered my thoughts, again, and continued where I left off. "Yesterday, when I hiked into the forest, I saw this man…"

"What man?" It was Billy and Robert glared at him for interrupting. "Sorry…"

"…I saw this man hiding behind a tree," I said. "At first, I thought you guys were right; that it was Ryan and he was going to jump out and attack me or something, but it wasn't. It was a man dressed in army fatigues. I thought he was spying on me and I wanted to find out why so, I followed him. Well, chased him is more like it.

"When I finally caught up with him, he wasn't alone." I said. "He had Barker with him. I asked who he was, and he told me his name was Colonel Albert Young and he was with the United Stated army. Have any of you ever seen or heard of an army guy living in the woods?"

"Not me," answered Billy. "Is he really an army guy?"

"Yes, Billy, he is," I answered. "How about anyone else? Army guy; about forty, forty-five? Kitten?" Kitten lived in Pig's camp for a long time. Maybe she knew things that we didn't.

"No, I don't know about an army guy," she spoke so softly that I could barely hear her.

"I've never heard of him either, Nicole," said Robert.

"Nor I," added Cornelius.

"Don't look at me," said Emma Lee. "I haven't been here that long. I didn't know you guys existed six months ago."

"So, who is this Colonel Young?" asked Robert.

"Well, Colonel Al told me he was sent down here by the American government with a mission to complete," I explained.

"What mission?" asked Billy.

"The mission to send us all back home," I answered. I looked around and saw confusion and disbelief on all their faces. "He's been working on it for years."

"And you believe him?" asked Robert.

"I didn't at first," I said. "But he took me to this old abandoned mine where he's been working and I saw what he's been doing and I think he could be legit or, at least, *he* believes he's legit."

"You followed him to an old abandoned mine?" asked Emma Lee. "Nicky, are you crazy? You don't know who this man is, what he intended?"

"He's perfectly harmless," I said. "Besides, I can handle myself."

"I'm afraid I must agree with Emma Lee on this one, Nicole," said Robert and I felt hurt that he didn't trust my instincts. "It was rather foolish to follow a strange man anywhere. You should have waited until one of us was with you."

"Well, I didn't have time to wait for anyone," I said, getting angry. "He had Barker and wasn't going to let him leave with me. I had to go with him."

"How come he had Barker?" asked Billy.

"Because Colonel Al told me that Barker belongs to him," I said. "Well, he refers to him as Private, but whatever. Apparently, Barker's been living with him for a few 360s."

"He thinks the dog is a Private?" asked Robert. "That doesn't sound very sane to me Nicole."

"I don't think he thinks Barker is a real Private." I said, laughing. Of course, he thought Barker was a real Private, but

I couldn't tell them that. That would totally give the wrong impression of Colonel Al. "I think Barker's been his only friend over the years and he just talks to him like he's a person that's all. He does understand it's just a dog."

"So, what you're telling us is that there's a member of the United States army sent down here by his government to get us all out of this place and back to the world we came from and he's been doing this since…"

"1967," I said.

"Ok, he's been doing this since 1967 with the help of a dog whom he refers to as 'Private'," Robert said. "Is that correct?"

"Yeah." It sounded pretty bizarre when Robert said it.

"Okay," Robert said. "So, he took you to his workshop?"

"Yes," I answered. "It's in this abandoned mine. He has a room set up with a bunch of clocks that are wired together, and he has a generator and batteries."

"He has a generator?" asked Robert, suddenly sounding interested.

"Yeah, but it doesn't work," I said. "Nothing works down here."

"Why all the clocks?" asked Cornelius.

"Because he's convinced that time doesn't exist down here," I explained. "He figured that if he could somehow get the clocks to work, he could get time to work and then that would get us back home."

"Well, that *is* what's happened down here isn't it?" asked Emma Lee. "Time has stopped, right? That's why we don't age."

"That's what I thought, too," I said and then explained why I thought this was wrong.

"I don't understand," said Emma Lee. "Aging takes time and we don't do that; so, no aging, no time."

"Nicky is right," said Cornelius. "But I daresay so are you darling."

"What do you mean, mean, mean?" asked Marshal. I was curious about Cornelius's answer too.

"You see, we do have day and night and seasons, proving that time exists," he said. "But we never age. Quite the conundrum."

"And do you have the answer?" asked Robert.

"It's simple really," Cornelius felt a bit of superiority that he had thought of something no one else had. "We're stuck."

"We all know we're stuck, Cornelius," I said, not understanding what he was saying.

"But we're not just stuck here," he said. "We're stuck in some sort of time wheel; repeating the turn of the wheel over and over again. That's why we don't age; we can't. We can only go so far and then we're back to start the turn of the wheel again."

"That makes sense!" said Robert, excited by this.

"See? I knew you guys were smart," I said, silently saying a *'hah'* at Colonel Al. I was right my friends *can* help with the mission. "You guys have to meet the colonel and tell him this. You'll really help him in his mission."

"What else has this man been doing besides trying to get a clock to tick?" asked Cornelius. "Surely, he's worked on other things over the years."

"Yeah," I said. "He has some old circuit boards hooked up to radios and he's working on some kind of simulator. I think he's trying to establish communication with his government. He has a chemistry lab too, with tubes and beakers full of different kinds of liquid."

"A scientist?" Robert seemed happy about this. "Does he seem to know what he's doing with these beakers and tubes?"

"I think so," I said. "He told me that things break down differently down here."

"How would he know that?" asked Robert.

"I don't know," I started, "but he was looking through a microscope when he said it."

"Humph!" mumbled Robert.

"What?" I asked.

"It's just odd that a colonel in the army would have scientific training," he said.

"I don't know," I said, shrugging my shoulders. "All I know is that he says he's from the army. He's dressed like a soldier and he's been living out in the woods for over forty years and nobody even knew it. Nobody's ever seen him or heard of him so, he's pretty discreet. He seems a bit weird, but I figure that's probably because he's had no one to talk to for so long. I think he genuinely believes that he knows what he's doing but, I don't know if I believe he's been sent here or if he just fell and can't come up with any other explanation for being here. But I think he could be on to something. Maybe we can go back home if we work at it. I think you guys should come with me and meet him and tell me what you think. We can go tomorrow if you want. What do you think?"

"Sure, Nicky," said Marshal. "I'll come with you." The rest nodded their heads and agreed to come too.

Chapter 6

The next day we all made our way to the abandoned mine. I was glad everyone agreed to meet Colonel Al. I was interested to hear their opinions of him. Even if they thought he was crazy, it was a good idea to look for a way out of here. At least he was doing something. It was hard to accept the fact that we were stuck here, forever. I felt more alive today than I did yesterday just thinking about it. I didn't like it here. I didn't like playing the game of survival of the fittest. It screwed with your mind and made you do things you would never have even thought of doing before. If there was even a chance I could leave, I was going to take it.

It was chilly again today, guaranteeing that whatever snow was on the ground was going to stay there for now. I wore gloves and a hat and kept my face deep within the collar of my coat. The wind was strong across the fields, stinging my cheeks and making my nose run. We left Cocoa back at

Marshal's, grazing on the grass before it was completely covered with snow. Billy and Kitten seemed to be the only ones that enjoyed the cold. They kept running around, playing tag and trying to gather enough snow to make snowballs. It was fun to watch them.

When we finally got to the mine, Barker was sitting outside the entrance waiting for us. I walked over to him and scratched him behind his ears. He wagged his tail and licked my face obviously happy to see me. The others looked at him with surprise.

"How'd he know we were coming Nicky?" asked Marshal.

"Barker has more secrets than any of us I think," I said.

"That he does," said Cornelius.

I made sure that we brought a lantern and I lit it as we entered the mine and its maze of tunnels. Barker led the way and kept looking back to make sure we were all there. When we finally made it to the clock room, the others looked just as confused as I was the first time I came here. After coming up empty again in the radio room we went on to the lab and, sure enough, that's where he was, sitting at the table and staring into the microscope. He didn't appear to notice our presence.

"Colonel Al?" I asked. He never looked up. "Colonel Al? I've brought my friends to meet you." Still, he kept his eyes on the microscope, not even nodding his head to acknowledge that we were there.

"Sir? Nicole has told us about your research…" Robert stepped forward.

"Nicole?" Colonel Al lifted his head and looked at us. "Why do you get to call her Nicole when the rest of us refer to her as Nicky?"

"Sir?" Robert was surprised by this question. It wasn't the greeting he had expected.

"It's okay colonel," I jumped in. I really didn't want our first encounter with everyone present to start with a stupid argument. "Robert can call me Nicole. We had this discussion a long time ago."

"Really?" He returned his gaze to the microscope, silent once again. The others looked at me as if it was my fault the colonel was being rude. I rolled my eyes and shrugged my shoulders. Then, all of a sudden, Colonel Al stood up and walked over to where we were standing. "Nice to meet everyone. Robert, Marshal, Cornelius, Emma Lee, Billy and Kitten." He nodded and shook their hands as he said each name. They looked stunned that he knew who each one of them were. "Max, I've been told, is off to find blood people. I'm sorry I'm not able to meet him right now."

"Colonel?" I said. "I've told my friends about your mission and they said they'd be willing to help."

"Is that right?" he smiled and folded his hands behind his back. "Actually, I was just studying a bit of what I thought was coal under my microscope when you came in. It's quite fascinating and a little confusing. You see, coal is supposed to burn at a high temperature, causing water to boil into steam, which can power a turbine, therefor creating electricity which is really what I'm after here. If I had power, I could finally make my instruments work but every sample I've analyzed has proved useless."

"What's wrong with it?" asked Billy, his ten-year-old mind full of questions.

"Well, Billy," he leaned down so he could speak directly to the boy, "every sample I've analyzed is not what it appears to be."

"What is it?" asked Billy.

"I don't know," said the colonel. "It's some kind of rock that I've never seen before. The Private keeps bringing me samples, insisting that I study it, but I haven't been able to figure out exactly what it is."

"An unknown substance?" It was Marshal, now and I looked at him. Did he know about this? He didn't look like someone who knew about rocks and minerals. "That's weird, weird, weird."

"No weirder than your need to repeat yourself," Colonel Al laughed and turned back to his microscope. Marshal looked down, embarrassed that his habit of talking in threes was spoken out loud. I didn't know why Marshal did that, I'd never asked him, and I certainly would never chastise him for it or call him out on it, which is what I felt the colonel just did.

"Don't be such an ass!" I scolded him. "He only made an observation."

"Did he?" He pulled his army cap down and took in a deep breath. "My apologies."

"It's okay," said Marshal. "It's strange, though, that there should be an unknown rock here don't you think. I know that the mountains around here are mostly shale and limestone. If there's a foreign substance, that would be something new."

"Yes, yes that's what I thought too," Colonel Al seemed excited that Marshal knew about the rock that made up the mountains. I, too, was surprised that the crazy red head knew so much. "Come, look here." He urged Marshal to the microscope to take a look. "This is sample number 11, 376. See if you can make out what it is. I took this from rock I dug up two weeks ago just north of here. It was really the Private that started digging it up, but I thought it was a good idea to analyze it with all my other samples."

"North? How far north?" Marshal sat at the table and peered through the microscope. "Oh my, this is not right."

"I know, I know," exclaimed Colonel Al.

"Careful," said Marshal. "You're repeating yourself."

"Hah! You caught me." The two of them became immersed in talk of rocks and minerals. I was lost and by the looks of everyone else, so were they. Then Colonel Al looked over to us and smiled. "Nicky, why don't you show them the clocks. I'm sure that might interest them."

"We've seen the clocks," I said. "It isn't really that interesting. I thought, maybe, you could…"

"Nicole, I don't think we should interfere with them right now," said Robert and I looked at him confused. "We can go look at the clocks. I'd actually like to have a closer look at them."

"Really?" There must be another reason I thought. "Okay, then. Marshal? Are you going to be okay in here?" They were back at the microscope and Marshal was looking over notes that Colonel Al had taken.

"Yes, yes, yes, Nicky," he said with a note of excitement in his voice. "Me and the colonel will be fine. You guys go." He went back to the notes and began talking away to the colonel again.

"All righty, Robert, let's go." The rest of us turned and headed for the clocks.

"This is really not where I wanted to go," said Robert when we got there.

"That's good," said Cornelius, "because I don't think I could be of any help in here. I've never really lived by the tick tock of a clock."

"I don't get it," I said. "Why'd you want to come here then?"

"Because, I thought we could look around while they were busy talking about rocks. Maybe search for information about this mission the, uh, colonel is on," he explained.

"Oh, I see," I said. "Hey, does that mean that Marshal doesn't really know anything about rocks? Was this something you guys planned?"

"On the contrary, Nicole," said Robert. "Marshal's knowledge comes as a complete surprise to me as well. I just saw it as an opportunity to find out more about this Colonel Albert Young."

"Yes, he does seem a little off, doesn't he?" Cornelius pointed out.

"Maybe he's a spy!" exclaimed Billy who, surprisingly had been quiet up until now. "That would be so cool."

"Yeah!" added Kitten.

"Oh, I don't think he's that," said Emma Lee.

"Whatever he is, let's not waste time talking about it," said Robert. "Let's look around while we still can."

We broke into two groups: Robert, Cornelius and Billy in one group; Emma Lee, Kitten and I in the other. Barker stayed with me which I didn't mind at all. He knew these tunnels better than anyone and if we got lost, he could guide us back.

I had already been to Colonel Al's living quarters, so I headed the other way. I had the lantern we came in here with and I kept an eye on the flame. I was still a little scared that the oxygen would run out if we went too far into the side of the hill. The tunnel went for a long stretch and was starting to get narrower by the time we came to another room. It had a small doorway and we ducked to get inside. It looked freshly dug out with walls of dark gray and pieces of rock strewn all over the floor. Other than that, there really wasn't anything in here and I wondered if this was where Colonel Al was getting his samples from. I picked up one of the rocks and sniffed it. It had a faint smell of sulphur like everything else in these tunnels.

"What on earth do you think this is?" asked Emma Lee and I turned to see her holding up some kind of chisel.

"I think it's a chisel," I said as I examined the rather large tool. "A big one at that. He must have used it to get the rock out of the wall. There's probably a hammer around here somewhere, too. It looks like he just dug out this room not long ago."

"I would say so," said Emma Lee. "It's done rather haphazardly though."

"What do you mean?" I asked.

"Well, when we built our town in the mining tunnels," she said. "we made sure it was well ventilated and had supports everywhere, especially in the doorway. He hasn't done any of that. He just seemed to have burrowed into the wall at random with no thought of collapse." I had forgotten that she had experience with tunnels and mines. She knew what she was talking about and that's what worried me. If she said there were no supports for this room, then we probably shouldn't be standing in here.

"Let's go," I said. "I think we should just head back. There's no way we should be wandering these tunnels without any knowledge of what's here."

"I agree," she said. "Come, Kitten, hold my hand so I don't lose you." The little girl grabbed Emma Lee's hand and we headed back to meet the others.

"I don't think we learned anything, maybe the others did," I said.

"I think we learned a little," said Emma Lee.

"Like what?" I asked.

"Well, for one thing, Colonel Young is starting to lose his sanity," she said.

"Why do you think that?" asked Robert as we met in the clock room once more.

"Because the room we found was hastily built," explained Emma Lee, "with no supports or ventilation. It's like he's in a rush to finish his experiments."

"Or, he's desperate to find answers," said Robert.

"What did you guys find?" I noticed that Robert was holding some kind of paper in his hands.

"I got this from his trunk," he said, handing me the paper. I looked at it and tried to figure out what it was.

"What is this?" I asked.

"You tell me," he said. "It looks like some kind of order from the American government, but he's crossed things out and added his own writing in here and there. It looks like he's changed whatever was written there to describe what he's doing here." I looked at the document and noticed how much force was used to cross out some of the typewritten lines. What had been written here and why did the colonel change it? If he was sent here on a mission wouldn't he have orders written clearly, maybe even a list of procedures he was to follow? I turned the paper over and held it up to the lantern, trying to see if I could decipher some of the typewritten words.

"Was this all you found in the trunk?" I asked.

"No," said Cornelius, "there were more uniforms, some medals, his identification papers that say he is who he says he is; Colonel Albert Young. He has no weapons. There are a few pictures of him with some other soldiers that look much younger than him and these orders."

"Hmm," I said.

"Nicole?" asked Robert. "What year did he say he started this mission?"

"1967," I answered.

"What was happening in the world in 1967, Nicole?" asked Robert.

"I don't know," I said. "I wasn't even born yet. I don't even think my mother was born yet!"

"Yes, but surely you know of the world's events," Robert urged. "Did you not learn about it in history? Was there a war or some other tragic event?"

"Oh, yeah," I said, remembering some of the movies my dad watched about it. "Vietnam happened in the '60's. Vietnam and lots and lots of hippies."

"Vietnam? Do you mean French Indo-China?" asked Robert.

"I don't know," I had never heard it called that before. "I just know there was a war in Vietnam in the '60's. I think Russia was involved and so were the States."

"A war?" asked Robert.

"Yeah, but the States didn't do so good," I said, trying to recall any information I had stored in my memory about the Vietnam war. "I think they lost."

"Lost?" asked Emma Lee and I could see the disappointment on her face for her country.

"Yeah," I said, "but it's not like the Vietnamese conquered the States or anything. I think Vietnam's divided into north and south and the Americans were over there helping the south and they lost so all the soldiers came home."

"How long did this war take?" asked Robert.

"I don't know," I said. I felt kind of dumb but American history was not a big priority in school. We spent most of our time on First Nations, the economy and World War I and II in Social Studies. "I think it wasn't over until the mid '70's."

"So, in 1967, the United States was at war in Vietnam and they chose to send a colonel down here instead of to a war they were losing?" Robert asked no one in particular.

"It makes no sense," said Cornelius. "Why would they send such a high-ranking officer down here?"

"I don't know," I said. "but there are lots of conspiracy theories about things the American government is involved in."

"Like what?" asked Robert.

"Like hiding aliens, selling weapons, creating diseases. Some people even think they shot their own president," I said.

"Aliens?" said Billy, suddenly excited. "Like UFO's and Roswell?"

"Yeah," I said, surprised that he new about Roswell. "How'd you know about all that?"

"My dad told me," he said. "He said that there was a flying saucer that crashed in the States and that they had these aliens and they were trying to cut them up and do experiments on them!"

"That's right," I said. "Roswell happened around the same time as you lived up there."

"You mean there are actual living things from the sky here?" Emma Lee seemed scared by this.

"It makes sense that the stars and planets have creatures on them," said Cornelius. "The universe is so vast it would be a shame if we were alone in it."

"This still doesn't help us with Colonel Al," I said. "Is he really here to get us out or is he just another person who fell down here and is trying to make sense of it?"

"We could just ask him." We all stopped talking and looked at the little girl who, until now, barely ever spoke and never gave an opinion on anything.

"Kitten's right," I said. "That would be our best bet. No more questions or assumptions; we'll just ask him."

"Well, you should ask him," said Emma Lee. "He knows you best."

"She's right, Nicole," said Robert, "you should ask him and the sooner the better. We'll go get Marshal and go back.

You stay here and talk to the colonel and try to get some answers."

"Me?" I asked and they all nodded. I felt my stomach flip with the thought of questioning Colonel Al. He didn't exactly have a stable personality. "Okay, whatever, I'll talk to him, but I don't know how much information I'll get. He doesn't seem very open to sharing secrets." Barker came to my side and licked my hand. "Are you going to stay with me?" I looked down into the brown eyes of my dog. He licked my hand again and gave out a whimper. I guess he wanted me to talk to the colonel too.

Chapter 7

I sat at the small table in Colonel Al's living quarters, staring into the cup of coffee he had just made me. The others made up excuses and left over half an hour ago. I helped clean up the lab and tried to show some enthusiasm as the colonel rambled on about the rock samples. Barker stayed by my side and was now lying at my feet. I think he realized that I needed his support. Now, if I could just find the courage to ask Colonel Al about Vietnam and why he was here instead of there.

"I have a feeling you have something on your mind," he said before I could ask him anything. I guess I should just plow ahead with the interrogation. Either he would welcome the chance to answer my questions or he would get angry and throw me out. "What is it?"

"I-or, rather, we wanted to ask you some questions," I started, turning my cup around and around.

"We?"

"Yeah, me and the others," I said. "Well they asked me to ask you."

"Go ahead," he urged me. "You know, you were right about them; it *was* a good idea I met them and enlisted their help. Take Marshal, for instance. I had no idea the young man knew so much about rocks and minerals."

"Yeah, Marshal kind of amazes me with a lot of things," I said.

"So, ask your question," he urged me. "I don't mind."

"Okay, I-uh-I wanted to, uh, we wanted to know…" I took another drink of coffee.

"Spit it out!" He was starting to lose his patience. I should just go ahead and ask.

"Tell me about Vietnam," I said, looking him straight in the eye. He let out a long breath and got up from the cot. He walked over to the kettle and started making himself another coffee.

"What do you want to know?" he asked. "Vietnam is a country in Asia and we, we being the United States of America, are involved in their civil war, trying to keep freedom from being destroyed."

"And…" I prompted.

"And...what?" He returned to the cot and calmly sat down.

"And, did you fight in this war?" I asked.

"Of course, I did," he said. "I'm a colonel and I commanded my men proudly."

"And, in 1967 the war was still going on?"

"Yes," he answered, narrowing his eyes.

"So, why did the government all of a sudden decide to send you down here instead of back there?" I got it out and waited for the fallout.

"I don't ask why the government does anything," he answered but, somehow, I didn't think he was telling me everything. "I just know they wanted me down here."

"How long were you in Vietnam?" I asked.

"What does that have to do with it?"

"I just wanted to know," I said. "I've heard stories of how bad it was over there."

"Stories?" he laughed, hesitantly and I thought I could see his hand shake just a little. "Who told you stories?"

"I don't know. We learned in school and there were movies made about it."

"Movies?" he laughed again but there was no humour behind it. He was upset. "Did you hear that Private? Movies were made. Well, that proves it then; the war in Vietnam was bad. Sweetie, war is always bad."

"I know," I said, trying not to let his sarcastic attitude get to me. I asked my questions as tactfully as I could. "But the Vietnam war was particularly bad wasn't it?"

"Why are you asking me this?" he asked, and I could see some of his bravado cracking.

"I-we wanted to know if your work down here is genuine," I said.

"Why wouldn't it be?" he looked confused now like I had caught him off guard.

"You know there's a difference between being sent down here and falling down here," I said, looking him straight in the eye.

"You don't believe me," he said and leaned his head down.

"Maybe you don't remember how you really got here," I said. "And that's okay. Waking up and finding yourself in a whole other dimension when you didn't even know that other dimensions existed and finding out that no one you know is here really sucks. It's even worse when you find there're others here from all over the timeline and that there's no way back. It plays tricks with your mind; makes you do things you never would have done before."

"Is that why you killed people?" he asked, turning the tables on me. I didn't like it.

"People?" I asked. "I only killed Butcher and that was in self-defence."

"You set fire to an entire camp," he pointed out. "That caused people to lose their homes, live in the wild and, maybe, die from it."

"That's a stretch," I said but inside I knew he could be right. I struggled with these thoughts everyday.

"Is it?" he looked doubtful. "I think you know better."

"Okay," I said. "Let's say what I did led to people getting hurt or possibly dying. Don't you think I've thought of that? Don't you think I live with that everyday? Don't you think I toss and turn at night, not able to sleep without thinking about it? Believe me, it eats away at me. It makes me question who I am; if I'm even good enough to be alive." Barker pushed my hand with his nose, making me pat him and feel the warmth he held for me. "But that's what I mean by it screws with your mind!"

"So, you've punished yourself, proving your human." He got up and put his cup on the table. "I haven't been able to do that yet."

"What do you mean?" I said. He didn't answer. "Tell me more about Vietnam. How long were you there?"

"You're not going to give this up, are you?"

"No."

"I did three tours," he answered me, still standing, his back to me. There was no emotion in his voice. "Three very active combat tours."

"That must have been hard," I tried to sympathize.

"Hard?" he laughed and spun around to face me. I was surprised by the pain I saw on his face. Had I finally broken through the barrier that held back his emotions? "How they expected anyone to keep returning to a country they knew very little about and command young men to kill..." He stopped himself and did his habitual lift his hat, rub his hand through his hair then return the hat. When he regained his composure, he continued.

"My first two tours went good. My men suffered small losses but nothing that was unusual. I liked my men and felt pain for the losses, but it was war and I could accept that men would die. Dying in war is acceptable, honorable." He was pacing now.

"And your third tour?" I asked.

"I had a platoon of boys," he said, and I could hear the pride in his voice; like a father's pride for his son. "I say boys because that's what they were, young, maybe eighteen, just out of high school. Mostly poor and uneducated because those were the ones who couldn't avoid the draft. It was my job to command their battles; ensure their success and, hopefully, keep them alive."

"And did you?" I whispered out the question, regretting what I felt the answer would be.

"Almost." He sat down, his shoulders deflated, ready to tell me everything and emotion dripping out of every word. "I sent them into the jungle, knowing it was probably full of traps. I had no choice; that's where the Viet Cong bastards hid." He let out a sigh before continuing. "The boys were making their way through, almost made it too, when it happened."

"What happened?" I asked, scared of what I might hear.

"The Viet Cong, that's what!" He looked down at the ground shaking his head; reliving every moment of the memory. I could see sweat forming on the back of his neck. "There was a girl, not much older than seven or eight, sitting at a fire, cooking something. She didn't look up at the soldiers, she just sat there stirring the pot. She looked scared, lost, alone. The boys tried to get her to talk; they put their weapons down and took off their helmets, so they didn't look so intimidating. Then Private Sanchez reached out to her, offering her a stick of gum. He got so close." He stopped and looked blankly into nothing, but his mind was seeing the scene as if it was being played out right in front of him. Then he took off his cap and crumpled it in his hands, pain contorting his face.

"What happened?" I asked.

"It was so fast," he went on, the truth obviously still too hard to believe. "Nobody could've predicted it."

"Colonel Al?" I wanted to comfort him, let him know that it was over, and he was safe now. I went to get up, but Barker sat up, wagging his tail and laid his head on my lap. I pat behind the ears and stayed sitting.

"It was the pot," he said. "It had to be."

"What was the pot?"

"The pot was where the explosives were, of course," he looked at me matter-of-factly, like I should know what he was talking about.

"Explosives?" I asked.

"When Sanchez leaned forward with the gum, he tripped a wire and the whole thing blew up," he laughed in a crazy sort of way. "The pot, the girl, Sanchez and anyone who was within ten feet of that fire got blown into pieces. Then everything became a blur."

"Tell me," I urged. I felt like it was helping him to talk about it.

"Well, my boys panicked of course," he said. "They were so young, you see. For most of them it was their first tour. How could they possibly know that a little girl would lure them into a trap?" He looked at me like he wanted me to answer. I shrugged my shoulders in a silent 'I don't know.'

"Well she did all right, and it caused all hell to break loose. The Viet Cong were there, you see. They were hiding, waiting for someone to approach the girl. They wanted to catch soldiers off guard, and they did." He looked at me and smiled.

"They came from everywhere," he continued, "from the trees, the ground, the sky; everywhere you looked was a VC. My boys started shooting. Every sound, every movement became a target." He got up and squeezed his head, trying to block out the noise that only sounded in his head.

"They were so young! Fresh out of high school, and out of their mama's arms. Christ, some of them didn't even shave yet!" He wiped the back of his arm across his sweating forehead, turning his back to me. "Bullets were flying, and men were falling quicker than blinking your eyes. My men, their men; what did it matter? Death doesn't give a rat's ass. There're no sides, no colour, no country, no race in death. There's only you and whatever god you pray to and the rest of the universe doesn't matter.

"Then, as quickly as the craziness started, it ended. Do you know what that means?" he asked, and I shook my head even though I knew he couldn't see me with his back turned. "It means that all the men from one side, every single one, was dead because men that are still alive make sound. They moan or groan or curse, but I heard nothing. That kind of silence can be deafening. I asked myself why? What the hell were we doing there? How could we hate a human being so much that we could kill them like that?" He snapped his fingers. "Especially ones we had never even met. We knew nothing of their lives, their dreams, their families, the women they loved and the ones they didn't, and they knew nothing of ours. Yet, we pulled out guns and knives and slaughtered one another without even batting an eye."

"What happened next?" I asked, knowing there was more to the story.

"The heat was so intense and the smoke from all the gunfire and explosives was thick as it settled onto the jungle floor. You could barely breathe. The putrid smell of blood from the fallen made you nauseous, wanting to puke up whatever was in your stomach." He stopped and put his hands on his hips and lowered his head. I could see his body shake and I felt for him. When the personal stories of war are told it's hard to imagine that anyone could live through the nastiness of it.

"And then what?" I asked.

"There was a sudden rustle of the bushes in front of us," he said. I could hear the turmoil in his voice; he didn't want to go on.

"And…"

"The bushes rattled, I raised my gun and fired without thinking." His face twisted in torturous memory and I could see tears forming in his eyes. "I fired and two little girls about five and six lay on the ground in front of me; I had killed them."

"Oh my god!" I put my hand to my mouth, not knowing what to say. I never expected this.

"I could only think of one thing; one reason why there were now three dead little girls."

"What?" I asked.

"The little girl by the fire was not a willing participant. The VC used her as bait and, if she didn't cooperate, they threatened to kill what must have been her sisters. So, she sacrificed her life believing it would spare her sisters. She would have, too, if I hadn't killed them." He finished his confession and looked like he had run a marathon with a thousand pounds strapped to his back. I got up and reached out to him. Barker stood to let me up. I wrapped my arms around Colonel Al and held him like I held Robert when Madge died. At first, he stood rigid, not knowing how to accept my compassion.

"I killed them, two little girls!" he said as he broke my embrace and tried to regain his composure. "I didn't even look; I just blindly pointed my gun and shot. What kind of commander was I?"

"You didn't know," I tried to console him. "How could you ever know that there would be two more girls in the bushes. It was war and so many crazy things happen in war. Just like down here; I didn't know Butcher and I just walked up to him and shot him."

"But he was an evil man intent on killing you. He deserved to die," he said. "These were two innocent children. They didn't deserve to die."

"It doesn't matter who you kill," I said. "It's the act of killing, itself, that destroys us. To actually believe, even for a second, that you have the power to decide that a life should end is arrogant and selfish of us no matter what you believe in."

"I didn't know what to do," he continued. "I told the men that survived to go back, and I ordered them not to tell anyone. I didn't want the government to know what I had done; to know what they had trained me to do. They *knew* what it was like there and yet they persisted in sending more and more men to fight their war. I didn't want to give them the satisfaction that they could use my horrible crime to force me back into battle."

"So, what did you do?" I asked as I sat back down at the table.

"I finished my tour and went back home to Fort Lewis in Washington," he said. "My tour was over, and I could finally be at home."

"And…?" I knew there was more.

"And they ordered me to go on a fourth tour," he said.

"Another tour?" I couldn't believe they would do that to him. He had already served three tours. Was that not enough?

"Yes," he said, "but I didn't go."

"What did you do?" I asked.

"I came here," he said.

"What do you mean?" I asked. "Is that how you got the assignment to come down here to rescue us?"

"No," he paused and then let out a sigh. "It means I left the army. I packed up a duffel bag and headed north to Canada."

"Wait a minute," I said. I was having a hard time understanding what this all meant. "You mean you didn't tell anyone? You just up and left the army? Are you allowed to do that?"

"No," he said. "I went AWOL and I'm pretty sure that I'll probably go to jail if I were to go back."

"So, you weren't sent down here?" I asked, knowing that he wasn't. Knowing that he had come up here to escape his government's orders to go back to war. I knew now that those orders were what was typed on that paper that Robert found.

But I still wanted some of it to be true. "Everything you told us about your mission is a lie? There is no secret government department and there are no people up there trying to get us out?"

"I think you know that I made that all up," he said, with just a tiny hint of regret.

"Then all these experiments, this mine it's just a lie?" I asked. "Then why'd you stay hidden? Why did you lie about finding a way back home?"

"I didn't lie!" he exclaimed. "This *is* a mission; *my* mission and I *am* trying to find a way home. I thought I was close a few times, too. I stayed hidden, at first, because I thought I had to. I didn't realize that I'd even entered another dimension. I was hiding from my government. I didn't leave the woods for months. I had no idea everything I knew was gone. I thought I would be arrested if I ever showed my face."

"So, why'd you finally come out to see this new world? Who explained to you where you are?" I asked.

"It was the Private," he said, pointing at Barker. "He found me about five years after I came here. He showed me the tunnels and told me about my mission."

"Colonel Al," I started, "you know that the Private is a dog! He can't talk, he can't give you orders. He can only bark and growl and that's about it."

"You're wrong," he said.

"I'm not wrong," I was angry that he still insisted that Barker was some kind of Private in his army telling him what to do. He'd admitted to all his other lies, why not tell the truth about Barker? "I'm pretty sure dogs don't talk."

"What if he's not a dog? What if he's only disguised as a dog?" he asked.

"What else could he be?" I asked. "I think you've been through some traumatic things and your mind plays tricks with you sometimes. It's okay, well, I mean it's not *really* okay. You lied to me and all my friends, but we can forgive that. But this belief that Barker, this dog, can talk and is giving you missions to accomplish has to stop."

"Ask him!" he said.

"I'm not going to…"

"Ask him!"

"Fine!" I turned to my dog who was sitting in the middle of the room, watching us argue. "Barker, can you talk?" Nothing.

"Call him Private."

"Private?" I rolled my eyes and let out a sigh. "Can you tell me why you gave this mission to the colonel?" Barker looked at me and tilted his head with his ears cocked. He let out a small whine and came and started licking my fingers. I looked at Colonel Al, "See? He's just a dog."

"Very well, Private," he stood up, "if that's the way it's going to be then I suggest the two of you leave. I need time to assess the situation."

"You want us to leave?"

"That's what I said isn't it? Or can you not understand English all of a sudden?" He was angry now.

"Okay, I'll leave," I stood up and made my way to the tunnels. I turned to say goodbye. "I'm sorry for what happened to you in Vietnam. I hope you can learn to forgive yourself because you can't change it. It was an accident and it's over; you have to go on."

"I will try to heed your advice but it's going to be hard," he said, and I found myself feeling sorry for him again. He had to stop punishing himself.

"I hope so," I said. I still thought that his pursuit of finding a way out of here was not so crazy. Maybe we could do it. We came down here, didn't we? That proves that somewhere, somehow, there is a way to cross the line between dimensions and we needed to work together to find it.

"Thank you," he cleared his throat and pulled on the skip of his cap. "Will you be back to work on the experiments?"

"Probably," I said. "I think Marshal enjoyed himself. Maybe, despite all the lies, we can find a way home." I made my way through the tunnels with Barker leading the way.

Chapter 8
Max

Max left Marshal's over a week ago and, surprisingly, he actually missed being there. It shouldn't be too much of a shock to him. After all, it was the only place he was able to call home since he had dropped down to this hell world. Oh, sure he had spent long periods of time in one place or another, but they were all just temporary; a place to sleep until he grew tired of it or whoever was there grew tired of him. Marshal's was different. He felt a sense of belonging there. He was a part of something. He worked hard with the others over the past few months. They built an addition onto Marshal's house so there was room for everyone. He fished and hunted for food for everyone and he spent hours bent over in the hot sun tending to the crops and gardens. He didn't help much with the canning and preserving of the vegetables, but he did help with the harvest.

There was also the added bonus of having Cornelius there. The Englishman had become like a brother to him after pulling him out of the ocean when he fell from the old world. They had been on many adventures together over the years, most of them ending with Max getting into some kind of trouble and the two of them fleeing in the middle of the night to escape somebody he had ticked off. It wasn't Cornelius's fault. He was a well-behaved proper Englishman who doted on the stars and wrote poetry. The trouble always started with Max.

Max had been raised a pirate, having joined his first seafaring crew at the age of thirteen. All he knew was thieving, drinking and women. Coming down here didn't change anything either, especially the women. He was always looking for a pretty face to impress and he couldn't do that without looking good and bearing gifts. So, he stole whatever he could as long as it looked good and fit properly. He always had a bag full of shirts and pants for himself; jewelry and lace for the ladies. It was his other habit, drinking, that usually ended every rendez vous. For some reason, though, Cornelius always stayed with him. It was like the Englishmen felt it was his duty to look out for the young scallywag and was continuously saving him from jealous boyfriends or possessive women. But one particular escapade proved to be too much for Cornelius and the two went their separate ways.

It happened about eight or nine summers ago. The two had come across a little group of about eleven men and women. Of course, Max found one particular girl to be to his liking, but she had a boyfriend. He was a big man and Max would never stand a chance against him. So, after he got what he wanted from the girl, her undying love and devotion, he and Cornelius fled before big bad boyfriend could get his hands on the young Scott. They were forced, once again, to abandon the hope of fitting in with a stable group. Before they left, though, they learned about a local gang who were terrorizing the countryside. They called themselves the 'Punks' and the girl who had fallen for Max warned him and Cornelius to be on the lookout for them.

These 'Punks' were making a name for themselves and it seemed there were more than a few people who didn't want to run into them. Rumour had it that they attacked small groups of two or three, stole their food and water and anything else they wanted. They had attitude too. If anyone tried to fight back, the 'Punks' were not afraid to use violence. They beat two men nearly to death and they shot another in the foot. Now that they had to leave so suddenly, Cornelius did not like the idea of he and Max being alone with no protection from what a bigger group could give them.

"I've told you over and over," said Cornelius who was still steaming at Max for having their lives threatened once again by a jealous lover. They were sitting around a fire that they had built. "Leave the ladies who have boyfriends alone. It never comes to any good."

"I can't help it," Max laughed at his friend. "Did you see the fire in her eyes? It almost matched the colour of her hair."

"Yes, I'll admit, she was a handsome woman," said Cornelius, "but she was already spoken for and to a man who could kill the both of us with one swipe."

"Oh, Cornelius, how you exaggerate," Max said as he pushed the embers of their fire with a stick. "You know I'm a fool for a pretty lady."

"Yes, well, you've gone and done it now, haven't you?"

"What do you mean?" Max looked at his friend, waiting for an explanation for his panic. They had been chased out of groups before; why would he be so afraid now?

"You heard what they said about the 'Punks'?"

"The gang who's been robbing people?" Max laughed. "Why would you be afraid of a bunch of fools?"

"You heard what they said?" Cornelius was angry that Max wasn't taking it more seriously. "These guys are bad. They beat a man and his son half to death and shot another!"

"You really believe that?" Max stirred the fire again. "I bet they weren't beat as bad as everyone's saying and, think about it, shot in the foot? How bad do you have to be with a gun to shoot someone in the foot. I've robbed a lot of people and, believe me, if I had to shoot, it was never at the foot."

"Yes, I know about your past, Max," Cornelius said, "but, still, we should be a little more cautious while out here. On our own. With no group."

"I get it," Max said. "You're pissed at me, again. Tell me, Cornelius, what does a lady have to do to spark your interest?"

"I am very particular when looking for a prospective mate," he said, trying not to look too embarrassed by the question.

"Prospective mate?" Max laughed. "Come on, lad, is that how you see women? No wonder you haven't caught one yet or are you more interested in the stronger sex?"

"What?" he seemed shocked by Max's suggestion. "I'll have you know that I have a very keen interest in women. In fact, I've had more than one triste in my day!"

"Okay, okay," Max laughed, "I didn't mean to offend. I just wanted you to know that, if you *were* interested in a stronger more masculine partner, that would be okay. Not with me, mind you, I still love the ladies, but I did know some pirates that weren't as manly as they wanted everyone to think and they were pretty good guys. Saved my life once, one did. Nice guy, Reginald was."

"Reginald?" Cornelius raised his eyebrow.

"What? It's a name." The two of them continued talking about women and life and the differences between this world and the world they came from and eventually the night came, and they fell asleep and there was no attack from the 'Punks'. At least not that night.

The next day the two hiked all morning and into the afternoon. They had been lucky, too, snaring two rabbits and stumbling on a row of untouched blueberry bushes. They picked blueberries for an hour, filling a couple of sacks, before moving on. Finally, after filling their canteens with water and skinning the rabbits, they decided to make camp. They gathered firewood and fashioned a spit for the rabbits and started to cook one. All was going good today. They shared stories and talked about where they were going to go next. Cornelius never mentioned how they had to flee, and Max never bugged him about finding a girl.

"Who's that?" asked Max. He had spotted a small group heading towards them, but they had the sun at their backs and Max could only make out their silhouettes.

"I don't know," said Cornelius as he held his hand over his eyes to shade them from the bright sun. "Looks like they're headed this way." The two stood and waited for the group to approach. When they finally came into focus, Max could see that the group was made up of five boys ranging in age from thirteen to seventeen. They were dressed rather roughly in jeans and leather and they carried an air of arrogance with every step they took. They were dirty and greasy and Max knew immediately that these must be the

'Punks'. He was right, they didn't look intimidating despite how much they tried. He looked at his friend and saw that Cornelius did not share his opinion. The Englishman looked wide-eyed and more than just a little alarmed.

"It's them!" he whispered.

"I know," said Max. "I'll take care of it."

"No," Cornelius pulled Max's hand away from the knife he was reaching for. "Perhaps if we gave them food and water, they won't find the need to steal. Look at them, they're just boys, not much younger than you."

"Your heart is too kind my friend," said Max as he left the knife in his belt and, instead, reached out a hand towards the group. "Hello, friends. How goes the journey?"

"Awe, a European," said the boy who looked like the oldest and, from the way he stepped to the front, the leader. "Haven't met too many Europeans. Where you from?"

"Scotland," answered Max, not liking the way the boy was eyeing him, "and my friend here is from England."

"Two Europeans!" said the boy. "Even better."

"Are you boys hungry?" Cornelius spoke. He could sense that there was tension between Max and the boy already. "We have food and we don't mind sharing."

"I don't know," the boy turned to the rest of his group. "What do you say boys? Are we hungry?" They all nodded, obviously not doing anything without the approval of their leader. The boy turned back to Cornelius. "I guess we are. Thank you."

That seemed to have broken the tension. The group gathered around the camp, sitting and relaxing. Cornelius cooked both rabbits and brought out the bag of blueberries they had picked earlier. They all ate and talked and shared stories of their arrival to this world. It turned out that the boys were all young. The leader, Keith, was seventeen, Steve was sixteen, Troy was also sixteen, Chad was seventeen and the youngest, Tommy, was only thirteen. They had all fallen down here at different times over the last thirty years. Of all the boys, Tommy looked the weakest. He was quiet and shy, only talking when he absolutely had to. Max didn't trust any of them. He saw them for the punks that they really were; trouble seeping from their veins. But Tommy was different. He liked Tommy, even felt sorry for him to be mixed up with these losers.

"Well," said Keith. "It's been real nice sitting and chatting with you guys. The food was good, but I think it's time we said goodbye."

"Are you sure?" asked Cornelius even though he couldn't be happier that they were leaving.

"Yeah, we've taken too much of your time and food," Keith reached out a hand to help Tommy up. The boy shyly took the hand and got to his feet. "It was nice meetin' the two of you. Maybe we'll cross paths again sometime. We should go before the sun goes down; find ourselves a place to hunker down for the night or keep walkin'. Sometimes you find cool things in the dark."

"Sometimes," Max said as he got to his feet. He reached out to shake his hand. Keith obliged but squeezed just a little harder than was necessary, never taking his eyes off of Max's. Max stared back, not showing any sign of weakness, until Keith felt the intimidation and looked away. Max's face broke into a wide grin. He was not intimidated easily.

"Okay, boys," Keith addressed his group. "Let's go. Thank the Europeans for their hospitality and let's header." They did as they were told and thanked Max and Cornelius, each avoiding Max's eyes as they shook his hand. The pirate knew how to be formidable. When Tommy whispered out a barely audible thank you, his eyes cast on the ground, Max softened and put his hand on the boy's shoulder. Tommy looked up for a second and saw only kindness in the eyes of Max.

"You guys be careful," he spoke more to the young boy than anyone else. "It can get ugly down here."

"Oh, we're always careful," smiled Keith. "Aren't we Tommy?"

"Yeah," Tommy looked down at the ground again and put his hands in his pocket. Then they left; just as quickly as they had appeared, they disappeared leaving Max and Cornelius alone once again.

"They weren't so bad," smiled Cornelius. He was happy they had fed them and looked after them. That had to mean something.

"Is that your official opinion?" asked Max.

"Well, now that we fed them and treated them like decent human beings," he explained. "Maybe, just maybe, they won't pick us to steal from now. Don't you think?"

"I think you're a smart, kind man," said Max. "And I hope you're right." But inside, he knew this was wrong. They would be back; he could guarantee it.

Hours later, as the sun dipped below the horizon, Cornelius unrolled his sleeping bag and laid it out a few feet from the fire. When he noticed Max wasn't doing the same, he questioned him, "Why aren't you getting out your bed?"

"I'm not sleeping," he stated.

"Not sleeping?" asked Cornelius. "Why not?"

"Because, mate," he looked at his friend. "I don't trust those boys."

"Really?" Cornelius didn't agree with his friend. They had a good time with the boys earlier. They gave them food and water and he felt they had come to some kind of silent understanding. If they were given the things they wanted, they wouldn't want to come and rob them. "I think we're fine. They probably moved on to something else, someone else."

"You're wrong," said Max, disappointed that Cornelius wasn't more concerned. After all, wasn't it him who was so paranoid of the 'Punks' before? "They'll definitely be back."

"Aww, you worry too much," Cornelius said as he lay on top of his sleeping bag and stared at the stars. "Go to sleep. You'll be tired tomorrow and we need to hunt for more food."

"Hmph," was all Max would give him. He knew that by we, Cornelius meant that Max would need to hunt for more food. It didn't matter, though, he intended to wait all night if he had to. "I promise; they will be back." He remembered the look in Keith's eyes. It was the look of greed and evil and he knew exactly what the seventeen-year-old would do.

"Suit yourself, but I'm going to sleep and sleep soundly," he rolled over and within minutes a soft snoring sound could be heard. Max put another log on the fire and pulled out the sword he had taken from a dead civil war soldier he had killed when the man challenged him to a duel for a girl he didn't even remember the name of.

Two and a half hours later, Max heard a shuffle. It was the sound of boots sliding across the dirt. He sat upright and listened again. More shuffling. They were here! He looked over at two large boulders that blocked the north. There was just enough room between them for him to squeeze into. He got up and snuck over to them, not making a sound. The shuffling was getting louder meaning the boys were getting closer.

"Over there," it was Keith. "I saw the English one put the leftovers in that bag. It must have the rest of their food as well."

"What about that one?" asked one of the others. Max couldn't tell who.

"No, that's nothing," said Keith. "I think it has fishing gear or something." Max raised an eyebrow. Fishing must be beneath them. "That one over there, it has clothes. Take that one." Max was raging at how these boys thought they could help themselves to whatever they wanted. And they were doing it so quietly, almost too afraid to wake them. It was as he thought, these 'Punks' were foolish little boys.

"Keith?" asked one of the boys.

"What?" the leader sounded angered that one of them was asking a question.

"Where's the other guy?" the boy asked. "There's only one here." Max would have to act fast before they realized that he was hiding somewhere waiting for them.

"What the…?" Keith couldn't get out the rest of the sentence before Max popped out from between the boulders.

"Looking for someone?" He gripped his sword ready for any action.

"You shouldn't have done that," said Keith as he reached for his belt.

"No?" Max lifted the sword, forcing Keith to raise his hands in the air. Then Keith shifted his focus behind the Scott. It was so quick; Max barely caught the movement. He quickly spun around, sword up and caught two of the boys across their stomachs. Blood flowed out of their wounds and they went to their knees. They wouldn't recover from such gaping cuts. The soldier's sword was sharp. He stepped a few paces to the right, never breaking contact with Keith.

"What the hell, man?" said Keith. "Those were good guys, asshole!"

"They couldn't have been that good if they were willing to follow a boy like you," Max smiled. Keith didn't like being called a boy.

"Steve don't let this jerk get away with killing our friends," Keith still held his hands up. Max could see Steve start to raise his hand. He had a gun that he must have retrieved when Max spun around.

"I wouldn't," Max warned.

"You just killed two of my friends," cried Steve. "Keith's right, I'm not going to let you get away with it." Before he could pull the trigger, Max reached his hand behind his back and pulled out his own gun from his belt. He pulled the trigger without hesitation and Steve fell to the ground. The sound woke up Cornelius.

"Max?" he said through a sleepy haze. "What are you doing?"

"I told you they'd be back."

"You die now!" Keith was filled with blind rage.

"No, I don't." He aimed his gun at the 'Punk's' leader and shot him between the eyes. A sound came from behind and he turned on his heel. He didn't even realize he had raised his sword, but he must have because Tommy stood before him holding his throat, trying to stop the blood that shot from his cut jugular. He had no idea the boy was even there. Why would Keith let someone so young and timid join in his plundering? He watched helplessly as the boy reached out for help, his eyes wide with terror. Tommy fell to his knees, then his eyes rolled to the back of his head and he fell face first onto the ground.

"Oh my god, Max," Cornelius was standing now, looking at the carnage that surrounded them. "What have you done?"

"I told you they'd be back," Max said with no emotion. He stared at the body of the young Tommy. What had he done? "I had to stop them."

"But kill them?" Cornelius was shocked at how violent it all was. "Did you have to kill them? My god, Max, they were just boys!"

"They wanted our stuff," he said. "They wanted to take everything."

"I can't," Cornelius started to roll up his sleeping bag. "I can't do this anymore, Max."

"Do what?" Max turned to his friend and watched him pack his things.

"I can't stay with you," Cornelius was shoving things into his bags now. "I think it's time we part our ways old friend. You go your way and I'll go mine. You can have all the women you want and run from as many angry boyfriends as you like. But I'm done. I just can't..."

"That's it? You're just going to walk away in the middle of the night?"

"Yes" he zipped his bag and strapped it onto his back.

"You can't be serious," Max reached out to his friend and grabbed his shoulder. "You can't just leave in the middle of the night. I told you they'd be back. I didn't want to kill them, but I had to! Don't you see? They were going to take everything."

"And the boy?" Cornelius searched Max's eyes. Nothing. "That's what I thought. Goodbye Max, I wish you well." He turned towards the west and headed off. Max watched him in disbelief.

"You won't survive all by yourself," he called but Cornelius didn't turn back. "I've done all the hunting and fishing. You'll starve without me!"

Max stood and watched his friend until he was absorbed by the night. He turned and looked at the camp. The fire was dying so he grabbed another log and laid it on top. He sat down as close as he could to the flames. He was getting cold. He laid down his gun and sword and rubbed his hands together. He stayed like that until the sun came up. Then he got up and looked at the bodies that surrounded him. He had no shovel so he couldn't bury them. Instead, he lay them in a straight line, one beside the other. He had found some wildflowers and picked them. He placed them on Tommy's chest and placed the boy's hand over them to keep them from flying away. He left the camp and hiked about half an hour away. He wanted to wait for Cornelius. He knew his friend would be back.

Three days later, Max gave up any hope that the Englishman would return. He packed up and headed south. What did he need with a pompous Englishman anyway? There must be someone out there that needed a strong pair of hands in their camp. Deep down he knew he would miss his friend who had become his brother and he wondered if he would ever see him again.

Chapter 9

It was the January before the last 360 that Max ran into Cornelius again. He and his horse, a beautiful black mare he had found while crossing Wyoming, had been making their way north when a blizzard put a stop to their travels. Max found himself at a little makeshift trading post that included a warm barn full of horses, some cows, a sheep, a few chickens and lots of hay, a small house where the owners and a couple of their friends lived, a drinking house stocked with bottles of alcohol, mostly whiskey and rum and a store that included food like fresh fruit and canned goods and supplies like shovels, rope and the occasional box of bullets. The store operated on the barter system; you brought in something you didn't want anymore in exchange for something you could use. The drinking house was more of a bring your own booze establishment and everything was shared no matter what. Surprisingly, it seemed to work; the owners only had a handful of fights break out because somebody didn't want to share their liquor. If you didn't have any liquor in the first place, then there was always some kind of chore to do to work off your shot. There was no money in this world, and everyone wanted to keep it that way.

Max was happy he stumbled across the little hamlet and he exchanged some of his supplies for warmer boots and thick mittens, but he really didn't want to stay there. For one thing, he was curious about this part of the world and wanted to explore more of it and, secondly, he really didn't want to be tempted by the drinking house. He was trying to change his ways and that meant keeping far away from alcohol. It had gotten him into too much trouble over the years. The sooner he got away from it, the better. The weather, however, was not cooperating. A blizzard had settled in and it looked like it wasn't going anywhere soon.

He didn't mind travelling in the winter, but he had never come this far north before. The snow wasn't any deeper here than anywhere else he'd been, but it was so much colder than he was used to, and the wind was relentless and howled like a banshee. Every time he attempted to continue with his journey, he was literally blown back to the hamlet, frozen, his toes and fingers nearly succumbing to frostbite twice. His horse wasn't doing much better either. The cold was making the mare's breathing laboured. She needed to rest and store up on hay and Max found an old blanket in the barn to throw over her back in an attempt to keep her warm. He kept away from the drinking house and, instead, made a bed in the hay in the barn next to his horse to wait out the storm. The owners didn't mind as long as he didn't mind the smell of all the animals.

Five days went by before the cold snap ended, and the warm winds blew in from the mountains to the west. The temperatures seemed to climb the scales in minutes, going from several degrees below freezing to warm, balmy weather. You didn't even need to wear a coat when you went outside. Max had never seen anything like it. Chinook was what the locals called it; a First Nation's word for 'snow-eater' which is exactly what it did. The wind was so warm that the frozen landscape became dripping puddles in a matter of hours. It was nice to say goodbye to the blizzard, but Max was not used to such drastic weather changes and found himself suffering a terrible headache from it.

He took refuge in the barn once again but let his mare out in the little corral behind the barn to enjoy the warm weather. He traded a can opener, he had two of them, for a bottle of headache tablets labeled extra strength Tylenol. He swallowed three of them and found a dark corner to lie down and sleep. He stayed like that for three or four hours, until his headache was gone, and he was ready to move on.

He had a satchel that he carried his guns in, two pistols, one rifle and a revolver. It wasn't much but it made him feel safe just knowing the weapons were there if he needed them. When he fell asleep a few hours ago the satchel was beside him, now, it was gone. He got up and started searching for it. It had to be there somewhere. Nobody even knew he had the satchel; he had been careful to hide it the first night he arrived at the trading post. It was never a good idea to show all your weapons when approaching any new situation but now, he couldn't find it anywhere and anger was starting to rise in his gut. Someone must have stolen it but who would be so brave as to take it right from his side while he slept?

He made his way out to the corral. At least he could get his horse and leave this place. Now that his possessions had been taken from him, he couldn't trust these people anymore. He needed to leave as soon as possible. His horse was no longer in the corral. What the hell was going on? First, his guns and now, his horse? His anger was starting to boil inside.

He started to make his way to the front of the barn when he spotted his horse through the open doors. There were three men across the way, all with horses of their own, trying to tie a lead from his horse to one of theirs. They were dressed in clothes that were dirty and falling apart. Their hair was greasy and tangled and their faces were sweaty, muddy and unshaven. Clearly, these men were not the trusting kind. They were the type of men who would steal or kill without reason. They had no moral compass to live by. Like the 'Punks', though, Max was not afraid of them.

"Hey," he shouted, "just what do you think you're doing?"

"'Scuze me?" said the one that looked to be the leader.

"I asked what you're doing?" Max approached them slowly. He didn't have his guns, but he still had a knife tucked into the back of his belt and a smaller one down the side of his boot. "That horse you have belongs to me."

"Is that so?" The man smiled and gestured for his men to stay back, which they did. "I was under the impression that it didn't belong to anyone. She was just wandering around out in that field, no rider in sight and no bridal or anything."

"She was in the corral," Max said through gritted teeth. With any man who relied on intimidation to get what he wanted; Max knew not to back down. "I was in the barn and let her out for some air. She's been stuck in there for a few days to weather out the storm. I took her bridal and saddle off because she didn't need it out there."

"I see," said the man, scratching his head. "Then it looks like we need to do some negotiating."

"Negotiating?"

"Why, yes," he smiled at Max and the Scott fought back the urge to punch him. "You see; I like this horse. She looks like a real good horse. We could use a horse like her back home, but if you take her, well then, I have nothing. I came here and got nothing. My men wouldn't like it if I returned with nothing. I am their leader, after all, and they expect great things from me. Do you see my dilemma?"

"Yes, yes I do," said Max. "But, you see, I don't give a shit. This is your dilemma not mine. Give me back my horse."

"Why, that's not how you negotiate," the man laughed. He signalled his men and they rushed at Max like trained dogs. "Let me teach you."

Max was ready for the attack; he was expecting it. Actually, he was surprised that it hadn't happened sooner. The man on the right got to him first so, he was the lucky one. Max waited until he was right up in his face and head butted him right between the eyes. The man fell to the ground, unconscious, blood pouring from his nose. The second man wasn't so lucky, he would probably need some kind of medical attention because Max had time to retrieve his knife for this one. He slashed once and opened a gash across the inside of the man's right arm from elbow to armpit as he tried to throw a punch. The man went down to his knees, staring at his wound in disbelief, blood streaming out.

"Your dogs are weak," Max smiled at the leader.

"Christ! What the hell? You frickin' asshole!" He was angry but he was also disappointed in his men and he could see that there was no use to try and win this fight. He needed this trading post; it was the closest one to his camp. The next closest store was up north in the 'Northerners' territory and he already had issues with that group. "Take the goddamned horse." He ripped a piece of his shirt off and tied it around his man's arm. "Get up and get that shithead up too. Lay him across his horse and let's get the hell out of here."

"Good choice." Max went to get his horse. As he was untying her, he noticed his satchel of guns sticking out of the saddle bag of the leader's horse. That did it. He went over to the leader, who was now strapping shithead, still unconscious, to his horse. He came up from behind, pulled out his knife and laid it across the man's throat. "I see my horse is not all you took. Tell your wounded friend to get my guns out of your bag and toss it over on the ground."

"Jesus Christ!" This man was good; disagreement would probably get him killed. "Do it!"

"But..."

"You heard him! Get the goddamned guns!" The man with the cut arm reached into the saddle bag, got the satchel and threw it on the ground.

"Thank you," Max put his knife back in his belt, untied his horse and retrieved his guns. "Nice negotiating with you boys. Hope to see you again sometime." The other two men got on their horses and rode away, leaving Max standing there shaking his head and laughing to himself.

"Max? Is that you?" Max cocked his head; it was a voice he hadn't heard in a long time. He turned around and saw Cornelius standing outside the tiny store.

"Well, I'll be damned!" He wanted to be angry at the Englishman for walking away eight years ago but he wasn't. All he could feel was relief and joy. Cornelius had very little survival skills and Max was almost positive that he would never make it on his own; it was one of the reasons he waited so long for him to come back. He could see now that he was wrong, and he couldn't be happier. "I think a ghost has appeared before me."

"Yeah, well, I suppose I could say the same," said the Englishman as he walked over to Max and the two embraced as two long lost brothers would. "You know, I never thought I'd say this but, I've actually missed your wayward ways. Life is so boring without some excitement."

"Well, I am the life of the party," Max laughed. "Once I'm gone, the party ends."

"But the hangover lasts a long time," Cornelius smiled. "Tell me, how has life been? How many more boyfriends have you pissed off?"

"A few," Max answered. "But less and less as time goes on. You can only go through so many ladies before you start to question your real purpose in life."

"I wouldn't know; I'm still searching for my perfect woman," he said. "I thought I had her, but she was taken from me before I got the chance to find out."

"I'm sorry to hear that," said Max, feeling bad for his friend. "You're a good man and you deserve a good woman."

"Thanks," Cornelius said. It was rare for Max to give compliments out. Maybe he was changing and that would be a good thing. "I see you met Pig."

"Pig?" Max looked at him confused.

"The gentleman you were just talking to?"

"Ah, the horse and gun thief," Max said. "Yes, we just met. Pig, eh? Is he a friend of yours?"

"Oh, no," said Cornelius, "on the contrary. Come, let's get us a drink and I'll tell you all about Pig."

"No, no," said Max, "that's okay. I don't drink anymore. It's beautiful out. Let's go for a walk." No more drinking; that was a new one. Maybe the pirate really was changing.

Cornelius told him everything about Pig and his camp. He explained about the people who lived in the valley and how happy they were and how Pig had been terrorizing them for years. He also told him that it was Pig who took away the woman he was starting to fall in love with. He explained how

143

Pig dragged her behind his horse because she wouldn't give him the bag of m&ms she had brought back from the city when the 360 came. It was her favourite treat and she didn't want a man like Pig to have any. Cornelius had found her in the field a day later, her hands still tied together with yellow rope. She was badly bruised, almost beyond recognition. She had several broken bones, and, to Cornelius' horror, there was no more heartbeat and no more breath that would escape her delicate mouth. Max was heartbroken for his friend and ready to kill the man that did it. Cornelius was touched by Max's willingness to kill Pig, but he had a better idea on how to get his revenge. That's how the plan took form to infiltrate Pig and his men and get rid of them once and for all. He could do that and then be on his way, knowing that Cornelius was okay.

"But you could stay," pleaded Cornelius. "Life is good there. The people are nice and let you live however you want. They don't intrude and, yet, are there if you need them."

"That's fine for you, but I can't be confined to one place. You know that," said Max. He would go and take care of Pig but, then, he would have to leave. There was no way he could be tied down to just one place. He had no idea how wrong he was. How could he know that Nicky would walk into his life and change him forever? How could he know that one woman could mean so much to him?

From the first time he saw her, he was infatuated with her. He remembered seeing her on the ground wrestling with one of Pig's men and actually breaking his arm. He had never met a woman like her before. She had spunk and was stronger than most men he knew. She didn't seem to back down from anyone, even someone as intimidating as he knew he could be. She was brave enough to kill Butcher and smart enough to get away with it. People seemed to like her; she fit in with Cornelius and his friends easily enough. And she was beautiful, more beautiful than any other woman he had met down here.

Her brown hair was long and smooth, and he loved the way the sun picked up the lighter shades in it. Her skin was soft and delicate, and her eyes were a pale blue that he had trouble turning away from. She was small, maybe a hundred pounds soaking wet, but she was tough. That's probably what he liked most about her. Her feistiness and quick temper were a challenge to him. Most women down here were scared of their own shadows, too afraid to do or say anything wrong. Oh, some were mouthy and liked to fight but rarely did you find those attributes in one so beautiful.

He and Cornelius would meet every few days so he could report his progress with Pig. When the dam was blown and Pig was killed, they met once. It was when Cornelius and Marshal were trying to make their way back home. Marshal was busy doing something and Cornelius made an excuse to need the bathroom and made his way through the trees. Max met him there and the two exchanged information on what was happening. He was told of Madge's death and their plan to attack the camp. It was important information, but all Max wanted was information about Nicky.

"Love stricken my boy?" Cornelius had teased.

"No!" It was a quick answer, filled with anger. The last thing he wanted, was to let his friend know how much the girl drove him crazy.

"Whoa!" Cornelius looked into his friend's eyes. "You like this girl, don't you?"

"What?" he stammered. "Of course not. She-she's dangerous. Her quick temper could get all of us killed."

"Oh, I see," the Englishman laughed, "you're worried about her temper?"

"Never mind," Max turned to leave. He could feel his face burning red.

He didn't like what Cornelius was insinuating. He didn't like Nicky that way. No woman had ever made him feel 'love stricken'. That's not to say he didn't love women because he did. A lot of women had him feeling things; he just didn't feel love or anything close to love. Nicky was not an exception to this rule; she couldn't be.

That changed the day the camp burned down and he kissed her. He had never felt such stirrings in his body from a kiss. Could he be stricken? No, he just hadn't had a woman in a long time. That was a yearning he felt, nothing more. Then he watched Nicky trying desperately to put out the fire and when she collapsed under the guilt, she felt for killing Butcher he remembered the things he had done. He saw the boy's face from the 'Punks' flash in his memory. He had struggled with his own guilt over the years. He knew how she felt, it was a connection he had never had with anybody before. He held her then and he knew that he was, for the first time, in love with a woman. If only she could love him too.

He tried over and over to win her heart, but she denied him. She told him she needed time; time to figure things out. Time to deal with her guilt. Time to understand how she could ever be interested in a man like him. After all, he was once a pirate and had a long list of ex-girlfriends. If time was what she wanted, then he would give it to her, but it was becoming more and more difficult to be in the same room with her; to see her everyday. His heart was aching to hold her and kiss her one more time, but she kept turning away from him. It was so damned frustrating. When the opportunity came to leave and scout the Blood Demons, he took it. It would get him away from her presence and give her time to realize that, yes, she did care for him. He felt her yearning when he kissed her.

Besides, scouting the Blood Demons would be easy. Nobody else knew, not even Cornelius, that Howling Wolf was an old friend of his

Chapter 10
Howling Wolf

Howling Wolf lightly blew on what was left of the fire, lighting up some of the dying embers. He could feel the warmth against his face and reached over and grabbed some splinters he had sliced off of a log with his hatchet. If he was lucky, he could get the fire going again without having to waste a match. Lighters and matches were so precious in this world. You never knew if you had enough to last until the next 360. He tried his best to stockpile but some of his followers were not too bright. Just last week a group of his men had fallen through the ice while fooling around on a frozen pond, acting like children and forgetting they were grown men. Each carried their own supply of matches, water and dried meat and now it was all ruined; only the water could be saved. For this act of stupidity, Howling Wolf had banished them from enjoying the fire and now they were all running fevers, growing weaker and weaker. Serves them right if they die.

Besides, it would only help him keep his numbers under control.

Ever since the blonde boy had been sacrificed to the gods a few months ago, it had grown unbearably cold. Too cold to move further north into the richness of the northern Rockies where the water was pure and there were plenty of animals to butcher and eat, at least, that's what he had heard. No, they couldn't risk travelling with their horses and supplies through the deep snow, in sub-zero temperatures and freezing dry winds. They had to retreat to milder conditions and wait out the winter.

They had just managed to store their food, make warmer clothes and set up their winter huts when the first snows fell. But it was cold, and he knew their food would not last. With over a hundred men in camp, it wouldn't be long before they ran out of supplies. So, he had to cut his numbers down, get rid of some of the men, but make it look like accidents. If they knew he was willing to kill them rather than save them, they may rise against him and he didn't want that; not when he held so much power down here.

So, he had sent them out on "missions", missions he knew they would never come back from. One group was sent after a small herd of deer, chasing them with so much speed, wanting to please their leader, that they never saw the cliff at the end of the small forest the deer ran through. All the men were killed instantly when they fell the sixty feet to the rocks below reducing the camps numbers by ten that day. All was not lost, though, the deer had jumped the cliff too and were scraped off the rock, butchered, smoked and stored in barrels. Another group of four were sent into a makeshift house made of leftover lumber and freshly sawed logs, a common sight down here. They were meant to gather clothes and anything else that would be useful. The house was occupied, however, by a woman and two men who hid behind furniture with rifles and killed Howling Wolf's men as soon as they entered. It was an admirable thing to do, trying to save their belongings, but Howling Wolf sent more men who killed the trio easily. Now, his camp was down another four and they had new supplies. Everything always worked this way if you paid the gods properly. At least that's what he told his men.

Howling Wolf was one hundred percent Lakota Sioux which meant absolutely nothing to him. Born in the Black Hills of the Dakota territory in 1870, he was dragged away from his family when he was only ten years old. The American government was trying to "assimilate" the natives into the white man culture and thought the best way to do that was to strip the Indian youth of their identity and bring them up in special white man schools. Howling Wolf was told he had a new name, Frank, and was forbidden to use his Indian name again. His father had named him Yelping Pup when he was born because of the way he cried. It was a name he never liked, in fact the other children often teased him about it, but it was his name and still better than Frank. His hair, which was so important to the Lakota people, was cut short and he was forced to wear some kind of white man uniform, making him hate himself even more. These were the people that were moving into his family's land and killing his sisters and brothers and now he was forced to look like them. The shame he felt was almost unbearable.

He was also told he could never use his native language again and he had to relinquish the old stories and traditions of his people. At first this made him angry and he refused to do as they asked but as his days in the Pennsylvania school continued, his anger turned to his own Lakota people. They had given him willingly to this school. They had wanted him to get educated in this new world. They had agreed to this, waving goodbye to him with smiles on their faces. He decided that any group of people that could give in so easily to such a corrupt band of people was not worth learning about. He began to learn English quickly and studied hard but, despite all of his hard work, the men that ran the school still found reason to punish him. He was whipped and beaten almost daily. He was deprived of food and sleep and he watched the children around him grow sick and die. Despite all of this, his determination remained steadfast. If he wanted to beat these people, he would have to learn their ways and study their weaknesses.

Then a new man came to the school and changed Howling Wolf's life forever. His name was Mr. Santini and he was fat and greasy and smelled like sour milk. He had dark hair and a thick moustache and seemed to hold great authority. He had been sent to teach the boys physical fitness, work their "laziness" out of them. He was a vile man, trying to do things with boys that boys should never be made to do with each other.

He remembered the day Mr. Santini had come to him. It was forever etched in his memory. He was fourteen and had just finished a class of Bible study, something he hated but found fascinating. Religion was something that always intrigued Howling Wolf. How could people believe such crazy stories? To think that there was some kind of god-man out there, ruling over everything, making such bad things happen as floods and fires. It seemed like some kind of magical tale taught around fire circles to scare the children not something to obey as law and, yet, still people prayed and paid tribute to their gods. His head was full of these thoughts when Mr. Santini caught up to him after class. He was on his way to the mess hall for lunch. Mr. Santini had been sent down from New York and had only been there for a little over three months. He was a strict man in the gym but seemed friendly when not throwing balls and forcing the boys to do push ups. The boy didn't like him, but he was part of the authority here and that meant punishment if his requests were denied so he reluctantly followed the man to his office on the main floor.

He should have known something was not right when Mr. Santini locked the door. There was no reason to do this, everyone was down in the hall eating lunch. Besides, a closed door meant do not disturb and everyone obeyed this rule. The boy sat down in the chair offered to him by Santini and faced the huge walnut polished desk thinking the man would go to his own leather chair behind the desk. That was not the case, however. Instead, Santini sat on the edge of the desk directly in front of the boy, his right leg to the side and his left leg hanging down.

"Frank," he said and smiled an oddly disturbing smile. "I wanted to tell you that I've been watching you and I find your devotion to your studies admirable."

"Thank you." The boy didn't know what to say. No white man had ever complimented him before.

"I wanted you to know that. Not many of the children seem to be doing as well as you in their transitions," Santini began shaking his head. "It makes me wonder if this little experiment of bringing the Injuns into our world is even going to work. What do you think?"

"I?" The boy looked at the man. Could this be a trick to get him to say something mean about the school and then punish him for it. "What do I think?"

"Yes," smiled Santini, "I respect what you have to say. It would be nice to know how the students feel about this whole assimilation process. Surely you have an opinion."

"Well," started the boy. He had to be careful what he said. "I think it will take time to adjust to all the changes for most of the students. A lot of them are missing their families. They are so young, some of them."

"Right you are," and he reached down and placed his hand on the boy's knee. Something done so quickly and easily that a less suspicious boy would have just let it pass but he jumped and swatted the hand off without thinking. This was the wrong thing to do. Santini rose, showing no emotion, and looked down at the boy. "I do believe you may have interpreted my intentions wrongly, young Frank. I was only showing you a friendly gesture. I apologize if I scared you."

"I-I'm sorry for my uneasiness," said the boy, looking down at the floor. If he showed submissiveness, Santini would be reassured that he still held the upper hand. "I'm not used to kindness."

"No? I find that hard to believe," Santini walked behind his desk and sat down. "You're such a good student. I can't see why anyone would have a problem with you. Are you combative?"

"Combative?" The boy raised his eyes to the fat man across from him.

"Do you fight with the teachers here?"

"Not anymore," the boy said, he bit his lip before he said the next bit. "I realize that my education here is important if I want to live with the white man. I want to become a good citizen."

"That is commendable," said Santini as he crossed his hands in front of him on the desk. "I wish others would be as agreeable. We've had some problems as I'm sure you know." The boy did not respond to this. He knew about the problems. Many of his fellow students had refused to eat and had fallen sick, others had tried to run away only to be brought back and severely punished for their actions. The school was a jail to the native children, and they were treated as if they were convicted felons. He, too, felt the atrocities here but had learned to hide his feelings. He had been beaten too many times for his smart quips so, he knew when to keep quiet. Santini took the boy's silence as compliance to his authority. The young boy seemed defeated; a wild horse that had been broken.

"I'm glad to see you have fit in so nicely," he said and rose from his chair one more time. "You are a strong young man and your people will be proud of you."

"My people have left me to your care," said the boy. "They have little to do with my future now."

"You can't possibly know how happy I am to hear this, Frank," he made his way around the office and stood behind the boy now. "You are a handsome young man and will be very successful in our world."

"Th-thank you." For the first time he was unsure of what was going to happen. This man was big and could probably hurt him badly but somehow, he didn't see him as someone who would beat him. But something was not right. Something felt wrong about Santini and he could feel a chill run through him.

"Yes, I would say your future looks very bright," Santini clapped him on the shoulder. The boy could feel the warmth from the other man's hands as he started to massage his neck. It seemed so innocent and yet he felt his stomach squirm. "My, you are a fit young man, aren't you?"

"Sir?" The boy tried to pull away but Santini held firm, sliding his hands down his chest and towards the front of his trousers. Terror gripped the boy's insides as he realized the sick intention of Santini's touch. The other boys had whispered rumours about the new teacher, but he didn't believe them.

How could a man do such things with another man? It seemed impossible to him but, he realized now, that the rumours were true.

"Don't try to fight it," the words came out as warm breath on the back of his neck. "If you do as you're told and relax, we can make your stay here something to remember forever. I can teach you so much more than throwing a ball around."

"Sir," the boy tried once again to pull away, but the big man was strong. "I do not wish to do this."

"Of course not," he said. "I'm sure your people have kept many things from you. It's why you can't trust them. Why you can never tell them what we can do with each other."

"No!" The boy was desperate now. He needed to get away from this man.

"No?" Anger filled Santini's voice and the boy could feel his hands ball into fists. "You will not deny me Injun. You have no rights here. Your obedience is commanded." And then several things seemed to happen at once. Santini reached, once again, for his trousers; this time with a strength that was not there before. The boy, who was now more desperate than ever, turned his head and bit down on the big man's arm as hard as he could until he could taste blood in his mouth. Santini howled with shock and pain and pulled his arms away. This gave the boy time to stand and whirl around, facing his attacker.

"You will pay for this," screamed Santini. He looked to the corner of the office where a filing cabinet stood. He walked over to it and yanked open the top drawer from which he brought out a thick leather strap about a foot long. The boy had seen this before. He had been whipped with it for punishment on several other occasions and he knew that a man as big as Santini could do a lot of damage to his slight fourteen-year-old frame. He leaned against the desk and fumbled his hands behind him, searching for something that would help him. His hand fell upon something long and thin. It was cool to the touch, metal, pointed at the end. He knew this tool. It opened letters; he had seen the secretary using one while sitting outside the principal's office. His hands tightened around it. He could feel his heart race and the sweat start to form on his face.

"I will show you who is in charge," Santini came towards him brandishing the strap. "Pull out your arm." The boy just stood there. "Pull out your arm boy! Or, by God, I will strike your face!"

"No, I don't think I will." The boy felt his heart slow and a calmness seemed to flow over him.

"You dare to defy me..." Santini reached for his arm and as he did this the boy saw his opportunity to strike. With the speed of a snake, he swept his arm out, letter opener gripped tightly in his hand and plunged it into the side of Santini's neck. He watched as the man's eyes seemed to bulge out of their sockets. He made no sound, the boy must have pierced his larynx, there was only a groan that caused the blood gushing from his neck to sputter. The boy watched with a look of triumph on his face as Santini slowly dropped to his knees, dodging out of the way as the big man reached up for help.

"You picked the wrong boy to play your tricks on. I will never be any man's slave." He bent down and wiped his bloodied hands on Santini's shirt. The big man's breathing was becoming more desperate and the boy knew he was dying. He had killed a man and felt nothing, well, maybe a slight feeling of delight crept through his insides. Now, he knew, he must leave. He had to get to his room and take whatever he could and flee the school. There was no way they'd ever believe that this was self defence. They would put him in jail and who knew what else. He had to get out of there fast before anyone discovered Santini's body.

Yelping Pup lived on his own, travelling through cities and making his way back to the Black Hills where his people lived. He didn't know what he'd do when he got there but it was home and the only place he knew to go to. A destination that he could strive for. It took him months to find his way back home. Having no money and being a fugitive made his travels almost impossible. His picture had been posted everywhere and there were several people out searching for him. He lived on the edge of different towns, only venturing among the houses when his search for food in the forests left him empty handed. He would go in at night and rob the root cellars of canned goods and root vegetables. He lived on old potatoes and dirty beets, but he lived.

He learned how to survive in the woods, remembering everything his grandfather had taught him when he was a young boy. He made himself a bow and sharpened rocks to make the arrows. He had makeshift weapons and tools that he carried in a satchel he stole from the school when he left. He began to flourish in the wilds and in the spring, he finally reached his people. He was looking forward to seeing his mother again and couldn't wait to see the pride in his father's eyes when he told them what he had done to the white teacher.

It was a warm day and Yelping Pup approached the settlement with caution. He noticed that the white man had left his mark on his home and it made him angry. He could see one trolling around right now. They came disguised as god-men, but he knew they were lying. He knew that this was how they made their way in and he knew that, once they were in, they would bring his people down. Soon there would be no more Lakota. He saw how his people were changing already; slowly turning into a white man settlement. Sure, there were tipis but there were also houses built with wood and nails. He watched as his mother came out of one of these houses and he silently cursed as he realised, they, too, were falling into the white man ways. He watched his family from a distance knowing it would be unwise to make himself known in the light. Surely, the god-man knew of his crime at the school and would try to capture him. So, he waited until dark.

At midnight Yelping Pup snuck down to his family's house and looked through the window. He saw his grandmother asleep in a bed small enough to fit a baby and he felt his heart ache. There was no way his grandmother's old bones would be comfortable in a bed like that. If only his grandfather was still alive, he would have never allowed his wife to be treated like this. He moved around to the back of the house and came to a window that looked into his parent's bedroom. His father and mother were wrapped together in a bed not much bigger than the one his grandmother was in. He could see that they were asleep.

He reached up and lightly tapped on the window. There was no need to scare them. His father was a light sleeper and heard the sound right away. He rose out of bed and searched the window for the source of the noise. His movement woke his mother and she, too, stood up to peer out the window. Yelping Pup stood to his full height and his parents saw him clearly through the glass. It was not the reunion he had hoped for. With anger on his face, his father opened the window and stared down at his son.

"What are you doing here Yelping Pup?" There was no welcome in his voice.

"I came back to you father," the boy said. "I have left that school so that I may come back to you."

"Yes, you have left the school," his voice was starting to rise in anger. "You ran from the school because you killed a man. You ran like the small mouse that you are!"

"But the man was..."

"...your teacher and you killed him." The boy felt his heart stop beating. His father was angry at him. He never expected this. "You have brought shame upon your family. Your mother cries for your soul. There is no place for you here."

Yelping Pup looked past his father and saw his mother still standing beside the bed. When he sought her face, she turned her eyes away from him, not able to look at him. So, it was true. His own mother was ashamed of him. Without hearing his side of the story, they had made their decision to believe the white man. They thought that he had killed Santini only to get away from the school. They thought him a murderer; a man of evil. He looked back at his father to plead his case one more time and that's when he saw it. Hanging above the bed was a cross with the god child Jesus pinned with his arms spread out and his head hanging down. He knew what this was; there was one similar to it in the school. They had taught him about their new religion, and he knew their symbols.

"You hang the cross on the wall?" He looked back to his mother and she slowly raised her head.

"Yes, we have found truth in the teachings of this Jesus," she said and lifted her chin, proud of her new faith.

"But..."

"But what?" asked his father.

"It is a white man's religion," said the boy. "It's not our teachings. It's not our way."

"It is now," his mother said, and the boy knew there was no longer a place for him here. His family had turned on their own people. They had given their souls to the white man. Slowly he let go of the window ledge and backed away. He had to leave before his father turned him in. He knew that he would do that now.

"I thought I could come back here to you," the boy whispered. "I thought you would welcome me back, but I can see it's not possible now. I will leave you now so you can bow to your white god child. I will not be your son anymore and you can wash the shame of me off your skin."

"Yelping Pup," his mother cried. "We want what is best for you. Please, turn yourself in. What you have done is very bad and you must seek forgiveness so your soul can be free."

"I will never seek forgiveness from anyone mother; never." He turned from them, knowing he would never see their faces again. He walked towards the tall grass where he could sneak away into the night and never look back.

"Boy." He was startled by the sound and turned to see his grandmother standing only feet from him. She was dressed in her sleeping clothes and the wind was blowing through her long graying hair.

"Grandmother," he braced himself, awaiting her scolding.

"I am not like your mother and father, but I am old and have no strength to argue with them. They provide me with food and shelter and that is all my body needs right now." She stepped closer and took the boy's hands in hers. He noticed how soft the wrinkled skin was and felt calmed by this. "I am proud of what you have done. Your grandfather would have been proud as well. It was wrong to send you away and I know they treated you badly. I have heard the stories. You must be strong now and go your own way. If you stay here, they will kill you. Our people will rise again but not until we are stronger and smarter. Prepare yourself for this. Remember what your grandfather taught you and stay safe."

"Yes, grandmother," the boy felt a peaceful resolve come over him. His grandmother believed in him. All was not lost. "I will go and make grandfather proud."

"Thank you," she kissed his hands and he felt the moisture of her tears. She let his hands go and reached inside the folds of her sleeping dress. She pulled out a necklace he knew his grandfather used to wear. It was a thin leather rope holding the arrowhead of his grandfather's first arrow. His grandfather had been a great hunter and he knew his grandmother always kept the necklace close to her after he had died.

"Grandmother, no, I cannot take this from you," he said. "It means so much to you."

"Take it and always know that I am with you and that I love you." She pressed the arrowhead into his hands, and he could feel the sharpness of the rock it was carved from. "Now, go. Leave before your parents alert them that you are here."

"Yes, grandmother," he put the necklace around his neck and reached for his grandmother's hand. "I will never forget what you have given me. You are the only one who believes in me."

"Our people will come back," she said with tears in her eyes. "Our gods will not allow us to be destroyed. Our people will come back and the white men will pay for what they have done to us."

"Yes, grandmother." He said the words to appease her. He didn't want any arguments but, to him, the belief that there were any gods anywhere was a lie. How could there be gods out in the sky and earth when there was so much evil in the world? No, the idea of god was man's idea. A way to make people do what a man wanted. A way to make people bow before some invisible authority and obey blindly. How stupid people were. It was foolish to believe in such an obvious lie.

The boy turned and left his home and his people, vowing to never make the same mistakes they made. He spent that first night high in the hills and listened to the howls of the wolves. The moon was full, and the packs of wild dogs talked to each other with conviction and power. The boy was mesmerized by the sounds and changed his name to Howling Wolf. He became his own god, living by his own set of laws and beliefs. He returned to the forests and spent months making his way to the Mexican border. He wanted to leave this white man country, go where he felt safe, live the way he wanted.

Five years after seeing the tears in his grandmother's eyes and accepting the arrowhead necklace, he learned of the wounded knee massacre. His grandmother was among the dead. She had believed in the words of Wovoka and believed that performing the Ghost Dance would shield her from the white man's bullets. She was shot in the head. Again, religion had played its cruel trickery on a people and they had paid with their lives.

Seven years later Howling Wolf fell with the 360. This was not a bad thing. Down here he could be god. It was easy.

So many that had fallen were lost and confused. He showed them how to survive but only did so if he could acquire complete servitude from them. He got that by preaching a religion that was violent and merciless. At first, he wondered if he could get away with it, but man's need to believe in something was his good fortune and he started to collect followers. He had so many followers now that he knew he would have to go to richer lands. Lands that could provide everything necessary for them to live. This was why he wanted to go north and conquer the lands in the mountains. There he could relax and not worry about his supplies and food running out.

He couldn't wait for the snow to start melting and the cold to ease up. Soon he could gather up his followers and start their trek. He smiled at the thought of all the people enduring the cold northern winter only to be slaughtered in the spring by his Blood Demons. He took no pity on them. Their loss would be his victory and would make his religion even stronger. Such was the way of the gods. Mercy was something that man mistakenly gave their religions. There was no room for mercy in the land of the gods. That was a mistake he was not going to make.

He was interrupted by one of his men and grunted his impatience. "Sir, a man approaches from the north." Howling Wolf dropped the arrow he had been working on and stood so he could scan the horizon. Sure enough, a lone man approached their camp. He walked alone and waved his hand in greeting.

"Hello, and greetings to you and your men," the man reached up and took his hat off and bowed his head. Howling Wolf smiled at the lilt of the Scottish accent. He shook his head and held out his hand in welcome.

"Maxwell, how nice to see you again. Please, make yourself at home. My camp is your camp as always."

Chapter 11

It's been over six weeks since the first snowfall and winter has its grip tightly wrapped around us. By my calculations, Christmas should be soon, but no one seems to be preparing for it. I don't know if it's because nobody's keeping track or because nobody cares. It's okay, though, I don't really feel like celebrating it anyway. Besides, there's still no word from Max. Not that I'm sitting by the door, holding my breath until he returns, but I would still like to know if he's okay and I'd like to know if he actually found the Blood Demons. Maybe the old saying was true; no news is good news. It would be nice to finally catch a break in this world.

We were working hard with Colonel Al, trying to figure out how to get back home but it wasn't going very well. Every sample of rock that we've collected so far is made up of the same unknown substance. It was driving both the colonel and

Marshal crazy. We started going through the books in Robert's collection and found one on rocks and minerals of the Rocky Mountains. It was no help.

"Nothing in here resembles any of our samples," exclaimed Colonel Al one afternoon as he slammed the book shut and tossed it on the table in the laboratory. It was warm outside, and Marshal and the Colonel had been working since the early morning without any breaks.

"Maybe, maybe it's a new material, only found in this world," Marshal was grasping at straws. He was frustrated just as much as the colonel, but he didn't want to upset Colonel Al any further. The man was a little intimidating when he was angry.

"Maybe, maybe! Of course, it's new, you idiot!" Colonel Al said. "I know that, and you know that but why would such a material exist here and nowhere else?"

"Because nothing here makes sense," I said as I entered the room. I was returning from a rock gathering mission with Billy and Kitten. We had hiked up past the pond and Marshal's cave hideout to excavate some of the rock from a cliff that reached at least thirty feet into the sky. Billy wanted to scale the cliff, but Kitten and I talked him out of it. It was mostly Kitten who convinced him; the boy was more willing to take advice from someone his own age than from me. "What are you guys talking about?"

"What we're always talking about," said Colonel Al, sounding angry and fed up with being a scientist. "What the hell is this rock and where did it come from?"

"Still haven't found anything, huh?" I regretted the question as soon as I asked it. Colonel Al shot me a death glare. I held up my hands in surrender. "Whoa, only asking a rhetorical question. If it helps any, we went to the cliff and brought back samples for you." I held up a bag filled with rocks.

"Not that it will be any different," said the colonel. "Bring it here and let's have a look." I brought the bag over to the table and spilled out a couple of small rocks that we chipped out of the cliff. Colonel Al took one and used a small chisel and hammer to break off a piece small enough to put under the microscope; rock dust flew up in the air causing Barker to whine. I gave him a scratch behind his ear, reassuring him that the rock was still okay. Colonel Al looked through the lenses, focusing on the material.

"Anything?" I asked.

"It's the same," he said as he looked up at me. His frustration was replaced with defeat. "I give up. I don't know what this is, and I don't know what it does. It's like this rock is from a different planet."

"What about everything else?" asked Billy and I could tell he'd been wanting to ask this question for a long time.

172

"What do you mean, Billy?" asked Marshal.

"You know, like the snow and the grass," he answered. "Did you look at those things under the microscope?"

"I could," said the colonel, "but I'm not a biologist. I dabbled in rocks not plants. I wouldn't know what I was looking at."

"I might be able to help you with that." Cornelius said. He and Emma Lee had just walked into the room. They, too, had been on a rock finding mission and were carrying a bag with a couple of rocks in it.

"Cornelius?" I asked. "You know about biology?"

"Well I didn't study at Cambridge for six years and not learn anything," he said. "I studied a bit of every science while I was there."

"You went to Cambridge?" Colonel Al sounded impressed by this. "No wonder you can navigate through the night sky. Some of the best astronomers went there."

"Yes, well," Cornelius seemed embarrassed by this. "If you have any grass or leaves or anything organic, I can have a look at it and see if it's the same as the grass from our world."

"Um," said Billy, "there's snow all over the grass. How about a pinecone or something?"

"That would be fine," said Cornelius. Billy took off to find something for Cornelius to look at.

"Will this work?" Billy was back, holding his hat out to Cornelius. It was full of pinecones, pine needles, a couple of twigs and a clump of grass he must have dug under the snow for.

"Wow, mate," said Cornelius as he looked into the hat, "this will do just fine."

We all waited as Cornelius took the hat and its contents over to the table so he could study them with the microscope. He was aware of us staring at him in anticipation and he let out a nervous cough. I guess we shouldn't put so much pressure on him, but it was hard not to. The thought that things here, in this world, were so chemically different was hard to comprehend. What could it mean for our survival or our chances to get back home? I went over to the wall and sat on the floor, leaning my back against the cold stone.

"Hmmm," Cornelius was looking at the pinecone. "I didn't expect that."

"What?" asked Colonel Al. "What didn't you expect?"

"Well, it isn't even the right colour!" Cornelius looked up and met the colonel's eyes. "Let me try the grass." He reached into the hat and pulled out the grass.

"What the...?" He looked up and rubbed his eyes then returned his gaze to the specimen. "No, this shouldn't be!"

"What?" Colonel Al asked. Cornelius moved away from the microscope and let the colonel have a look. "What am I looking at?"

"You see how the cells are moving?"

"Yeah?" The colonel didn't understand what this meant.

"Well, first of all they're pink when they should be green," Cornelius explained. "Secondly, they shouldn't be moving at all."

"What do you mean?" asked the colonel.

"Billy?"

"Yeah?" asked the boy.

"Where did you get this grass?" asked Cornelius.

"Outside," explained Billy. "I had to dig under the snow, but I got a good handful."

"Yes, you did thank you," Cornelius said then turned to the colonel. "You see? The grass was buried under the snow, in freezing temperatures. It should be frozen, dormant. There should be little or no activity in the cells and, if you look, they're dancing up a storm. This is not how grass behaves! The other things he brought, the pinecone, dirt, pine needles, they're all wrong! None of them are the right colours or are behaving as plants should behave. They are not the same as the world we came from."

"I don't get it," said Marshal who had been strangely quiet until now. "What does it mean, mean, mean?"

"It means that nothing down here is the same," I said as I stood up and walked over to the table. "What that means for us and how we get out of here? I don't know. Does it mean anything? Maybe the colonel was right. Maybe we're not really on Earth anymore. Maybe we've, somehow, fallen to another planet, one that nobody else knows about."

"But that would be impossible," Robert had quietly entered the room while we were talking. "If we were on another planet, we probably wouldn't be able to breathe because the oxygen would not be at the right mixture for our lungs. Besides, our night sky would look totally different, wouldn't it, Cornelius?"

"Yes, of course it would," said Cornelius. "We would be viewing the stars, the moon, the sun from a different angle. Everything would change for us. No, we most definitely are not on a different planet."

"Well, then, where the hell are we?" I asked. "If none of this stuff is the same as where we came from, then why? What's the purpose for changing it all?"

"I told you before," said Colonel Al. "It all has to do with time. The time dimension has been tampered. Changes in that dimension must account for the changes in every substance here."

"But I told you," I explained, "time does exist here; it has to! Everything we do or say is measured in time. It takes me ten seconds to walk across this room, five minutes to study things under a microscope, twenty minutes to walk to the cliff; it all takes time. Time exists, otherwise, we'd all be frozen, not able to move, stuck in one endless time frame."

"Wait a minute," said Robert, "you think that time is a dimension?"

"Yes, I do," answered Colonel Al.

"How?" Robert asked, wanting to know more about this dimension.

"Because it is," Colonel Al answered with no further explanation.

"We touched on this at the University," said Cornelius. "Well, at least, the philosophers did. They didn't exactly communicate with us lowly scientists. Their studies were above mere earthly sciences. They wouldn't even give me a nod of hello until they saw me gazing through a telescope. You see, my stargazing put me on the edge of their precious club."

"Geez, touchy," I could see the built-up anger in Cornelius' face. "I know what it's like not to be part of the popular kids, but you need to get over it. It's over. Those guys are all dead now and look at you. Still alive and kicking and living in a world they never even knew existed." Cornelius looked at me and laughed, shaking his head.

"When you're right, you're right," he said.

"Will someone please explain to me what you're all talking about," Emma Lee seemed confused by all the scientific talk. It was no wonder, though, women from her time weren't allowed to be educated, let alone know about anything to do with science.

"Allow me," I said because I actually knew a little about dimensions. I read a lot of fantasy novels over the last five years. "The first dimension is a line. The second dimension is a flat drawing on a piece of paper. The third dimension is like a sculpture; you can see all sides of it and the fourth dimension is time. We can't have anything without the fourth dimension, but Colonel Al thinks that the fourth dimension is screwed up down here and that's why we're stuck."

"So, if we can figure out what messed up the fourth dimension, we can get out of here?" asked Emma Lee.

"Give the lady a prize," exclaimed Colonel Al. "See, Nicky, she gets it. Why can't you?"

"I get it," I said, angry that he was making fun of me. "I know the fourth dimension is messed up, but I don't know why or how we can fix it and I don't see how studying rocks and plants is going to help us."

"Maybe it won't, but it's interesting how different things are down here," admitted Colonel Al "And the rocks? What if they're the fuel we need to power our clocks?"

"I really don't think starting the clocks will do anything," said Robert.

"Won't do anything?" Colonel Al was mad that someone was questioning his theory. "Of course, it will do something! We start the clocks, we start time. Don't you see?"

"No, I don't," said Robert. He sounded so calm and logical compared to the hysterics the colonel was displaying. "If we start the clocks, we start the clocks that's all. Clocks are merely machines that report the time. They don't actually create time, nor do they make time work. Although it's mysterious that wind up clocks don't work here, it would mean absolutely nothing if they started ticking the seconds away. It doesn't help us if we figured out how to start them." The words came to the colonel like a slap in the face and he just stood there staring at Robert.

"Robert's right," I said trying to break the silence.

"Yeah, yeah, I suppose he is." The colonel looked defeated and lost; his military professionalism gone. He turned away from all of us and headed for the door. "I suppose he is. I have to go now."

"Colonel? Are you okay?" I asked but he walked right by me, not hearing a word I said. "Colonel?" He kept walking out of the room and down through the tunnel.

"What's wrong with him?" asked Billy.

"I think he just realized that Robert's right and all the effort he put into starting those clocks was pointless," I tried to explain. "I think he's in shock. Robert, I think you opened his eyes to something he refused to acknowledge."

"I don't know how he could have thought that starting a clock would change everything," said Robert. "He seems to be somewhat intelligent, but this wasn't a very smart assumption."

"At least he tried," I said softly, looking down at the ground. I knew that Colonel Al was a little on the extreme side, but I liked him, and I admired that he was trying to get back home. He wasn't just sitting around and accepting that this was where we were going to be stuck for eternity.

"Nicole?" Robert waited until I looked at him. "I didn't realize that getting home meant so much to you. I thought you were getting used to being here."

"I am," I said, "and, don't get me wrong, I really like you guys, but I miss my home. I miss my mom and dad and even my brother. If I could go home, I would in a heartbeat. Colonel Al may be a little out there, but he believes there's a way back and I want to help him find it."

"Okay," said Robert, "then we'll all help. The clocks were a bad idea but his attempt at communication makes sense and his discovery of these new rocks is fascinating. Marshal? What do you make of it?" He squeezed my shoulder before turning his attention to Marshal. I breathed a sigh of relief that I hadn't offended him.

"The rocks, rocks, rocks?" Marshal asked and Robert nodded. "I don't know what to think. It's weird, weird, weird. They don't seem to match any of the rocks in your book. I don't know what they are."

"The plants are different too don't forget," added Cornelius.

"But different how?" asked Robert. "Is it something you've never seen before or is it something that doesn't belong here?"

"Isn't that the same thing?" I asked.

"No," answered Robert. "Something you've never seen before means that it could be new to this planet; something that doesn't belong here means it could be plants that are only found in, say, Africa."

"Or sometime else," said Cornelius, suddenly excited by something. "Let me take a look at that grass again."

"Why?" I asked. "What's wrong?"

"Oh, damn," said Cornelius as he stared through the microscope. "I can't tell from this and I can't bloody well remember what the professor said."

"What are you talking about?" I asked as I walked over to the table that the microscope sat on. Everyone else slowly made their way to the table too. "Cornelius? What can't you remember?"

"It was a class I had, something about plants…but I can't remember," he looked up and was startled to see us all staring back at him. "I'm sorry, it just evades my memory."

"What does?" I asked.

"Well," he explained. "What if the reason the plants look differently, and the rocks seem foreign is not because they're from a different place but because they're from a different time?"

"What do you mean?" I didn't get what he was suggesting.

"Are you saying that this world started years ago and that's where all this is from?" Robert seemed to be getting it. Why wasn't I?

"Not just years ago," said Cornelius, "but centuries maybe millennia. We have no idea how long this world has been here. I know I've been here for four hundred years and I knew a few men in Europe who have been here longer. How about you guys? What's the longest you've heard of someone living here?"

"Well, I knew a few down south who have been here for a couple of hundred years," said Emma Lee. "But no one who came earlier than that."

"I think you'll discover it's like that in this part of the world," said Robert. "We are a continent that didn't have a great population until about 250 years ago. There were indigenous people, but I haven't really seen that many since I came here and, if I did, it was in passing. I never got to know them long enough to ask how long they'd been here."

"I think any other continent would have the oldest citizens of this world," I said.

"It doesn't matter because I think that this world," said Cornelius, "has been here for a long time, longer than any of us. I also think that it hasn't changed since it was created and that's why all the confusion with the plants; they've been here since the beginning and are probably ancient ancestors of the plants in the world above. They haven't changed; nothing here has changed."

"And the rocks?" asked Robert.

"I can't explain that," answered Cornelius. "Maybe they're supposed to be different. Maybe they have a purpose, but we just haven't found it yet."

"What kind of purpose?" asked Marshal.

"Well, when I lived in England many years ago," said Cornelius, "alchemy was very popular. Great myths were born of it. Perhaps looking at the rock from the eyes of an alchemist would solve the mystery."

"That makes sense," I said. The others seemed confused by what Cornelius said. I, on the other hand, had a real curiosity in anything based in fantasy; books, movies, video games. So, I knew about alchemy. I always thought it went hand in hand with witchcraft and wizardry which was pretty cool. "But it still doesn't answer the big questions."

"What's that?" asked Robert.

"Why was this world created and how do we get back home?" I asked. Silence filled the room and I could tell that everyone was thinking the same thing.

"I don't know," Cornelius finally answered quietly, sounding ashamed that he didn't know the answer.

Chapter 12

I found Colonel Al in the small room I discovered with Emma Lee and Kitten the first day I brought them all here. He was sitting in the dark with his back against the cold stone wall. I held up my lantern to get a better idea where he was so I wouldn't trip over him. Barker was beside him, all curled up against his leg. I wasn't surprised that the dog was there. Although I hated to admit it, Barker seemed to have a good relationship with the colonel.

"Colonel Al?" I walked into the room slowly.

"Hello, Nicky," he said. "The Private told me you would come. He thinks highly of you and I think he's right to do so."

"I just wanted to see if you were okay," I said. I sat down, cross-legged, in front of him. "So, are you?"

"Am I what?"

"Are you okay?" I asked. "I know that you've worked hard at getting the clocks to work and I know that what Robert said was upsetting."

"He's right," he said. "I just couldn't see it. Of course, the clocks don't control time! I must be an idiot not to have seen it earlier. I've wasted so much time and now I'm back to square one."

"I don't think you've wasted time," I tried to console him. "The other things you're doing are important."

"Do you mean radios and circuit boards with no power?" he asked sarcastically. "Or discovering rocks that don't exist?"

"Well, if you put it that way, it does sound kind of pointless," I said.

"You see? You see Private?" he was addressing Barker again like I wasn't there. "I told you she didn't want to help; that she would be judgmental."

"Stop talking to my dog like I wasn't here!" I exclaimed. "I'm right here. You know I'm right here and can hear every word you say to the dog! I never said it was a waste of time to study rocks and try to communicate with somebody to come help us. You're the one who's questioning it, not me." Colonel Al looked at me, blankly. He turned to Barker and started to say something, then stopped.

"I'm sorry," he said. "Maybe you're right, maybe it's not a waste of time but I think I'm lost. I don't know where to go from here."

"That's why it's good that you found us," I said. "We can work together to figure it all out. In fact, that's one of the reasons I wanted to find you."

"Why?" he asked.

"After you left, we talked about everything," I explained, "and came up with some sort of an explanation as to why the plants are so different."

"Why?" he asked with a hint of skepticism.

"Cornelius figures that they're plants that existed hundreds, maybe even thousands of years ago," I could see that I had piqued his interest. "He thinks that, maybe, this world has been here that long and that nothing has changed since then. Except, of course, that people keep dropping through some kind of portal here."

"But why wouldn't the vegetation change over all those years?" He looked like he was trying to understand this new concept.

"I don't know." The lantern started to dim, and I reached down to turn it up. I had turned it down for the colonel's benefit. I didn't want to embarrass him by shining a bright lantern in his face but, now that we had talked a bit, he seemed a lot better. I felt it would be okay to turn the flame higher to light up the room. When I did, I noticed marks all over the walls. They were vertical lines in groups of four and a long horizontal line through each group. It was obvious that the colonel was keeping track of something. I got up and walked over to the wall and held the lantern up so I could see the lines better. There were little drawings over some of the groups. I saw a sun and what looked like rain coming out of a cloud. There were trees with leaves and trees without. Then I saw a block of ten with what looked like a cloud blowing gusts of wind over top of them.

"Colonel Al what is all of this?" I asked.

"It's my calendar," he said. "I started it after I found this place. The room was too small to do anything with, so I used it as a calendar."

"And what are all these pictures?" I asked.

"The weather report," he said it like it should have been obvious to me what they were. "I kept track of significant weather changes."

"Wow," I said. "There must be…"

"16,317 days," he finished for me.

"You know exactly how many days?" He nodded. "You must be bored." I looked over the wall, finding it hard to believe that someone would take the time to document everything so meticulously and, on a wall, no less. He had actually carved out each line, I thought as I ran my fingers over the indented markings. Why would he do this? It wasn't like anyone was going to see this. I looked at the little sun over one of the groups of five and smiled. He wasn't a very good artist, I laughed to myself.

As I looked, I began to see a pattern. He seemed to have separated his years into blocks of about two feet by three feet. His lines were nice and neat, and his drawings were small enough not to interfere with any of the groupings. I looked around the room and saw block after block; forty-four in all. Then something caught my eye and I went to each block, studying it carefully. I had to be sure I wasn't just seeing things, but I wasn't. There was definitely something strange happening in this world and, although Colonel Al had documented it, I didn't think he noticed it.

"Hey, did you know that there's a pattern here?" I asked.

"Yes, I know. I have them grouped into years," he said, "and each year into months and months into days. It's almost like a calendar that way."

"No, no more than that," I said. "Look." I pointed at the sun above one of the groups of five and then I went to a previous year and pointed at another sun. "See?"

"Yes, it was sunny on those days," he said, still sitting on the floor and not understanding or caring what I was trying to tell him.

"No! Look!" I tried to stress that this was important. "It was sunny over this group of five here and it was sunny over the same group the year before and the year before that and so on. In fact, in every year over that group of five there's a sun…"

"Yes, I know," he was getting angry with me. He obviously thought I was wasting his time. "It was summer when those days occurred so, it was sunny. Not much of a mystery there."

"Yes, but…" I went from block to block pointing at the different pictures, "…it rained on the same group of days year after year and it snowed at the same time every year. See? Look! I can see where the wind days have changed each year with the 360 but every other weather condition happens on the same day every year. Look!"

Finally, I had gotten through to him. He got up and walked over to the wall with skepticism. He stared at his pictures and then looked at the different blocks. I could see his expression change as he realized that I was right. There was a pattern!

"You're right!" he said. "The weather does repeat in a lot of places."

"Not a lot," I said, "more like every single time!"

"Yes," he said. "Private? Come take a look at this. The girl has discovered something." Barker wagged his tail and barked as if he knew this all the time and was just waiting for someone to find it. "Now, tell me. What does it mean?"

"Haven't the foggiest," I said, shrugging my shoulders and shaking my head. "But it must mean something. You've never seen this before?"

"No," Colonel Al said as he kept studying his wall of ticks and lines.

"I think we should tell the others, don't you?" I asked.

"You go," he said. "I'll stay and try to figure this out."

"You sure?" He nodded and I left to find the others, Barker following behind me.

"Where is everyone?" I asked when I got back to the lab, seeing only Robert and Marshal. Marshal was still looking through the microscope and Robert was sitting at the end of the table reading some sort of textbook.

"Cornelius and Emma Lee took the children back home," said Robert as he looked up from the book. "They were hungry, and they wanted to make sure Cocoa had enough hay. How is the colonel. Is he still upset?"

"No, I mean, he was but I think I've found something else for him to think about," I said.

"Oh, is that so?" Robert smiled. He knew me too well. He knew that I had something to tell him, but he also liked to tease me. "I guess I'll wait for him to come back to find out what it is." He returned to his book.

"Robert!?" I pouted my lip and put my hands on my hips. He looked up again and laughed.

"Go on," he said, "tell me what you found."

"Okay! Marshal, you should listen too." Marshal looked up from the telescope and came to the end of the table to join us. "Okay, you know that room that Emma Lee, Kitten and I found when we were searching the mine?"

"I've not seen the room, but I remember you telling us about it," said Robert. "It wasn't very big, right?"

"Right," I continued. "It was small and dark; we had to duck low to get through the door. Anyway, that's where I found Colonel Al. He was all upset and sitting on the floor, Barker right beside him. Well, I turned up the lantern to see better; I hate talking to people when I can't see them. So, I turned up the lantern and noticed all these marks on the wall."

"Marks?" asked Marshal. "What kind of marks, marks, marks?"

"They were lines; all neatly carved into the walls and grouped into nice little blocks," I explained. "It seems Colonel Al was keeping track of the days he's been down here."

"That seems normal," said Robert. "He wouldn't be the first to check off days. I even did it when I first came down here, but I gave it up when I came out west. It was too hard to keep track of days when I spent every one of them in a different place."

"Well, Colonel Al kept a pretty good account of all his days here," I said. "He's made a perfect calendar in there. He has his years separated and his months are in their own groups. That's not the only thing, though. He's kept track of the weather too."

"The weather?" asked Marshal.

"Yeah," I said. "He's drawn little suns when it was sunny, rain clouds when it's rainy and so on and so on. He even blocks out the days when the 360 comes and the winds blow."

"That sounds pretty detailed," said Robert and I could tell he was impressed by it.

"I thought so too," I said. "Then I saw it."

"What?" asked Marshal.

"There's a pattern," I explained. "He didn't notice it, but I did. It's probably because he's been looking at it every day and I just saw it for the first time. He's probably too caught up with carving in the lines and keeping them grouped properly that…"

"Nicole!" Robert interrupted me. I guess I was rambling on. "What was the pattern?"

"Sorry," I said. "The weather repeats itself." I waited for their oohs and ahs, but nothing came out of their mouths. They were staring at me, not understanding what this meant so, I continued to explain. "You see, every year has the same weather on the same days, year after year. If it rained on the third day of July this year, then it rained on the third day of July every year since he came down here; every day is the same as that day the year before. It's like the year just repeats itself over and over."

"Are you sure?" asked Robert and I could see his mind was working something out. I nodded.

"That's weird," said Marshal. "It's like, it's like…"

"A time loop," whispered Robert.

"A what?" I asked.

"I have to go," Robert sprang from his stool and headed for the door.

"Wait a minute! Where are you going?" I asked as I ran after Robert.

"I have to go back to my place," he answered.

"You mean back to Marshal's?" I asked, knowing that he meant the place where he and Madge used to live. I had no idea he still had anything left there.

"Yes, yes," he answered. As he walked down the tunnel to the entrance he called back, "I'll explain everything later."

"Hmph," I went back to Marshal and his microscope. "That was weird. I wonder why he went back to his place. I thought we moved everything out of there."

"We did, did, did," said Marshal. "But he still has some books that he's stored away in a trunk. He didn't want to move them because he thought they'd take up too much room and he didn't think he'd be reading them anytime soon."

"Books, eh?" Now, it made sense why he wanted to go there. He probably had a book that had information about repeating time over and over. I laughed to myself. It was like that movie where the guy kept waking up on the same day and repeating it over and over again. He was stuck in the same day for the rest of his life. Could that be what's happened to all of us? Were we all stuck in the same year, repeating it over and over for the rest of our lives? It was too much to comprehend right now so, I turned my attention towards Marshal and the rocks.

"Anything new?" I asked.

"It's all new, new, new," he said. "That's the problem. I can't identify any of it. Every single rock we've collected is made of some kind of material that I've never seen before. I don't get it." He went back to the microscope and I stayed in the lab and helped him break apart some of the samples so he could study them better. Colonel Al never came back and neither did Robert. Finally, I told Marshal we should go and the two of us packed up everything, put on our coats and bundled up. We said goodbye to the colonel and headed back home. Barker decided to go with us. He'd stayed with us the whole time we studied the rocks, barking every time we broke one apart to put it under the microscope. I guessed he didn't like the dust we created when we did this.

I was surprised to see how dark it was when we left the mine. I knew the sun disappeared in the early afternoon at this time of the year but, still, I didn't realize it was so late. Despite the absence of the sun, though, it was still relatively warm out and the walk back to Marshal's would actually be nice; we wouldn't freeze for once. That's probably why Barker decided to come back with us, I thought to myself. Marshal and I didn't talk very much on our walk. We'd just spent the last two hours with each other; there wasn't that much more to talk about.

We got back home half an hour later and I was surprised to see Robert there. I was convinced he would be lost in a book in the underground home he used to live in, but I was wrong. He was sitting at the table, drinking tea and flipping through the pages of a book that must have been three inches thick. Cornelius and Emma Lee were playing cards with Kitten and Billy in Robert's new house. They had been out making snowmen and having snowball fights all afternoon and were now enjoying being inside. I took off my coat and boots and put them out to dry. Despite it being warm, there was still lots of snow and snow was wet and my boots were damp inside.

"So, Robert," I walked over to the table and sat across from my friend. "What ya' reading?"

"Physics," he said and closed the book.

"Done already?" I asked.

"You could say that," he said and took a sip of his tea. "I thought I'd look up some theories I knew were in this book."

"Theories, eh?" I smiled. "Anything interesting? Anything to do with repeating weather conditions?"

"Yes, I think I've found some of my answers," he smiled back at me.

"Well, come on! Tell me what you found," I pleaded with him.

"Okay, okay. Marshal do you want to hear my theory as well?" Marshal nodded and Robert waited for him to sit down. "Nicole, when you told me about the calendar the colonel's been keeping and how the pattern of weather has been repeating itself year after year, I was reminded of something I had read in this physics book years ago. You see, when the world above imprints on this world for a few brief days, I make it a priority to collect as many books as I can. I try to take a variety of books, you know, some current textbooks, novels, manuals even some cookbooks. It's my way of trying to keep up with things."

"It's a good thing, too, Robert," said Marshal. "I know you've learned a lot from those books, and I have too. You've been kind enough to lend them to me. That's one of the reasons I know so much about rocks."

"Yes, well, sharing knowledge is far better than sharing wealth," Robert said. "Wealth comes and goes but knowledge will stay with you forever."

"Anyway," I said. They were getting off the subject and I was losing my patience. "Tell me what you found!"

"Okay," he said. "I think I've figured it out."

"What do you mean, mean, mean?" asked Marshal. "What have you figured out?"

"Why the weather keeps repeating," he said. "Why the plants are from a different age, maybe, even why the rocks are posing such a headache. I think I can explain it."

"So, explain," I said.

"I think we or, rather, this place is caught in some kind of temporal loop," he said.

"A temporal what?" asked Marshal and I could tell that he didn't know anything about the subject. I knew about it from watching movies and TV shows, especially Anime. Anime dealt with temporal or, rather, time loops all the time in their stories.

"I think you're right," I said.

"You do?" Robert seemed surprised that I was agreeing with him.

"Well, yeah," I said. "I think we're in some kind of parallel world with the real world and, you're right, I think we're caught in some kind of time loop, repeating the same year over and over."

"Yes," said Robert, amazed that I knew what he was talking about. "That's what I was going to say but a little more scientifically."

"I don't know the science behind it," I explained, "but I figure it's like any good rpg game except *I'm* actually living it."

"What's a rpg game?" asked Marshal.

"Role playing game," I answered. "You see, in the world today, this kind of thing; dimensions and time loops, are everywhere. There are books about it, movies and TV shows revolve around it and everyone I know has at least one video game that has some kind of paradox being played out in it. Having said that, though, doesn't mean I know exactly how it works or how we can fix it."

"I've no idea what these games are that you talk about but you're right about books," said Robert. "I know the writer, Jules Verne, talks about time travel in his books. If it's become commonplace to speak of these things, then it doesn't surprise me that you know so much about it."

"Well, I don't understand it," said Marshal, obviously angry that he didn't know what we were talking about.

"Let me try to explain," said Robert. "You know what dimensions are, right?"

"Yes, yes, yes," said Marshal. "2D is a painting, 3D is a sculpture."

"Yes, that's the simplest way to explain it," Robert smiled at Marshal's elementary description. "Scientists believe that there are many more dimensions. They state the fourth dimension is time and that subsequent dimensions involve multiple timelines, multiple worlds and even multiple universes. To get from one dimension to the other there must be a fold in the dimension." He picked up a sheet of paper he had been writing notes on and bent it so that one side touched the other forming a wide tube. "You see, we come from a four-dimensional world; length, width, depth and time. There must be some sort of fold that happens every 360 days that allows some of us to jump from one dimensional world to another. Now, here we are in this new world and we don't know its origins; how it was formed. We do know it's different from our world and that the principles that govern it are foreign to us. This could explain why you can't identify the rocks. They must be made of material that is only found in this world. I think, however, they may have the same function as similar rocks from our world."

"Which is?" asked Marshal. He was anxious to solve the puzzle of the rocks.

"Well, the mountains contain coal and other rocks that can be manipulated to create power, right?" asked Robert.

"Yes, yes, yes," said Marshal, excited that he could finally understand something.

"Right," said Robert. "We must be able to manipulate the rocks here to produce power. We just have to figure out how."

"You're right!" Marshal sat back and thought about the possibilities. "You're a smart man, Robert."

"What about the time loop?" I asked. This concerned me more than the rocks.

"The same as the worlds," Robert explained. "I think there's a fold in the dimensional timeline here. The start of the year follows a line until the end of the year, and it should keep going; year after year, decade after decade, but it doesn't. Instead there's a fold that happens at the end of the year creating a circle and this world keeps going around this circle again and again year after year. I have no idea when or how it started but, by the age of the plants, it's been going on for a long time."

"If that's the case," I wondered, "shouldn't *we* be repeating everything year after year as well? I mean, our memories should be erased at the end of each year and we would start the year doing the same things over and over."

"I don't think so," said Robert. "I think we are merely observers here; visitors if you will. If we were born of this world, perhaps, we would repeat ourselves, but we are here by mistake and the only thing that remains the same year after year or, in reality, fold after fold, is our age. Not really a bad thing if you think about it."

"Or a good thing if you're Kitten or Billy," I said beneath my breath.

"Oh, I don't know," said Robert. "It would be nice to be ten forever. I wouldn't mind."

"Yeah, but you're never taken seriously, and you can't physically do things for yourself," I said, "and you never get to fall in love and be with that person forever."

"No one gets that," Robert said and quietly stacked the papers in front of him. How stupid of me to be so inconsiderate. Robert was still hurting over Madge and what I had just said was so cruel. I'm an idiot.

"I'm sorry," I whispered and reached out to touch his hand. He pulled it away and stood up.

"Now," he said, "the only thing we have to do is figure out how to reverse the fold."

"The time fold?" Marshal looked surprised at this. "But, Robert, if we do that, we'll start to age. I don't think that's a good idea." Marshal must like being young and innocent.

"No, not the time fold!" exclaimed Robert. "The dimensional world fold. If we can figure out how that works and reverse it, we should be able to get back home."

I sat back in my chair, not any more at ease than I was before Robert explained everything. Reverse the dimensional fold. Just how the hell were we supposed to do that?

Chapter 13
Howling Wolf and Max

Max hated to admit it because he never wanted to admit any weakness, but he was exhausted and frozen and finding Howling Wolf and his men, once again, was a blessing. He knew the Lakota warrior and his men weren't a group you just strolled up to. They were savages in every sense of the word. When Emma Lee described what had happened to her people, he knew it could only be the work of Howling Wolf except he didn't know them as the Blood Demons and there was a lot more of them now. The fact that they had a name now meant that they were more organized; more dangerous. They wanted people to know who they were and to be afraid when they heard their name.

Max met Howling Wolf five years ago, after he had killed the 'Punks' and before he found Cornelius again. The charismatic native American only had about twenty men then;

a large group but not large enough to take over some of the makeshift towns down here. Howling Wolf lived by the rule of survival of the fittest. He knew that he who held the power held everything. Part of gaining that power was reinventing himself as a god. The warrior was smart and knew that the people who fell down here were vulnerable. He knew that they were alone and confused and fresh from a world that believed in a god that controlled their destinies. Howling Wolf convinced them that if there was a god there, then there was a god here and that he was the voice of this god. He was the prophet, the saviour the demi-god all wrapped into one. Follow him and you would be saved; disobey him or fight him and you would be sacrificed, and he was an expert at the sacrifice.

Howling Wolf was an expert at ritual killing; sacrificing those who disagreed with him or posed a threat. Every drop of blood spilled was consumed by him and his followers. He had them convinced that the blood of their enemies would give them strength to defend themselves, to conquer new land. So far, it had worked; they had beaten every enemy and conquered all the land they wanted. Max guessed that this was why they called themselves the Blood Demons. The name would intimidate anyone; except Max. He knew the real Howling Wolf. He had seen through his façade from the first time he met him. He knew that the god the warrior preached about was a lie used to control his men. What the warrior really was, was an angry little boy who wanted the whole sandbox to himself.

Five years ago, Max was a mess. His massacre of the 'Punks', especially the boy, Tommy, had filled him with shame. How could he kill such an innocent boy? His mind told him it was an accident; that when he turned, he didn't consciously slit the boy's throat. It was just a mistake; a horrible, irreversible mistake. But every part of him knew that he had ended the life of a helpless, innocent boy and the guilt took over his mind. He wandered for months, then years, from one group to another, from one empty relationship to another. He went through women, through friends and through bottle after bottle of alcohol. It was the alcohol that did the most damage.

He drank anything he could get his hands on, whiskey, vodka, rum, it didn't matter as long as it made him numb enough to sleep or numb enough to live. Each day blurred into the next until he didn't know where he was or how long he had been there. Then, one day, he hit the bottom of his self-dug pit. He met up with a group of newcomers, all women, who had been exiled by the communities from which they came, shunned for being new. If they could survive a year on their own, they would be welcomed back. They didn't want to go back. Instead, they wanted to survive as a group on their own. They had been doing a good job of it, too, until Max showed up.

A group of women only presented a new challenge for Max and his charming ways. Instead of wooing one woman, he sought the affections of three. He probably would have pulled it off too if his efforts hadn't been soaked in a bottle of Jack Daniel's. His drunken carelessness uncovered his prowess with each woman, their affairs no longer done in secret. This caused fighting amongst the women, each one wanting Max all to herself. Jealousy between desperate women is ugly and two of the women ended up shooting each other in an old-fashioned duel. Neither died but they did come to their senses and realized their only true enemy was Max. So, one night, they held a celebration and promised him that the three would share themselves with him. They pampered him and teased him and poured two bottles of whiskey down his throat until he was close to death by alcohol poisoning. But he didn't die; he only passed out. The women stripped him naked, took his clothes and left him in the middle of a field under the hot sun.

Max woke up a day later, sun burnt and sick from the worst hangover he had ever had. He could barely open his eyes, but he knew he had to get up and find some water and shade. He had no idea where he was and no recollection of what the women had done to him. He didn't care; his head hurt, and his stomach was turning violently inside. He wretched on the ground beside him and then struggled to his feet and staggered off to find water.

He hadn't gone far when he ran into a group of men led by a man with long black hair and strong native features. He had heard of the Native American population before but, until now, had never actually met one. He didn't know what to expect or if he should be afraid, but he needed water and clothes and maybe even a shot of whiskey. He held up his hand as a welcome but stood still, waiting for the group to approach him. He knew that if he walked over to them, it would put them on their defence. If he let them feel like they held the control over him, they would be hesitant to do him any real harm.

"Greetings," said the leader who sat upon a tall, black stallion. Max was impressed with his strong voice. This was a man that commanded with an inner power; more dangerous than those who seemed in control but weren't. This man would have followers that would do anything for him, no questions asked. That was the kind of power a man like him would have. Max knew he should be careful, but he was desperate and needed help.

"Cheers, mate," Max said, not caring that he was standing naked, with no weapon.

"You speak funny," said the leader. "Where do you come from?"

"Scotland," answered Max. "But that was a long time ago."

"Is that not across the great water?" Max nodded. "How did you get here?"

"I was working on a ship when I fell down here," Max explained, squinting his eyes in the sun and wincing at the pain this had caused him. "I landed in the middle of the great water and swam for the shore. I've been here ever since."

"Hmmm," pondered the leader. "I've never seen this before. Your arrival is unprecedented."

"I'd like to think I'm one of a kind," Max said bringing a smile to the leader's face.

"You are with wit, I see," the leader said. "Even in your current state. What happened to your clothes?"

"Well, you see there were these women…" Max started.

"Say no more," said the leader. "Women are the cause of every man's most trying times. You need clothes, water, food. We have all of that and will take care of you. You can not stay out here much longer or you will die." The man got off his horse and walked over to Max.

"I am Howling Wolf," he held out his hand, a gesture he learned in the white man school. Max shook it and felt the strength in the man's grip.

"I'm Max," he said.

"Men," Howling Wolf addressed his men. "We will stop here for the night and help Max out; give him the rest he deserves." Howling Wolf knew the Scottish man probably deserved what he got. He could smell the alcohol on his breath, and he felt the arrogance that emitted from his pores. It didn't matter; his blood would be just as good as anyone else's, maybe even better. He could make it seem like the sins committed by this man could be absorbed through each of them, making them stronger than ever before. First, though, he had to clean him up; cleanse his blood of the alcohol that poisoned his body. Nobody would want a taste of such tainted blood. They would make camp for three days; by then the Scottish man would be ready for sacrifice.

It didn't take long for Max to realize he had made a mistake letting Howling Wolf and his men help him. There was something not right about the native leader. For one thing, he had a real god complex. It wasn't like he struggled with god or religion; it was more like he thought he was a god. At least, he wanted his men to think he was a god.

Max could tell that Howling Wolf didn't believe in any of it but made sure that his men did. He saw the way he studied them when he gave orders. He was always judging how they talked to him; to see if they truly believed that he held the power of a god. He was always quick to turn their doubt into lessons and speeches that kept their attention on him and his word. He was good, Max thought, he knew exactly what people needed when they came to this world. They needed to feel safe; to feel like they weren't abandoned down here. They needed to know there was a god looking out for them. Men were funny that way. They just couldn't except that life just happened, for no reason whatsoever, life was just there. They needed to know there was an invisible force keeping them all safe and as long as they did what their god told them, *they* would be the chosen few who would be rewarded with riches for their loyalty.

Max saw all this but didn't say a word. He would stay one more day then he would sneak away in the middle of the night before Howling Wolf realized that Max could see right through him. It wouldn't be easy, though, his every move was being watched. Then, on his first night, he got an unexpected surprise that would guarantee his freedom.

It was the middle of the night and Max was feeling a little sick. He had come to rely on alcohol so much over the past few years that not having any made him shake and feel feverish. He knew it would pass but until it did, he would feel sick from the wanting. He lay in his newly acquired sleeping bag on his side, his eyes closed, trying to fight the nausea in his stomach. He could hear a few of the men talking. They must have thought he was asleep.

"Do you think we should?" asked one of the men.

"Would you rather wait for that crazy Indian to kill us?" asked another.

"No," said the first, "but if we get caught, he'll kill *us*."

"All the more reason to do it quickly," said a third. "We can wait until sacrifice night, that's only a day away. We do it while he's busy slitting the Scott's throat. We wait until he's dipped his cup then we shoot the arrows from our posts. Hopefully, we all hit the target but, even if just one of hits him, it should be enough to bring him down. If we have to, we'll finish the job with a knife. By then, the others will see what we're doing and, hopefully, help us."

Max couldn't believe what he was hearing. Sacrifice night? What was that? And what did they mean by slitting the Scott's throat? Was that what Howling Wolf had planned for him? He recognized that he was using a phony religious spiel on these men but human sacrifices? That was carrying it a little too far. He now knew that there was no way he'd be able to sneak out in the middle of the night. He had to come up with another plan to stop Howling Wolf from sacrificing him to his made-up god. He opened his eyes just a sliver to try and see who was talking. They weren't very far from him and he thought them fools to be hashing out a plan this close to him. Did they really think they wouldn't be heard?

"What if they don't?" asked the first one. Max could hear the fear in his voice. This was a good thing. If this man was so afraid of Howling Wolf, there must be a reason. Maybe he could save his life after all and still give the crowd a sacrifice. He knew what to do. All he needed was ten minutes alone with their messiah. He closed his eyes and tried to stop himself from shaking. He cursed the alcohol that had turned his body against him and swore that, if he got out of this alive, he would never drink again.

The next day saw Max receive gifts of food and water. Some of the men gave up some of their clothes for him to wear but, then again, why wouldn't they? They probably figured they'd get them back after the sacrifice anyway. He knew they were trying to fatten up the calf before the slaughter and he played along with them, pretending to be grateful for everything they gave him. He had stopped shaking by mid-morning and his fever had subsided. He still had a craving for a shot of whiskey, but he could control that. He wanted to meet with Howling Wolf while he felt good enough to. He got his chance after a supper of dried fruit and roasted rabbit.

"Your cook is good," Max said as he took a seat beside Howling Wolf. The man was finally on his own, the nearest follower far enough away not to hear them. This was his opportunity to tell him about the planned mutiny. "This food is pretty good."

"I'm glad you're feeling good enough to eat," he said. "You were not at your best last night."

"No," Max smiled. "I think I've dabbled with the liquor bottle too many times. Last night was a sign that I should quench my thirst with water from now on."

"That's a good idea," said Howling Wolf. "Alcohol is white man's poison. Eventually it will kill you. You are a smart man for learning your lesson before that happened."

"Yes, I am," said Max. "I believe you're a lucky man to have so many men under your command. It must be hard to keep them all happy."

"If you give them reason, men will do almost anything," Howling Wolf said as he looked over his men.

"Is that what you give them, reason?" Max asked and the warrior turned to look him in the eye.

"It's worked so far," he said.

"So, it has," said Max, "but, surely, there are some that question your authority?"

"Do you have something you would like to tell me young, Max?" Howling Wolf was staring into Max' eyes, looking like he could perform the sacrifice right here, right now.

"I wanted to let you know how grateful I am that you helped me," Max started. "I would also like you to know that if anything or anyone, was going to do you harm I would tell

214

you. I would have no reason to lie. You've saved my life and I am in your debt."

"Yes?"

"Last night I overheard a conversation that both disturbed me," said Max, "and, quite frankly, made me worry for your life."

"My life?" Howling Wolf looked angry and Max could see why the man who questioned the success of the assassination was so scared last night.

"Yes," he said. "Three of your men are planning to kill you."

"Three of my men?" Howling Wolf showed no emotion. Max couldn't tell if the information was a shock or if the man had his suspicions all along.

"Yes, they want to do it tomorrow while you're slitting my throat for the sacrifice," Max showed no sign of fear or anger at his statement. He just relayed the information as if his death was not a part of it. This took Howling Wolf by surprise. He had never met a white man who talked so bravely when his life was in danger.

"Who are they?" Max looked around the camp until he saw the three men. They were sitting together, finishing their supper and laughing.

"That's them," Max whispered and nodded his head towards the trio. "Over by the pile of blankets."

"What is their plan?" Still no emotion.

"Each has a bow and arrow," Max explained. "They plan to take positions on either side of you and one in the crowd. When you slit my throat, they'll shoot their arrows, hopefully hitting you from each position. They want your murder to be a rallying cry for the others so that, if they fail and you are still alive, they'll join in to finish you off."

"That's the plan?" Howling Wolf didn't seem impressed by it. "They'd be better off to wait until I'm sleeping and kill me then. Fools! Thank you, Max, for telling me this."

"Well, like I said, I owe a debt to you for all you've done for me," Max was feeling a little relieved, but something told him it was to be short-lived.

"I will wait until the ceremony," said Howling Wolf, "and I will catch them in the act. I will say nothing to them until then. Thank you, again, Max. You may go now."

"Wait, you're still going on with the ceremony?" Max couldn't believe that his head was still on the chopping block.

"Yes, Max, the ceremony will still take place," Howling Wolf looked the Scott in the eye and Max shuddered under the stare. This man was more terrifying than any other he had encountered, including some of the pirates he sailed with. "I know nothing of you. How can I trust a word of a naked drunkard? If you are telling me something false only to gain your freedom, I will still happily slit your throat and bathe in

216

your blood but if you are telling me the truth, I will be in your debt for the rest of my life. Now, go. I will see you tomorrow."

Max spent the rest of the evening and the next day searching for ways to escape. He didn't like the fact that the ceremony was still going to take place. What if the men got scared and didn't try their little coup de tat? He wanted to find an alternate way to deal with saving his life but everywhere he went there were two or three men watching him, following him. He wasn't left alone for a minute. So, he sat back and accepted their food offerings and gifts and kept an eye on the three men who held his life in their hands. In the evening, about a half hour after a huge supper that was practically shoved down his throat, the preparations for the ceremony began.

Two men grabbed his arms and tied them behind his back while a third bound his feet with rope. Then a huge man grabbed him and threw him over his shoulder. He was taken a little way outside the camp where an apparatus had been erected. He looked at it and wondered when they had built gallows; he never heard any hammers and they weren't that far from camp. Already about eighty per cent of the camp were there and the rest were arriving every minute.

He spotted Howling Wolf standing by the structure and got the feeling that he was going to go through with the sacrifice no matter what. He stood, shirtless, his long hair plaited into two braids and wrapped in beads. There was a table behind him with a clay bowl sitting on top, a small cup beside it. Max saw a knife laid out and decorated with more beads and feathers. This must be the knife that will kill me, he thought then shook his head, trying to rid himself of the thought. He wasn't going to die; the three men would make their attempt and his life would be spared.

He was carried up the steps of the gallows and wondered how his throat was going to be slit when he would have a noose around it, but he soon learned how that was going to happen. Two men were waiting for him when he was placed on his back on the platform. They took the noose he assumed was for his neck and wrapped it around his feet then swung him, dangling upside down, towards Howling Wolf who now stood with the knife in his hand.

Max felt sweat start to form on his brow. This was getting a little too close for his comfort. He searched the crowd for the three men, looking from left to right but saw nothing. If the men didn't make their move soon, he would be dead.

"Attention everyone," Howling Wolf started. "This man has come to us in a time of great need. He has appeared out of nowhere as if sent by the gods themselves. We have saved his life from the poisonous alcohol that filled his veins. Now, we must pay tribute to the gods and return his cleansed body back to them. We must take his blood and drink it as its newfound purity will give us strength and sustain us in our new life down here. Thank you, oh gods, for your gift of life-giving blood."

"Thank you, oh gods, for your gift of life-giving blood," the crowd all spoke in unison, repeating Howling Wolf's words. He then turned and faced the Scott. Max searched the crowd, frantically trying to locate the three men. There was movement to his left! He turned to see one of the men raise his bow. Max looked up at Howling Wolf and was surprised to see him already in the motion of throwing the knife at the would-be murderer. He had no intention on ever using the knife on Max. He just had to make his attackers believe he would. The knife hit the man between the eyes, killing him instantly. Chaos broke out as the other two men tried to hide their bows, but they were quickly surrounded and brought to Howling Wolf.

Max watched it all while he helplessly dangled upside down, hoping that Howling Wolf would keep his word and spare his life. The warrior ordered his men to take Max down and watched as they attached a second noose to the gallows. They then placed the nooses around the necks of the two traitors. Howling Wolf turned and addressed the crowd.

"It seems as if we have traitors among us. It was through the help of my new friend, Max, that I have uncovered their plan." He made it sound as if he and Max had been friends from the beginning and that they discovered the treasonous plan together. Max didn't care about the lies; as long as he was free. "These men have sin in their hearts and their blood has been tainted. We can not drink of their blood for it will only darken our souls. However, the gods would not want these men to remain in our family knowing that they wish me dead. I will give them a sentence worthy of their crime. Treason is punishable by death." He nodded to the man working the gallows who swung out the two men over the bowl that was intended to hold Max' blood. It was a slow death as they struggled to break free but, eventually, their bodies went still, and they were dead.

"I owe you my life," Howling Wolf said to Max as he untied him. "I will be in debt to you forever. If you want to stay and help me command, I will welcome you to our group."

"I appreciate the offer," said Max, "but I'm a man who likes to be on his own. I like the freedom that only solitude can give me."

"Very well," Howling Wolf said, "I will give you food and clothes for your journey. You may leave whenever you want, and I wish you luck wherever you go."

Chapter 14

Max entered Howling Wolf's camp cautiously. There were so many more men than when he was with them before. They had caused a lot of damage over the past few years, too. Emma Lee's community was not the only massacre they had conducted. He'd heard of a few more throughout his travels but none quite as devastating as the one committed against the peaceful group of people who were building their city in the caves. He knew Howling Wolf was a man of his word and would welcome him without any inclination of killing him. He also knew that if he started pleading with him to keep away from the land where his friends lived, his debt would mean nothing. Howling Wolf liked power and control. If he wanted to take over his friends' home, he would, and no one could stop him. Somehow, Max would have to turn him in a different direction, perhaps west towards the mountainous forests and the ocean.

"Well, if I wasn't seeing you for myself, I would not believe it," said Howling Wolf as he made his way towards the Scott, his arms held out for a brotherly embrace. He was happy to see his old friend. If it wasn't for him, the warrior may not be alive. "What brings you out in weather like this? Surely you're not living on the road in the middle of winter?"

"You know me, Mr. Wolf. I may have given up the bottle, but I will never give up the women. It's my biggest weakness and it always gets me into the sort of trouble one runs from," said Max, chuckling under his breath. It wasn't a complete lie. He did leave, hoping Nicky would discover her love for him in his absence.

"I told you before that women were trouble," laughed Howling Wolf, not questioning the lie. "I'm glad you've given up the bottle, but you should have given up the women as well. Both can poison your blood. Come, come meet some of my men and warm yourself by the fire."

Max followed Howling Wolf into the camp. He was introduced only to the men Max figured were the most trusted, the ones that obeyed every word the warrior spoke. The fire was in the centre of camp and its flames reached high into the air. There were logs positioned around it so, Max put down his pack and sat on one of them and held out his hands towards the flames. Oh, it felt so good to gain warmth back to his fingers. Howling Wolf sat beside him and presented a plate full of food to him.

"You must be hungry, hiking in such cold," he said.

"Well, I do have plenty of rations," he looked at the food longingly and took it from his friend. "But I haven't had a *warm* meal in a long time."

After he ate and was warm enough, Howling Wolf showed him around his camp, which was more like a portable village, and introduced him to more of his men. Max noticed how every man they passed would gaze at their leader in awe and, if they were so lucky as to get a nod of recognition from him, they would quickly bow their heads in reverence. Max realized, with great trepidation, that nothing had changed. Howling Wolf still had these men completely under his power. They truly believed he was a prophet, a speaker for the gods or, perhaps, a god himself. In fact, through their tour of the camp, Max didn't see one man show any sign of doubt in the warrior. It was worse than he thought; Howling Wolf had gotten better at his deception. If he didn't approach the suggestion of changing direction carefully, they would all turn on him.

"Well, mate," Max said after they returned to the fire, "you've grown yourself quite the army of men. How'd you do it?"

"It was really quite easy," said Howling Wolf proudly. "I speak of ideals that make their stay in this place bearable. I give them a reason to work together and survive."

"And what reason is that?" asked Max.

"To please the gods, of course," he said. Max looked for any sign of deception but saw none. Maybe he actually *believes* he's a god now, thought the Scott. "If the gods are happy, then life or death will be filled with pleasure."

"Of course," said Max.

"So, tell me," said Howling Wolf, "where are you going in such weather?"

"I told you," said Max. "I'm running from something not to something."

"Yes, the woman," Howling Wolf shook his head and smiled. "Tell me what happened."

"It's really not that exciting," Max explained. "I fell for a beautiful girl who had a problem she just couldn't or wouldn't get rid of."

"And what was that?"

"A boyfriend," Max said. Howling Wolf laughed at this. "He took offence to me kissing his girlfriend and chased after me with a shotgun. It's a good thing he had a lousy aim and it was snowing like mad otherwise I might not be here today."

"It serves you right," scolded Howling Wolf. "According to the white man's bible it's a sin to covet thy neighbour's wife."

"Hey, she didn't tell me she had a boyfriend!" Max held up his hands in defence.

"Would that have stopped you?"

"Probably, maybe," Max stumbled over his answer, "probably not. You should have seen her though! She was gorgeous! Hair down to here, eyes that were green like emeralds and a figure to die for."

"Which you almost did," said Howling Wolf, "and it would have been a wasteful death too. No woman is worth dying over."

"Never a truer word was spoken," said Max as he wondered if he would risk his life if this man and his 'Blood Demons' made their way north towards Nicky.

"So, tell me, my friend where are you thinking of going?" asked Howling Wolf again, convinced that the Scott had some kind of destination in mind. Max knew that this was the chance he needed to drop the seeds of doubt in the warrior's plan to head north.

"Somewhere warm," he said. "Somewhere where I can feed my belly without having to thaw it out first."

"Ah, the trials of winter," smiled Howling Wolf. "Was the cold season bad where you were."

"Bad is not the word for it," answered Max. "I don't know how anyone can live so far north. The snow comes early and never stops. I swear, I never once walked in snow below my knees the whole time I was there."

"How far north were you?" Howling Wolf asked the question without a lot of emotion, but Max could tell that the warrior was very interested in hearing about the north.

"Oh, about a week's journey," he had to be careful. He didn't want to reveal exactly where he came from, but he wanted it to be close enough that he could discourage them from going there. "A long week, too. I haven't seen anyone since leaving the little group with the jealous boyfriend."

"You've seen no one?" Howling Wolf found this interesting. Surely, in a land known for prosperity, there should be more people taking advantage of it.

"Nope," Max said. "Come to think of it, that group was heading west, themselves. Seems they'd spent the last five years there and were tired of working like dogs to survive. Do you happen to have any coffee? I've tried the brew a few times and drink it whenever I can find it. Next to whiskey it's the only thing that can warm you from the inside out."

"Yes, we have some coffee," he turned to one of his men. "Dolton will you get my friend here a hot cup of coffee." The man quickly left to retrieve the coffee. Max smiled his appreciation, hoping he was presenting a believable picture of what life was like in the north.

"You don't know how much I appreciate your hospitality," he said as he took the cup of coffee from the returning Dolton. He wrapped his hands around the cup and took a sip. "Ah, this hits the spot. Thank you."

"Nothing is too good for the man who saved my life," Howling Wolf said and then returned to his questions. "So, how long were you up there?"

"Maybe a year, maybe less," Max blew into his cup and took another sip. "I thought I had found the promised land. You've heard the rumours, right?"

"What rumours?" Oh, sure act clueless, thought Max. The warrior wasn't fooling him; why else would they be camped in the middle of nowhere waiting for winter to end?

"You know, that life is so pure in the north," said Max trying not to roll his eyes. "Especially by the Rocky Mountains. They say the water is plentiful and the wildlife is prosperous. It's the place to go and live out eternity in peace and harmony with the land. Blah, blah, blah."

"I have not heard these rumours," said Howling Wolf. "Is it so? Is it the promised land?"

"Not if you want to relax and enjoy life!" exclaimed Max. He had to make this sound convincing if he had any hope of changing the warrior's mind about his travel plans. "Hell, from the first minute I got there, I worked. There're hardly any people there and the ones that are there are half crazy. I had to do everything for myself: cut wood, build shelter, set traps, gather food, keep warm, so many things."

"You have to do that wherever you go," said Howling Wolf.

"True," said Max, "but at least you get rewarded every once in a while. Do you know I went two months straight without catching anything in my traps; I didn't even see a rabbit, or a squirrel, or anything. I had to forage for berries, which was fine until I ran into a bear foraging in the same bush. I've never seen anything so big!"

"Bears are good omens," said Howling Wolf. Max cursed inside. Who thought a bear was a good omen?

"Yeah, well it destroyed my pack and ate the bucket of berries I worked so hard to pick!" Max took another drink of coffee; it was almost gone now. "I tell you, everything I heard about that country was a lie! Serves me right for listening to rumours. I should know better."

"Where are you going now?" asked Howling Wolf.

"To warmer weather," said Max. "I think I'll head for the ocean that touches the western shores. I've been in the one that touches the east; I'd like to compare the two. Besides, I'd rather dig up clams in the sand and sun then dig through snow for frozen potatoes."

"That does sound pleasant," said Howling Wolf.

"You should come," said Max as if this idea had just popped into his head, "bring your men!"

"It is something to think about," the warrior's face showed no emotion and Max didn't know if he was serious or not. At least, the seeds were planted, he thought, no need to overdo it. That would only raise suspicion.

"Yeah, well, enough about me," Max said. "Tell me how've you been over the years besides gathering admirers."

"I've been well, as you can see," said Howling Wolf. It seemed that was all he was willing to say.

"That's it?" asked Max. "You've been well? No special someone in your life? No girl to drive you crazy?"

"I've told you before," said Howling Wolf. "Women are unimportant in your life. They only complicate matters."

"Well, I know they're unimportant," said Max with a look of disbelief on his face. "But, mate, they're a great distraction for the mundaneness of this world."

"That's a distraction I can do without," said Howling Wolf. "There are too many other things in this world to keep me occupied."

"I know that but every once in a while, it's nice to get your feather tickled," he elbowed the warrior jokingly, smiling and winking as if this was a joke they shared with each other.

"You are hopeless," Howling Wolf smiled back. "Someday, some woman will be the death of you."

"Well, may it be her lovemaking not her ex-lover that takes me out," said Max. "Then I shall die a happy man with a smile on my face." The two talked for a couple more hours about nothing in particular. They talked about snow and sun; what was the best fur to keep you warm, what was the best fur to keep you dry. They talked about food; what kind of traps worked best. Did they fish? They talked about life from their old world, both withholding important details; Howling Wolf didn't know that Max had been a pirate and Max didn't know that Howling Wolf had killed his teacher when he was just a boy. Finally, as the sun went down and darkness began to swallow the camp, Howling Wolf offered Max a place to stay for the night. There was a small tent that slept four but only had one man in it right now. He could sleep in there in a warm sleeping bag.

"That would be great," said Max. "I want to keep going but, I must admit, a night in a warm tent sounds pretty good right now."

"Then stay," said Howling Wolf. "You can continue your journey tomorrow."

The next day Max woke up feeling exhausted. Although he was given a warm and comfortable place to sleep, he couldn't keep his eyes closed for long. He didn't trust

Howling Wolf and kept himself awake most of the night. It helped that the man he shared the tent with snored so loud that the ground shook. How anybody within hearing distance of this man could sleep was beyond him. All night he struggled with whether he should re-emphasize how bad it was up north. If he tried to sound too convincing it would sound suspicious. He decided not to say any more. If the warrior asked, then he would offer more information, but it was probably a good idea to stay away from the subject. He lay awake, staring at the inside wall of the tent, waiting for signs that others were waking.

After about an hour, sounds started to rise from the camp. Max listened as men started to unzip tents, put on boots and head out to the fields to relieve themselves. That was something he'd had to do for a while now. In fact, his stomach was starting to hurt from such a full bladder. If others were getting up, then he would get up too. He sat up and looked over at heavy snorer. The man was on his back, mouth wide open, sucking in, with great force, all the air around him. Max doubted he would wake him by quietly getting dressed. He was right. Five minutes later he unzipped his tent and reached for his boots. They were freezing inside, and he winced as he squeezed his feet into them. His tent mate didn't miss a snore as Max pulled himself outside and then closed the tent door.

There were a handful of men awake, some relieved the lookouts who were always patrolling the camp, and some were sitting by the fire, which they never let die. It reminded Max of the fire in Pig's camp. He asked one of the men where he could go to empty his bladder and he was directed to the field outside the camp. He returned ten minutes later and was surprised to see Howling Wolf waiting for him with a cup of coffee in his hand. He was sitting on one of the logs in front of the fire. The warrior looked exactly the same as he did the night before and Max wondered if he, too, was awake all night.

"Good morning, mate," Max greeted his host with a wave and a smile.

"Good morning, friend," said Howling Wolf. "I've made coffee for you."

"Thank you," Max took the cup and sat down next to him.

"I've told my men to gather some more rations for you to help you on your journey," he looked at the Scott friendly enough but Max got the impression that the sooner he left the camp the happier the warrior would be.

"You didn't have to do that," he said, "but thank you. I was starting to run a little low. How far do you think it'll be before I leave the snow behind?"

"I think you have a couple of weeks yet," said Howling Wolf. "You should make your line diagonal, heading south as well as west. It will put you in sunshine quicker."

"I will," said Max. "Sure you don't want to come with me?"

"I have too many men," replied Howling Wolf. "My camp would take days to pack up."

"Well, if you change your mind," said Max, "look for me on the sand covered shores, digging up clams and browning my shiny white skin."

"I will keep that in mind." The two talked for a bit, eating breakfast and waiting for the sun to come up. Once the sky turned blue and there was no hint of any winter storm, Max could tell that his visit had come to an end. For some reason, Howling Wolf looked anxious to send him on his way. Maybe he was getting too many questions from his men and it would be hard to keep them satisfied with his answers.

"Thank you, again, for your hospitality," said Max. It was midmorning now and his pack had been replenished and his clothes had been dried and carried the scent of campfire on them. He was ready to go. Knowing how savage these men could be, Max didn't want to overstay his welcome. He knew that Howling Wolf owed a debt to him, but he wondered what he would do to him if he considered the debt paid off. Would he still be friendly and welcome him so easily? Max didn't want to stick around to find out.

"Safe journey to you, my friend," said Howling Wolf. He held out his hand to give him the white man handshake. "It was nice to see you again."

"It was nice to see you as well," said Max as he shook the warrior's hand. "I've always wondered what happened to you and now I know."

"Me as well," said Howling Wolf. "Maybe we won't have to wait as long between visits."

"Maybe," Max didn't know how to take this statement. Was this a hint that the warrior would be heading west in the future? If only that were the case, then Max' mission would've been a success. "Take care of yourself, mate."

"And you. Stay away from the women as much as you can," smiled Howling Wolf. "They will destroy you eventually."

"My weakness is sometimes also my power," Max said. "But I will try to cut down." They said goodbye once more and then Max turned and headed out of camp, southwest like the warrior had told him to do. He supposed he would follow this direction for a couple of days at least in case Howling Wolf sent spies after him to make sure he was going where he said he would. He would head that way and then we would double back and go home to warn the others that Howling

Wolf and the Blood Demons were only a couple of weeks' journey away. They should prepare themselves for a battle.

Howling Wolf waited until Max had disappeared into the horizon then turned to the two men who had been standing behind him, waiting for his command.

"Follow him," Howling Wolf said. The two men were dressed and waiting for this. They had packs of their own, filled with rations and clothing to last at least five days. They would follow the man until they were positive they knew exactly where he was going. Then they would return and report everything to their leader, hoping that this would please the gods and bless them with good fortune.

Howling Wolf watched his men disappear into the distance before he turned back to the fire. He knew from the first minute he talked about the north that Max was lying. The blond boy who they had sacrifice all those months ago had told him exactly what it was like up north by the Rocky Mountains. He bragged about how beautiful it was, about the food and waters. Max had lied and he didn't know why. Perhaps a woman had finally captured his heart and he wanted to protect her. If that was the case, he would use it to destroy the deceiving Scott. Howling Wolf hated liars, even if the man did save his life.

Chapter 15

"Oh my God! This is so frustrating!" I threw my pen down and looked at my calculations one more time. "Even if I forgot to count thirty-one days for August, it's got to be at least two weeks after New Year's and, according to Colonel Al's calendar, we still have another week before the storm comes, then, we'll get a really long chinook."

We were sitting around the table in Marshal's house, trying to get ready for the storm. If we could agree on the date, we could be more precise with our preparations. I thought we still had at least another week before being hit by the blizzard, but Marshal said that was impossible. According to Colonel Al's calendar, the storm would hit tomorrow or the next day no later. We finally convinced the colonel to leave the mine and come to Marshal's. He was sitting at the table with us, looking like he enjoyed watching us fight over his calendar and its accuracy.

Max was still not back, and I was getting a little worried. It must be over two months now and I thought, for sure, he'd be back already. I had talked to Robert about it and he agreed with me. If Max wasn't back by next week, we would have to put our assumptions in order. Did he freeze to death? Did he just bugger off somewhere? Or did he actually find the Blood Demons and fall victim to their savagery? By next week, I thought, finally admitting to myself that I missed him and that I cared what happened to him.

"I think you're wrong, wrong, wrong, Nicky," said Marshal. He took the paper from me and picked up my discarded pen. I didn't want to argue anymore. I thought I had counted the days correctly since I came here but, apparently, nothing was adding up. I was out by ten days to Colonel Al's calendar; ten days! Either I screwed up big time or Colonel Al did. Believing that the latter was unlikely, I had to admit that I'd somehow lost ten days of my life somewhere.

"See? Look," Marshal pointed to the paper where he had written a series of numbers. "If you take into account the winds and all the time we spent at Pig's, the storm should start the day after tomorrow."

"Okay, okay," I said, hands in the air. "I give up. You're right and Colonel Al's calendar is extremely accurate. So, I guess we should get lots of wood ready and put up some tarps to keep the wind out of Cocoa's shelter."

"Yes, yes, yes," said Marshal, "we should."

"Before you do that, though," said Robert, "we need to settle something. Colonel? I think you should stay here to weather out the storm. It's warmer and we have plenty of room."

"Oh, no," said the Colonel. "I'll be going back to the mine as soon as possible. My experiments can not be left unattended for too long. When that storm comes, I'll be fine inside the mine. I've done it before, and I'll do it again."

"I'm sure you'll be fine inside the mine," said Robert. "I just thought, if we move some of your experiments here, we could work on them together."

"That's not such a bad idea, mate," said Cornelius. "We have plenty of food and that stove can really keep you warm as long as it's kept well fueled with wood."

"They're right, you know," I said. "Stay; we'll get so much more done."

"Okay, I'll stay," he said, giving in to their hospitality. He had to admit, it was nice to finally have people to talk to.

That afternoon they took Cocoa with them to the mine and packed up some of the test tubes, the microscope, some of the rock samples and a few personal belongings. They filled up bags tied to Cocoa's saddle and went back to Marshal's. The temperature was already starting to drop, and the sky had turned white. It wouldn't be long before the snow came.

The blizzard showed up the next day, exactly when Marshal said it would. It was a horrible storm, too. The wind blew snow around so fast that it began to pile up into four, five and even six-foot-high snow drifts. If you were outside, it whipped your face like tiny little ice chips, stinging you like thousands of bees. Visibility was zero; you couldn't see across the yard to Cocoa's shelter which, thankfully, we had managed to extend and tarp before the storm started. Cocoa was safe inside out of the wind and covered with warm, dry blankets. We did have to go out and check her food and water throughout the day to make sure she had enough, and it wasn't frozen. This required us to tie a rope from the house to the shelter so we wouldn't get lost. The blowing white snow was so bad you couldn't see two feet in front of you. We also tied a rope to the trap door that led to the underground fortress in case we needed more wood or food.

The rest of us stayed inside where it was nice and warm thanks to Billy and Cornelius who kept feeding the stove with fresh wood. It was cozy inside and I found myself becoming lazy. I was comfortable in the tiny house. There were games to play, people to talk to and Robert lent me a small box of books and I found myself sitting on the couch or bed reading for hours at a time. I should have been trying to solve the problem of breaking through the dimensional veil, but all the calculations were driving me crazy. The blizzard seemed to have sealed us all inside a sort of cocoon and I felt safe.

Barker stayed by my side the whole time the blizzard raged outside. I think he wanted to protect me from the blowing winds outside. It was like the days down in Marshal's underground fortress after I had first come here. The winds raged then as well, and Barker stayed by my side just like he was doing now. I liked it; he felt warm and calm against me.

I went to bed on the last night of the blizzard thinking about Barker and how lucky I was to have such a good dog, even if he did tend to wander off from time to time. I was still not comfortable with the fact that Colonel Al had him for all those years before I came. I kept telling myself that it didn't matter; Barker had to survive down here the only way he knew how and if that meant being looked after by different people then so be it.

It was late and I could hear the winds howling outside. Emma Lee and Kitten had gone to bed earlier and were fast asleep by the time I crawled under my covers. I had stayed up a little longer, talking with Robert, Marshal and Colonel Al but now I could barely keep my eyes open; I was so tired. I gave in and called Barker up on the bed so he good lie next to my feet and keep them warm. I turned down the flame in the lantern until it went completely out, and the room was thrown into darkness. I lay back on my pillow and felt totally relaxed as I drifted off to sleep.

For what must have been the second or third time since coming down here I started to dream almost as soon as I fell asleep. I dreamt about the day I woke up for the first time in this world. I seemed to retrace every step I took that day, not leaving anything out; the walk to the school, back home, to the mall. Every moment being relived in my mind. My dream self was walking to the police station when I heard the barking in the distance.

'A dog,' I had thought. I wasn't alone, there was another living thing here with me. I felt so relieved. I heard him starting to cry and I started walking a little faster. There was no reason for him to be afraid, I wasn't going to hurt him. I turned the corner and looked down the street. I knew this block well, one of my friends lived here. There were a couple of parked cars, a mailbox and a fire hydrant. Trees lined the street, planted in the strip of grass that ran all the way down the block between the sidewalk and the road. I saw the dog sitting perfectly still, waiting for me to come to him.

I walked over to him and crouched down so I could pat him. He reached up his paw to me and something caught my eye just behind him and off to the right. The air seemed to be wavering like it does when it's really hot out and you can see heat waves rising from the surface of something. I hadn't noticed it before or hadn't acknowledged that I noticed it. I let go of the dog's paw and reached out to the wave. The dog jumped up and started barking again, this time wagging its tail, excited that I had finally seen this.

'What is it?' I asked. I looked at the dog and he looked back at me.

'It's the way out,' he said.

I sat up with a jolt, feeling at the end of my bed for Barker. He was sitting up, wide awake, wagging his tail. He licked my hand and gave out a little whimper. My heart was beating fast and I tried to catch my breath.

"What the hell was that?"

Chapter 16

Barker spoke to me! I mean, it was a dream but, still, he spoke to me. His voice was clear and direct. He told me that wavy thing I saw was the way out! It was a portal of some kind; it had to be. Maybe Barker was awake when he was dropped in this world. Maybe he saw the portal and knows how to use it. I didn't even look when I found him. I was more excited that I had found another living creature that I didn't even think to look at the air around him. Who would? The important thing was that there was a portal and Barker knew where it was and so did I now. Lot of good that did me, though. There was no way I could find it with the city gone. I would need the city to reappear so I could go to the same street again and find it and that wasn't going to happen until the next 360.

"You knew all along didn't your?" I pat Barker behind his ears and kissed his head. "If you could talk for real, it would be so much easier to ask you questions."

"Nicky?" It was Emma Lee; I must have woken her up when I talked to Barker. "Is everything okay?"

"It's better than okay," I said, not even caring that I woke her up. "I know how to get back home! I know where the portal is!"

"Portal?" asked Emma Lee, the sleep leaving her voice as she became more awake. "What is that?"

"It's like a door that brings you from one dimension to another," I explained. "If you go through one, you wind up somewhere else. I think that's how we came to this world."

"Well there must be a lot of these doors because people came here from every part of the world," she said. I stared into the darkness to where her voice was coming from, feeling all the wind deflate from me. Of course, there was more than one door. Why didn't I think of that? Either there was more than one door or the door, itself, moved around the world collecting people. If that was the case, then my chances of finding it again were pretty slim. I reached out and took Barker's head in my hands.

"Why can't you talk?" I asked. "You could probably tell me everything I needed to know about the dumb portal. It's not fair that animals can't communicate with us; they know so much more than we do."

"Nicky, are you all right?"

"Yeah, I'm fine," I said. "Go back to sleep. I guess I'll wait until the morning to talk to everyone about it."

"Okay," said Emma Lee. Within minutes I could hear her breathing grow heavy and I knew she was asleep. It took me longer, at least another hour before I finally calmed my mind and fell asleep. No dreams this time, though, just sleep.

In the morning I got up and dressed quickly so I could let Barker out for the bathroom and then go and check on Cocoa. The snow had stopped sometime through the night and the temperature had dropped dramatically. I knew what a Chinook was, who didn't? Living in Calgary or any other part of southern Alberta made you well aware of the warm winds that came in over the mountains. They were a welcome break of cold weather in our long winters. I could already hear the snow melting and it made me smile because I knew that this was the end, or pretty close to the end, of winter. We had maybe three weeks, at most, of the coldest season left. That was according to Colonel Al anyway. I would be glad not to have to trudge through the snow anymore, freezing my feet and hands and face.

Marshal was already up, sitting at the table and drinking tea when I came through and Robert was putting more wood into the iron stove. They both said good morning to me as I walked out the door and I told them I had something important to tell them when I got back. I returned fifteen minutes later and was happy to see that Colonel Al and Cornelius had joined them. Hopefully, I would only have to tell my story once.

"Okay," I started after getting a tea for myself. We all sat around the table and everyone was waiting for me to speak. "Last night I had a dream about when I found Barker. It was so real, like a memory that comes to you under hypnosis or something. Anyway, I recalled every little detail that happened the day I woke up down here for the first time.

"I heard Barker barking down the block and was so excited that I wasn't alone. I found him sitting on the sidewalk, waiting for someone to come. I bent down to shake his paw and that's when I saw it."

"What?" asked Cornelius.

"The portal," I said. "I didn't notice it the first time, the non-dream time. I was just happy to find Barker; I didn't look at the things around him. I must have subconsciously looked, though, because the memory is still in here." I tapped my head with my finger.

"Nicole?" asked Robert. "Are you sure that this wasn't just a dream?"

"I'm sure," I said. "Like I said before, there was too much detail for it not to be a memory."

"What did this portal look like?" asked Robert.

"It was wavy, like the air was full of heat of some kind," I explained. I could see that Robert was very interested in what I was saying. "That's when Barker told me it was the way out."

"Barker?" Cornelius tried to hide his laughter. "The dog told you it was the way out?"

"I know, I know," I tried to make it sound legitimate. "Dogs can't talk, it's impossible. Not here, anyway, but he did talk to me in my dream and I think that's quite possible."

"Yes," said Colonel Al, "the Private has spoken to me on several occasions. In fact, he's the one who convinced me to make my calendar."

"He did?" I was surprised to hear this. "I swear, there is more to this dog than anyone knows."

"So, the dog told you, *in* your dreams, that the wavy air you saw, *in* your dream, is a portal. Is that right?" asked Cornelius.

"Yes," I answered sharply and glared at the Englishman.

"Just checking," he said. "So, what do we do with this information?"

"I guess we go look for this portal," said Marshal. "Right, right, right Nicky?"

"We can't," I said.

"Why not?" asked Marshal.

"Because I don't know were it is," I answered.

"But you just said…" said Cornelius.

"I know, I saw the portal," I explained, "but that was in the city when there were streets to navigate from. I don't think I can find it without the city being there."

"I guess we wait then," said Colonel Al. "Until then, we keep doing the experiments."

"Oh, jolly," said Cornelius under his breath. I smiled and rolled my eyes at him so he would know that he was not alone in his thinking.

Chapter 17
Max

Max left Howling Wolf's camp and headed southwest. He was pretty sure the warrior would send spies out to see if he had been telling the truth about where he was off to. He wasn't disappointed. Two men were following him and if they were an example of Howling Wolf's army, it didn't say much about his men. Max was aware of their presence almost immediately. They weren't very discreet as they tried to hide behind trees or ducked down flat to the ground, thinking the snowbanks would hide them. What fools, he thought. They were dressed in black! Surely, they must know that they stuck out against the white snow. He could spot them from a mile away. To add to their lack of camouflage they were noisy. There were times he could hear every word they were saying. On one occasion they even got into a shouting match over their food supply; the whole countryside could hear them. Max kept going, though, pretending that he didn't know they were there. He kept marching in a southwest direction like he said he would. If he convinced them he was actually going to the west coast, they would go back and report it to Howling Wolf. Hopefully, this would convince the warrior that he was telling the truth. Whether or not it made him change his direction from the north and head west as well was another question. Somehow Max didn't think it would. As soon as his two little tag-alongs decided to go back to camp, Max would change directions and go back home to Nicky.

After three days of tagging behind, the two men decided it was time to go back. There was nothing unusual about where the Scott was going. He said he was heading to the coast and that was exactly where he appeared to be heading. He was on his own and, from what they observed, had no intention of meeting up with others. They could report to Howling Wolf that he had nothing to be concerned about; Max would be long gone before they packed up and headed north.

Max waited one more day just to be sure the men weren't coming back then he turned north and started to head back to Marshal's. He made sure that he was about a half mile away from his original path. The last thing he wanted was to run into Howling Wolf's group of men on his way back. He knew he could travel much faster than they could. He kept to the trees for the most part, knowing they would provide cover for him. There was more than just the warrior to worry about down here. Smaller groups of two or three could be just as dangerous if you didn't stay aware of everything around you at all times.

He just made it to where the Canadian border should be when the blizzard hit. It was bad and he knew he had to find a warm place to wait out the freezing storm or he would die. After, what seemed like hours, stumbling around in the blinding snow, he found a little cabin amongst the trees. It was owned by a couple in their twenties. The woman had fallen two years ago, and the man arrived in the 1950's. They met each other six months ago on the west coast and fell in love almost instantly. They wanted to explore this world together and left their coastal home not long after they met. When they got here, they fell in love with the quiet beauty that surrounded them and decided to stay for awhile. This proved lucky for Max, who would have frozen to death if he had not found them.

Sajni was a beautiful girl and Max probably would have tried to seduce her if he hadn't been thinking of Nicky all the time. Oh, how that girl had changed him! Sajni was exactly the type of woman he'd want for himself. Tall, curvy in all the right places, long black hair and dark eyes; she was beautiful. Her boyfriend, Phil, should consider himself lucky, Max thought. Phil wasn't built very big and he was lacking in any real muscle power. It would have been easy to take Sajni from him.

He stayed for five days with them, until the storm subsided, and it warmed up outside. They were gracious hosts and Max promised he would stop in to see them if he ever made it down this way again. He wanted to get back home as soon as possible. Nicky, Marshal and all the others had to make plans to either stay and fight or run. Although he'd only known them for a short time, he knew that they would stay and fight. Like himself, they would not give up what was theirs easily. They fought Pig and his men and won. There was no way they would give up everything they had worked so hard for to a man like Howling Wolf and his men. This scared him more than anything because the warrior was not like Pig at all. Howling Wolf was smart and trained in the art of brutality. Max knew men like the warrior; they thrived in the killing fields. Wiping out Nicky and her friends would be fun for him. Their army was big and willing to do whatever Howling Wolf told them and the warrior had no rules when a battle was being fought. They would just as easily kill Kitten as they would Max, himself.

He figured he was about five or six days away from Marshal's. If he had a horse, he would be so much faster. Unfortunately, he had lost his horse a long time ago. It had to be shot not long after he had reunited with Cornelius. On his way to infiltrate Pig's camp, Max and his horse had taken a path that led them through the foothills. They came across a small rockslide that was difficult to navigate through. Max got off his horse and tried to guide it through the rocks to a safer path. They had almost gotten through when the horse slipped, catching its hoof in a hole. Max could still hear the awful crack as it broke its leg and went down hard, crying in pain. Max couldn't bear to see the animal suffering, so, he took out his gun and shot it between the eyes, ending its pain.

They probably would have let him take Cocoa, but he couldn't leave his friends without the loyal horse. They needed her more than he did, especially when they gathered wood for the stove. In this weather they would need a lot of it and Cocoa would be able to pull huge loads for them. Besides, he was always afraid that something might go wrong and he couldn't bear the thought of having to shoot another horse in his care.

He knew that Howling Wolf had horses for himself and his men but, he also knew, that he didn't have a horse for every man, and he didn't see any wagons anywhere in the camp. Marching with so many men and having to go at a pace that matched the men walking, they weren't likely to get ahead of him if they did decide to head north. He also assumed they had to stop for the blizzard as well. They were probably a couple of days behind him at the very most. Just thinking about it made him hurry his pace and take less breaks.

It really had warmed up and he found himself walking through more puddles than snow. His feet were constantly wet, and he started to sniffle a couple of days after leaving Sajni and Phil. The last thing he needed was a cold. He stopped before he really wanted to so he could build a fire and dry out his boots and socks. He would be of no use to anyone if he were to get sick. It would slow him down, but he couldn't help it; he was soaked.

The next morning, he got up before the sun came up. His clothes were dry, and he actually felt better. His sniffles were gone and so was the feeling of a cold coming on. That was a good thing because he was only a couple of days away now. He felt a couple of butterflies' flutter in his stomach at the thought of seeing Nicky again. Maybe being away had confirmed his feelings for the feisty girl who had captivated him since the first moment he saw her. One of the reasons he volunteered to go find the Blood Demons was to, hopefully, let her sort out her feelings for him but, to his surprise, their separation actually strengthened his. Life had a twisted sense of humour, he thought. After so many years of going from one woman to another, he had finally found someone he wanted to spend eternity with, and she hated him.

Howling Wolf

When his men returned from tailing Max, Howling Wolf could see the relief in their faces as they told him that the Scott was, indeed, heading towards the coast. They saw no reason to bring him back and they assured their leader that he was no threat to any of them.

"I see," said Howling Wolf. He was disappointed in his men. Were they really that stupid? Did they really think that his old friend just happened to stumble across them in the middle of the icy winter? There was a reason Max tracked them down and Howling Wolf thought he knew why. There had to be someone or something he was trying to protect. "Thank you. You should go to the fire and warm up and have something to eat."

The two men looked at each other, not sure what to do. Howling Wolf had never been nice to them before. They knew better not to question him, though, and left before he could change his mind. Howling Wolf turned to look out to the west. He fumbled with his grandfather's arrow which still hung around his neck on a string made out of rawhide.

What was Max trying to hide? There must be something. Maybe he should ride out and ask the Scott, himself but he knew it would be a waste of time. Even if he did catch up to him, there was no way he'd be able to get any information out of him. If he was truly protecting something, he wouldn't talk, not to him, not to anyone. Torturing him wouldn't help either, not with Max. He wasn't your typical white man. He came from a land and time of strong men who could survive almost anything. Torturing him would only lead to one thing; the Scott's own death. No, Howling Wolf could not go after him. He turned to face the north. There was only one thing he should do; head north now as quickly as he could.

He made his way back to his tent. There was no way he could reach his destination quickly with this many men. He had to do something to cut his numbers. He figured he could take twenty, maybe twenty-five men at most. If he picked out his strongest fighters, that should be enough to fight any group they came across. That meant he had to get rid of eighty men but how? He unzipped his tent and crawled inside. He had wanted to stick with the traditions of his people and use a teepee, but the white man's tent was faster to set up and take down, so he begrudgingly gave in and used one.

He laid down on a pile of furs he had acquired from the animals he had killed. He closed his eyes and tried to clear his mind. He needed to think, and this was the only place where he knew he would be left alone to do so. He had to eliminate eighty men, make them disappear without causing any kind of dissention among them. How was he going to do that? An hour later he had his answer.

"Men." The whole camp had gathered around Howling Wolf who was now standing atop a pile of snow he had built up before calling his men together. "I have been thinking about my old friend who came to visit us. He told me that the north holds nothing. It has been cursed by the gods and bares no riches. I didn't want to believe him. I thought he was telling me lies to keep us away from his home, but I was wrong." A low grumble ran through the men.

"I have sent two of my best men," he pointed to the two men who had followed Max. They raised their heads, showing how proud they were to have been chosen for this task. Howling Wolf tried not to show his anger in their self love. He knew they had been fooled and should only feel shame for their stupidity. "They have returned today to tell me that my friend was telling the truth. He is on his way to the coast as we speak. I was wrong to assume he was lying." A murmur of shock rose from his men. Their leader never admitted his mistakes to anyone.

"Based on this information," he continued, "I have changed my mind. Tomorrow morning, at first light, we will leave this place and head towards the coast." The men erupted into confusion. This was a complete change. For months now, all Howling Wolf could talk about was the north and how rich the land would be. He promised that this was what the gods wanted for them; they would finally be able to settle and build their community. It was their promised land and now this. How could he change his mind so easily? Howling Wolf was expecting this, in fact, he had planned it.

"I see you have doubts." The men nodded their heads and voiced their concerns. Howling Wolf raised his hand for their silence and then pointed to one of the men in the front. He wasn't a good fighter nor was he very strong, but he was known by everyone; either hated or loved and was a perfect choice. "Come."

The man smiled and made his way to Howling Wolf, the men around him patting him on his back, congratulating him for being called upon by the prophet. He would be the envy of everyone today. He faced Howling Wolf and smiled as he looked into his leader's eyes. What he saw terrified him, but it was too late to do anything.

"You all have doubts about my decision," he kept his gaze on the man in front of him, evil reflecting from his eyes. "Let's see what the gods say!" He pulled out a knife and slit the man's throat, soaking himself in blood. The crowd of men gasped as Howling Wolf moved to let the dying man fall, terror painted on his face. Soon, the white snow was covered in red as the blood crept down the snow pile they were on top of. Howling Wolf picked up some of the red coloured snow and put it in his mouth then turned to his men.

"The blood flows to the coast," he pointed to the path of the blood. "The gods want us to go west. We must obey the gods." He looked out at his men with complete authority daring any of them to question him. The men stared in disbelief as their friend's blood ran out of his body until he was dead. They didn't understand what had just happened. There were no gallows, no rope or pot to catch the blood. What kind of sacrifice was this? Howling Wolf saw their doubts and knew they were questioning his actions.

"The gods have granted me permission to sacrifice one of my own," he explained. "It was how they wanted to show us the way. They will take this man's spirit to the skies where he will live as a prince for eternity." This seemed to calm the men down and they refocused on Howling Wolf and what he was saying. "We are the Blood Demons and we must obey the gods. Their word is final; we must go west to find the ocean. This is where the waters will wash away our wrongs, where we will build our community and live for the rest of time. We are the Blood Demons and we must obey the gods."

"We are the Blood Demons and we must obey the gods," the men started to chant.

"We are the Blood Demons and we must obey the gods," Howling Wolf said louder and with more conviction.

"We are the Blood Demons and we must obey the gods," they repeated again and again, getting louder each time. Soon, their voices could be heard from far away and there was no doubt that Howling Wolf had sacrificed their friend for a reason. Their prophet had done no wrong and his actions would never be questioned again. Finally, he raised his hands to bring silence to the camp.

"Tomorrow, we will pack our belongings and most of you will head for the ocean," he said. "I will ask some of you to stay behind with me. If we want a community that will thrive and last forever, we can not do it alone. We need women to help maintain our homes. We need women who will cook our meals, clean our clothes and keep our beds warm." The men gave out a small cheer. It would be nice to have a woman after all this time of travelling with just men. But Howling Wolf's plan was not accepted without question. Some of the men were still confused.

"Can't we look for women on our journey to the coast?" asked one of the men. He knew that Howling Wolf wouldn't like being questioned, but he didn't get it. It made more sense to collect women on their journey to the coast instead of looking for them here. The ocean was still far away; they could meet several women by the time they got there.

"We could look for women on our way, that is true. My friend informed me, however, that the people still living in the north are growing weak and will soon be following him," he explained. "The gods have told me that it would be better if we captured them here, as they flee. They will be too weak to fight and will be thankful to come with us. We can teach them their duties before we meet again." Now he would give the larger group of men their purpose, a reason for being the first to the coast. He had to make them feel important. That's what every white man wanted; to think the world could not exist without them.

"I, and the gods, have great faith in those of you that are going straight to the coast. Your task is the most important. You are the ones who will build the foundation for our community. You will be the ones to clear out anyone or anything that gets in our way." Howling Wolf was right; already he could see their evil pride possessing their minds. What he was saying made sense to them. They had their purpose now and returned to their tents to prepare for their departure the next day. Howling Wolf silently laughed at their foolishness. They would believe anything he said as long as he told them it was what the gods wanted. He shook his head and started selecting the men he wanted to take with him.

The next morning everyone was packed and ready to go. Howling Wolf had picked twenty-three men to stay behind with him and only kept a small amount of supplies. He didn't want to be slowed down with the weight of extra cargo. He took a dozen horses, enough so they could ride in pairs if they needed to. He let the larger group take the rest. He watched as the large group slowly made their way over the land believing that, one day, their group would be reunited on the wet sands of the coast. Idiots! Now, he had to convince the remaining men that they had to march north. He already had his plan worked out in his head, but it required one more night here. It was amazing what the gods could tell you in your dreams. They might even tell you to head north after all.

Chapter 18

The blizzard was over, the chinook was over, and winter was almost over, and we still didn't know anything about the foreign substance that created the rocks that exist in this world and I, for one, was done with it. I didn't know what else we could do. I think we tested a sample of rock from every square inch of the land in a fifty-mile radius around us. It was useless. Every sample came back the same, substance unknown, properties unknown, usefulness unknown. That's it and I'm over it. I say we give up and try to fix the radio or the clocks whichever was easier. I say the clocks; they didn't require any power. I wanted to take them apart, tweak the insides and put them back together again. Then I'd wind them up and they would magically tick away once more. If nobody else wanted to do it, then I would do it by myself.

So, now, I sat in the clock room with about ten different screwdrivers in front of me. Most of them were useless because they were too big to work on the tiny screws that held the clocks and its parts together. Still, I managed to take apart three clocks and now sat, staring at the parts, panicked because I had no idea what part came from what clock and how they all should fit together. I should have drawn diagrams and labeled parts as I took them apart, but I didn't think of that until after. I could just sweep everything onto the floor and start crushing the parts with the heel of my boot, but I was trying to control my temper and not give in to it.

Billy and Kitten sat at the table with me, but they seemed to be having way more fun than I was. They were taking apart the watches and I kept hearing oohs and awes coming from them like they were fascinated to see the inside of each watch. What made it worse, was that they managed to put all the pieces back after they were finished looking at them. What was wrong with me? Two ten-year old's could figure this crap out and I couldn't?

I felt a chill and zipped my hoodie up to my chin. The chinook had melted most of the snow covering the ground from the mine to Marshal's and, according Colonel Al's calendar, there wasn't going to be any more snowstorms. In fact, there wasn't going to be very much snow at all before we said goodbye to winter. That suited me just fine; intense cold and snow was not my forte. I was more of a warm weather girl; I thought with a smile and then shook my head. I was letting my mind wander and should get back to the clocks. I looked at the pile of gears and knobs and screws and sighed.

"Are you okay Nicky?" asked Billy. I guess I had sighed louder than I thought.

"Yeah, I'm okay," I answered. "It's just really hard to put this all back together. I can't remember where anything goes and it's starting to piss me off."

"Want some help?" he asked.

"Nah, I can do it. It's just going to take a whole lot of patience," I said, "and I think I've used my patience quota for the day. How about you guys? Anything, yet?"

"Nope, but it's fun to take them apart," he said with a look of excitement on his face. Kitten nodded her head in agreement. The girl still didn't talk very much unless your name was Billy; she seemed to talk quite a bit to the boy.

"Do you wanna keep working at it?" I asked.

"I don't know," he said. "What else do you wanna do?"

"I was thinking of going back home and getting something to eat," I said. "I don't like the food the colonel eats; it's all bland and yucky. We could go back, and I could make us some soup or something."

"That sounds good to me," Billy jumped off of his stool. "Come on, Kit, let's go eat!" The little girl smiled and jumped down from her stool to join her friend.

We went and told the others where we were going and were quickly joined by Emma Lee who didn't like doing these experiments any more than I did. The only thing she studied growing up was how to be a proper southern belle. All this talk of chemistry and physics confused her, and she found her lack of knowledge embarrassing. Robert sensed how she felt and gave her books to read that explained the basics of science. She appreciated Robert's help and read whatever he gave her and was starting to understand a bit of it, but it was still overwhelming. When I told everyone that Billy, Kitten and I were going back to Marshal's, she jumped at the opportunity to join us.

We took our time walking through the woods. Although the snow had pretty much disappeared in the fields leading to Marshal's, the woods still had a blanket of white covering its floor. The elevation was higher here and it didn't get as warm as it did on the prairie. Barker had come with us and Billy and Kitten had fun throwing snowballs for him to catch. This was one of the few times that I liked this world. It was peaceful. There was no buzz of a cell phone or rumble of a car passing by. I wouldn't have said it when I first woke up down here, but I actually liked that there was nothing hi-tech here. Instead of looking down at a screen full of text messages, I actually looked around and noticed all the beauty that surrounded me. It was nice.

By the time we got to the edge of the trees it was early afternoon and the sun was high in the sky, shining brightly in the clear blue that surrounded it. We walked through the fields talking about everything and anything as long as it wasn't about the mines or the experiments. Emma Lee and I talked about what we would make with the soup and decided we'd make biscuits. We still had a couple of big buckets of flour that Marshal had filled with bags of flour we brought from the city months ago.

"Hey! Who's that?" Billy was pointing at the house which was now visible. There was a man standing in front of the door, hands on his hips, staring back at us. I felt my heart begin to beat faster and my hands clenched into fists. Who the hell was snooping around our house? I was furious that there was an intruder hanging around what was ours. Being afraid didn't even cross my mind. I was ready to fight whoever it was and protect our stuff. We kept walking towards the house, and I could see that Emma Lee didn't share my fearlessness, she looked white as a ghost and her hands were starting to tremble.

"Hey! It's Max!" yelled Billy as he and Kitten started running towards him, Barker right beside them. I stopped and squinted so I could see the man more clearly. Could it finally be Max? I was starting to think I'd never see him again. Billy was right, it was him all right, I recognized the backpack strapped across his back. I felt my stomach flip and then *my* hands started to shake. What was wrong with me? I was starting to look just as scared as Emma Lee did a minute ago.

"It is Max!" exclaimed Emma Lee. "Oh, I thought he'd never come back."

"So, did I," I spoke the words with no emotion.

"Aren't you happy to see him?" she asked, surprised to see how little I reacted to seeing Max again. "I thought you had feelings for him. Isn't that why you've been working so hard with all those boring experiments; to keep your mind off of him?"

"No! I haven't got feelings for him!" I almost shouted the words at her which made her stop and look at me funny. Then I lowered my voice, "And I've been helping with the experiments because I really want to go home."

"Okay, if you say so," she said, "but I know he has feelings for you. Cornelius told me."

"Well, then, that's his problem," I said, feeling a rush of excitement to find out that Max had talked to Cornelius about me.

"Hmmm, I was so sure you liked him," she said, and I could see a bit of a smile lift the corner of her mouth. She was teasing me, and I could feel my face flush. I quickly turned my attention back to the group of three that had just reached Max. The kids reached out and hugged him, their faces buried in his coat. Barker was wagging his tail and barking his own greetings. We continued walking towards him and I felt the butterflies flying out of control in my stomach. Maybe I did like him just a little.

"You made it back!" Emma Lee wrapped her arms around him and gave him a kiss on the cheek. "I was so worried about you. Did you find them? Did you see the Blood Demons?"

"Whoa, hang on, I just got back. I haven't even been inside yet," he laughed at everyone's enthusiastic welcome. He looked at me with expectation in his eyes. His smile faded and his face turned serious when I didn't make any move to hug him or welcome him back with a kiss and a smile. "Hello, Nicky."

"Hello," I said, formally. "I'm glad to see that you're okay."

"Thank you," he turned to open the door, but I could tell he was disappointed in my lack of excitement for his return. Emma Lee could see it too and lightly elbowed me in the side. I glared at her and she looked back at me with raised eyebrows and nodded her head towards Max. I mouthed 'What?' to her and went into the house. I knew my reunion with Max would be awkward, but I wasn't anticipating all the anger. Whatever. Nobody could tell me who I should like and how I should like them.

"Did you find the demons?" asked Billy, anxious to hear about the diabolical group. "Were they mean? Did they, like, wear war paint and have necklaces made of human teeth?"

"Billy!" Emma Lee didn't like the way the boy was talking. It was like he was in awe of them. "Those men are not to be taken lightly. They're not to be admired."

"I was only asking Max if he saw them," Billy looked down at his feet. He hated when grown-ups tried to lecture him. He only wanted to know if Max had found them.

"Emma Lee's right kid," said Max. "These men are bad and dangerous. They don't care about you, me or anyone else. If you have something they want, they'll kill you for it without blinking an eye."

"Sounds like you found them," I said.

"I did," said Max. "I found them, and I talked to them."

"You talked to them?" gasped Emma Lee. "How'd you do that without getting yourself killed?"

"That does seem odd," I observed. How *did* Max establish a good enough relationship with such a diabolic group as the Blood Demons?

"What's so odd about it?" Max looked at me with a sarcastic sneer on his face and I could feel my heart racing. He made me so angry when he looked at me like that.

"It's odd that you were able to talk to these men so easily," I said.

"Who says it was easy?" Again, with the cocky sneer and this time I looked away from his piercing eyes. He smiled as if he had just won something. "I entered their camp knowing full well that my life was in danger. I needed to talk to their leader if I was going to get anywhere with them and to do that, I had to go to him because he sure the hell wasn't going to come to me with open arms."

"Did they know where you came from?" asked Emma Lee.

"I told them," he answered as he took off his backpack and sat down to take his boots off. He had been walking for over eight hours and needed to sit down for a few minutes to let his feet rest.

"You told them!" I couldn't believe it. Why would he tell them where he was from? Did he forget that these men wanted to come here and take the land from us, killing us in the process?

"Yes, I told them," he sounded angry that he had to defend himself. "It was all part of my plan."

"Your plan?" asked Emma Lee before I could say anything and make him angrier. "What kind of plan?"

"A good one," he said, happy that, at least, Emma Lee was willing to hear him out. "I told them that it was so bad up here that people were starving to death. I explained that all the talk about the north being the perfect place to live was a lie. I said the north was cold and frozen and it was impossible to grow any food before the snow came and, because of this, most of the wildlife had fled, leaving nothing to hunt. Oh, I laid it on thick, but not too thick. I didn't want Howling Wolf to think that I was exaggerating on purpose."

"Howling Wolf?" asked Billy. "Is he the leader?"

"He's the leader," confirmed Max.

"Wow!" said Billy. "What a cool name!"

"It is not cool," said Emma Lee. "It's a name for an animal which is what that man is."

"Anyway, I told Howling Wolf that I gave up on the north and was heading for the coast," said Max. "I told him I was tired of the hard work and the cold weather and that, if he was smart, he would go west as well."

"Did he believe you?" I asked.

"No," said Max and I started to say something, but he held up his hands to stop me. "That's why, when I left the camp, I headed towards the coast. I knew Howling Wolf would send some of his men out to follow me; make sure I was going where I said I would go and that I didn't have my own group of men ready to attack them."

"Did he?" asked Billy. "Did he send someone to follow you?"

"Yeah, two of them followed me," he answered. "They weren't very discreet about it either. I knew they were there the whole time. I ignored them, though, and for three days I headed south until they were convinced I was no threat and went back to their leader to report my whereabouts."

"And you?" I asked. "What did you do?"

"I turned and headed back here," he said. "I would have been here sooner, but I got held up by a blizzard."

"Do you think that this Howling Wolf believed you?" asked Emma Lee. Max shook his head and she gave out a small gasp. "Do you think he'll come anyway?"

"Yes, I do," said Max. "I think the man believes he has the right to take whatever he wants. He's used some kind of made up religion to convince his men that he communicates with the gods that control this world. Believe it or not they're convinced that he's a prophet sent to save them. As long as they do what he tells them to, the gods will take care of them."

"Really?" I rolled my eyes and shook my head. "Honestly, how can so many men let themselves be controlled by this guy? Gods, religion; those things don't exist here or anywhere else. I can't believe grown men would let themselves be scammed like this!"

"They're not as strong as you, Nicky," said Max. Was he complimenting me or being sarcastic? I couldn't tell. "They need the reassurance of believing that there's something out there that's watching over them. They need to know that they're not alone."

"But they're *not* alone!" I exclaimed. "There're lots of people here. Look at all of us, living together, helping each other out. Why can't they form *peaceful* groups and learn to live with each other *peacefully*; help each other?"

"Because they want it all," said Max, "and Howling Wolf has convinced them that they'll get it even if it means killing innocent people. He's tricky, this Howling Wolf, a very commanding man. He speaks with confidence and strength; I can see why so many want to follow him."

"Did you like him?" I asked. He looked at me and smiled and I could feel my heartbeat faster.

"I can admire a man who has both strength and pride," he said, locking his eyes with mine, "but not one who manipulates others to commit such savagery in the name of a god to benefit himself. I especially detest a man who wants to take away the things that I cherish most, and I have come to cherish everything about this place. I consider it to be my new home."

"That's, uh," I had to grasp the words as the smile returned to his face. I forgot that there were others in the room and felt my face flush a dark crimson, "good to know."

"So?" asked Billy who had no idea of the passion that was growing between me and Max.

"So?" Max repeated Billy's question, having no idea what the boy was asking and not taking his eyes from mine.

"So, are the Blood Demons coming here or not?" Billy asked angrily. Max looked at him and blinked his eyes and shook his head, trying to refocus on the conversation.

"Yes," he said, "I think so. I don't think Howling Wolf believed anything I said about the hardships of the land up here. He's coming and I think he's coming soon but there's good news and bad news."

"Yeah?" Emma Lee looked shocked to have her fears of the Blood Demons arrival confirmed as she blindly sat down at the table. "What's the good news?"

"Well, the good news is they'll take a few days to get here," he said. "They won't be able to travel very fast."

"What's the bad news?" Not that she thought slow travel was good news.

"The reason they'll be travelling slow is because there's over a hundred of them," he said. "A group that big can't travel too fast."

"Over a hundred men?" Now it was my turn to be in shock. There was no way we could defeat a hundred men! We barely beat the out-of-towners and they weren't half as evil as the Blood Demons. What the hell were we going to do? I felt the colour drain from my face. I had to leave, go outside and breathe fresh air into my lungs. "Excuse me," I said and walked outside.

A hundred men! Each one willing to kill us and take what we worked so hard for. How were we going to defeat that many? I stared out at the fields that I had walked across so many times over the last couple of months. I saw the mountains, covered in snow, reaching majestically into the sky. It was chilly and I saw my breath as it formed foggy clouds each time it escaped my lips. The door opened behind me and I turned and saw Max walking towards me with a look of concern on his face.

"Nicky are you okay?" he asked, and I was struck by how beautiful his voice was. The lilt of his accent sounded so reassuring right now.

"Max, a hundred men?" I felt the hopelessness of the situation strangling me and my face filled with pain. I felt my voice quiver and my eyes sting with tears. "There's no way we can beat them. We'll all die!"

"No, Nicky," he came to me and put his arms around me, holding me close and stroking my hair with his hand. I rested my head just under his chin and felt the comfort of his warmth. I could smell the sweat he had worked up on his journey here and it reminded me of how strong he was. I was scared and he was making me feel safe and protected and it was nice to let myself be vulnerable to him. Through his clothes, I could feel his heartbeat and was happy that it beat just as fast as mine. Maybe I missed him after all. "We'll figure it out, luv. I swear, I'll not let those men hurt you."

"You won't?" I sounded like a child and silently cursed myself, but I couldn't help it. In his arms, I felt all my doubt and anger disappear. I had been foolish for denying my feelings for him. I pulled away from him so I could tilt my head and look into his eyes. "How?"

"I-I don't…," he started but stopped, unable to continue as he looked at me. I felt his body tremble and that half smile that drove me crazy crossed his lips. Before he could say anything that would ruin this moment, I stood on my tiptoes, grabbed his collar and kissed him so hard I thought I had bruised his lips. I didn't intend to be so rough. I guess there was a reason that men usually initiated the kiss; they were so much better at it. He looked at me, surprised by my actions. "Nicky?"

"Shut up and kiss me properly like I know you want to!" He ran his fingers over my face, and I felt them quiver with his built-up passion. I closed my eyes at his touch and felt my body press against his and, even through all our winter clothing, I could feel the heat between us. I parted my lips, anticipating his kiss and felt myself get lost as he answered my plea. His mouth worked expertly over mine and I knew I had never nor would I ever be kissed like this again. I accepted him without even trying to deny my feelings. He was just as lost as I was and neither one of us wanted it to end but slowly, after what felt like an eternity and rushed by like a second, we broke apart. It took me a moment to open my eyes and look at him. He was smiling and I blushed.

"That was amazing," he said, his voice just above a whisper, trying to recover from the shock of my passion. "I, uh, I'm lost for words."

"Then don't say anything," I wanted to kiss him again and again. It felt so right, and I didn't want the feeling to go away. He didn't disappoint as our lips touched again and I felt his passion grow stronger and less guarded. His fingers tangled in my hair and I reached up and caressed the back of his neck, running my fingers up through his hair. He groaned and I responded by pressing closer to him.

"Max, Nicky?" It was Emma Lee who had just opened the door behind us. "Oh my, I'm so sorry! Please, forgive me. Continue. Oh my, I'll-I'll just go back inside." Max and I quickly broke apart and I covered my mouth and looked away, trying to catch my breath and not look too embarrassed.

"No, no, that's okay," said Max who held my hand now. When did he take my hand? I didn't remember but it felt natural. "We were just, uh, just…never mind. What is it that you want?"

"Well, the kids and I were just talking about what we're going to do," she stammered, still feeling bad that she had interrupted such an intimate moment. "We wondered if you and Nicky were okay and if you'd like to come back in and have something to eat."

"Oh, yeah, the soup," I said. "Sure, I'm game. Are you hungry Max?"

"Starving," he smiled and looked at me with mischief in his eyes, "but I guess I'll settle for soup for now." Heat and adrenalin filled my face and I giggled like one of those annoying girls in high school. He saw my reaction and I saw a trace of red cross his cheeks, too and then he leaned over and whispered in my ear, "We'll continue this later."

We both shared a knowing look and then followed Emma Lee back into the house. They had set the table with four bowls and four spoons. Kitten was stirring the pot of soup on the stovetop and Billy was opening a pack of crackers. Barker was lying on the floor in front of the stove, enjoying the heat that radiated from it. As I watched Billy with the crackers, I was reminded of when Marshal and I travelled out here from the city. We stopped and ate peaches and crackers that day and I thought Marshal was the craziest person I had ever met. I was so confused about what this world was and had no idea of the things that would happen in the months to come. I hadn't seen Marshal eat peaches for so long that I forgot how much he liked them. Maybe I'd go to the underground fortress later and get him a can.

"We really need to figure out what we're going to do," said Emma Lee. We were sitting around the table and eating our soup, vegetable as it turned out. "I think we should leave, maybe go further into the mountains."

"We could do that," said Max. "But you and I both know that won't solve anything. If we run or if we stay; it makes no difference. These men won't be satisfied with staying in one place. Howling Wolf won't be satisfied with it. He'll eventually grow bored of the routine he's promised his men and will convince them that they have to leave and find better land; kill more people. He enjoys killing; it's a game to him."

"What do you suggest we do?" I asked. I was thinking we should leave as well. I knew we could never defeat that many men.

"We stay," he said.

"And get ourselves killed?" Emma Lee asked. "We'd be foolish to do that. There's too many of them!"

"We don't have to fight all of them," he said, and I knew he had a plan.

"What do we do then?" I asked.

"We cut the head off the snake," he smiled.

"What?" asked Emma Lee but I thought I knew what he was saying.

"You think we should try to kill Howling Wolf," I said. He smiled at me with pride.

"Exactly," he said. "If we kill their prophet, they won't know what to do. They'll be lost."

"You don't think one of the others will take over and they'll continue to kill?" I asked.

"No," he said. "I think Howling Wolf picks his men carefully. He only wants men who will follow. He doesn't want men that can lead. Another leader would eventually try to take over."

"But how are you going to kill this man?" asked Emma Lee. "If he surrounds himself with men who think he's their saviour, how are you going to get close enough to kill him?"

"You can ask the colonel," said Billy who had finished his soup and was listening to our conversation.

"The colonel?" asked Max. I had been so caught up in his return and his news of the Blood Demons and our kiss that I had completely forgotten to tell him about Colonel Al.

"Yeah," continued Billy. "He's a real colonel, too, from the army. He's been to war and everything! I bet he knows how to do it."

"Who is this colonel?" asked Max.

Chapter 19

"I can't believe you want to go home so much," Max said. We had told him everything about Colonel Al and his experiments and were now making our way to the mines so he could meet him. I knew he'd have a lot of questions about the colonel, but I didn't think he'd be so upset that I wanted to go back home. I still couldn't figure out why anyone would want to stay down here and not return to the world we came from. I understood that it wasn't going to be the same as when they left but it still had to be better than here. There were so many conveniences there like heat, light, running water to name a few. I really missed my hot showers and I could guarantee the others would like them too.

"I'm sorry," I said, not really meaning it. "I miss my home and I want to go back. Don't you?"

"Nicky, I fell down here over three hundred years ago," he explained. "The home I remember does not exist anymore.

The way that world is now would be just as foreign to me as this world is to you. I've had glimpses of what it looks like each time the 360 happens and I don't think I'd fit in. This is my world now; I'm comfortable here, I know how to live here."

"I could show you around," I said, laughingly but I was upset that he really didn't want to come with me. "I could help you adapt to the way the world works now. It's better than here. You don't have to work so hard to survive."

"Nicky, I don't want to go," he said, and I could see the seriousness in his eyes.

"Okay, I guess I'll go alone," I said and picked up my pace, so I didn't have to walk beside him anymore. I was angry with him for not even giving it a chance. If he thought that I was going to stay here with him, well, there was just no way! My mom and dad were still alive; my friends were still there. I wasn't even gone for a year. For me, nothing had changed. How could he expect me to stay? I paused for a moment to consider *his* side. What was I thinking? How could I be so cold? Whoever he knew there died long ago. There, he had nothing; here he had everything. How could I expect him to leave? This was his home now. I silently cursed for letting myself care so much about him. If only I could ignore my feelings for him, I could leave without another thought. I looked back at him and realized he was watching me and, by the look on his face, was just as troubled as I was over this. I smiled and waited for him to catch up.

"I'm sorry," I said. "I guess it's not really a problem unless we actually figure out how to get back."

"You're right," he said sounding relieved, "but I do know what it's like to miss your home and your family. If you have the chance to see them again, I can't ask you not to take it."

"Thank you," I said. It was all we were going to say about the subject for now.

When we got to the mines, Max was surprised by how well it was hidden. With a few strategically placed branches, it could disappear altogether. He followed us with apprehension through the tunnels. I could tell he was a little antsy and wondered if he was claustrophobic. It would be out of character for him to be afraid of something. His demeanor changed, though, when we reached the 'lab' and he saw his friend with his head hovering over some kind of apparatus, his eyes completely focused on two round tubes.

"Max!" It was Robert who saw him first and came to him with his hand outstretched to welcome him back. "You're back! What a pleasant surprise. We were wondering how your journey was going. I'm glad to see you're okay."

"Mate?" Cornelius looked up from the microscope. "Well, I'll be damned; it is you! Back from the pit of blood I dare say."

"You could say that," Max said. He greeted each of them with a handshake and hug. They were all happy to see him, but they also wanted to know about the Blood Demons and if they were, indeed, on their way. Colonel Al stood in the background waiting to be introduced.

"You must be the colonel," Max said as he made his way over to him.

"And you must be the Scottish pirate," Colonel Al said as he stepped forward and saluted Max. "Colonel Albert Young, United States army. Very pleased to meet you. I have been informed of these Blood Demons and their plans for total destruction of our community. I admire that you have taken the responsibility to act as a scout to ascertain the position of said group and report back to us any information you have obtained."

"Well, I'll be damned! You are *definitely* a soldier all right," said Max as he shook the colonel's hand. "It doesn't matter what uniform a soldier wears; you all have the same rehearsed greeting. Yes, colonel, I have been on a scouting mission to find the Blood Demons and I have brought back information on their whereabouts and their plans."

"Well, sir," said Colonel Al, "I suggest we all cease our experiments and retreat to my quarters where we can talk, and I can make coffee for everyone."

"Geez, colonel, you don't have to be so formal," I said. "Max is just one of us. You can talk to him just like you talk to us."

"I'm sorry." I could see his expression change and he seemed more relaxed. "It's just habit to talk to a returning soldier with respect."

"But Max isn't a soldier," I said.

"No, but he was on a very important and dangerous mission like any real soldier," said Colonel Al and I felt bad for calling him out on the way he was talking. He was only being respectful towards Max. I probably should have let him.

"I'm sorry," I said. "You're right. Talk to him however you want."

"I don't care how you talk to me," said Max. "I heard you say coffee and I don't want to say anymore until I have a cup."

They were all sitting around Colonel Al's room; some on the edge of the bed and some on the floor. Max was drinking a cup of coffee and I could tell he was enjoying it because he smiled after every sip. Robert and Cornelius were having coffee as well but Emma Lee and myself didn't want one. The colonel didn't have a lot of coffee left and I wanted him to save it for himself. Besides, the colonel had made me a cup this morning.

"So, mate," said Cornelius, "tell us what you've discovered."

"Okay," he took in a deep breath, regretting that he had to tell them how much danger they were in. "Let me start by saying that, yes, I did find the Demons. I talked to their leader and I'm afraid the news is not good." He told the others what he had already told us; that Howling Wolf probably didn't believe his story about how bad it was here and that he was most likely on his way right now and was bringing an army of a hundred men with him. We were impossibly outnumbered and, if we stayed, would probably be killed. We needed to find a way to defeat them. That's when he told them about the plan to assassinate Howling Wolf.

"If we kill their leader," he explained, "maybe we'll kill the ideology that inspires these men. It's our only hope."

"Or we could run," said Emma Lee. "I know these men and what they can do. I've seen it. They want to kill people; they love it. It's what they live for. I don't think we can get their leader without getting ourselves killed first."

"But I'm willing to take that risk," said Max. "If we leave, we're giving them an opportunity to continue with their killing. There are others that live around here. I, for one, will not be responsible for leaving them to die under the Demons' rule."

"Then we'll take them with us," said Emma Lee.

"Or, we ask them to help us fight," said Cornelius.

"They won't help," I said. "Remember when we were gathering people to go fight Pig over the water? None of them wanted to help. They all wanted to stay in their own little bubbles and let us do the dirty work for them. I don't think they'll take this threat any differently."

"Nicole is right," said Robert who, until now, had been silent. "Nobody is going to help us, and we can't just leave and hope that the Demons will pass them by. I think we should try to kill their leader. Max is right, it's our only chance. Now, let's stop wasting time arguing about it and figure out how to do it."

We talked for another twenty minutes trying to come up with a plan to kill Howling Wolf. We all agreed that it would be almost impossible to get to him. Maybe a child would be able to infiltrate his ranks without suspicion, but Colonel Al was strongly opposed to such a ploy. This was what the Viet Cong did, and he refused to be like them. No child would be used as an assassin, not while he breathed the air around him. We couldn't use Max because he was supposed to be on his way to the beaches of California. In fact, using one of the men would be too risky. Howling Wolf would see any man from here as a threat. We were running out of options.

"I'll do it," I said. It was really our only choice.

"No!" Max was the first to respond. "Nicky, no, it would be way too dangerous. You don't know what this man is capable of."

"Yeah I do," I said, touched that he was worried about me and angry that he was worried about me. I wasn't some weak little girl. If a man could assassinate this guy, then so could I. "How could I not know what he's capable of? You guys keep telling me. This guy, Howling Wolf? He sees, he wants, he kills, he takes. That about sum it up?"

"Y-yeah," Max answered, always shocked with how I could get to the point so quickly.

"Ok, then, by process of elimination, I'm the only one left," I said. "So, I'll get close to him and I'll kill him."

"What about me?" asked Emma Lee and I could see that breaking into the Blood Demons camp was the last thing she wanted to do but I admired her attempt at volunteering.

"No," I said, "it can't be you. He'd recognize your accent and know that you're from the south and probably know about his attack on the mine community. He'll know you'll be seeking revenge."

"She's right, pet," said Cornelius who stepped forward to take her hand.

"Then, it's settled," I said. "I'll kill this wolf guy."

"Howling Wolf," corrected Max who still wasn't happy to let me do this. I could tell that he would have a lot to say the next time we were alone.

"Okay, now that that's out of the way," I wanted to change the subject as soon as I could, "let's go show Max what we're working on. Maybe he can tell us what the rocks are." Everyone agreed and we started to make our way back to the lab.

"We're not finished with this," he whispered to me on our way down the tunnel.

We stopped in the other rooms and showed him what we were doing with the clocks, the radio, the calendar. We explained it all to him earlier, but it was different to actually see it. I could tell he didn't have a clue what any of it meant. He came here so long ago. He didn't know what radios were. He practically grew up on a pirate ship and, unlike Cornelius, had never studied any kind of science. He knew how to fight and steal and that was about it. Never, in his life, had he ever looked down a microscope.

"What is that?" he asked while he stared at a sample of rock being magnified a thousand time.

"It's a piece of rock," explained the colonel as he adjusted the small flame under the specimen. It was the only light source we had to actually see the specimen and had to be constantly monitored. If it got to high, it could burn the specimen. If it got to low, you couldn't see anything.

"That's a rock?" He seemed fascinated with it. "Show me."

"It's here," said Colonel Al, pointing out a dish of crushed rock. He had pounded it down into a powder. "See? It's been reduced to this form so we could look at it easier."

"Wow, that's impressive." He reached out and gathered some of the powder in his hand. He looked at it closely and even smelled it. I watched him closely, amused by his child-like fascination with the rock powder. When he was finished, he turned his hand over to pour the powder back into the dish.

"What the...?" I started, silenced by what I was seeing. The powder in Max's hand was not going back into the dish. Instead, as he poured it out of his hand, it seemed to make a sudden ninety degree turn in the middle of the air and head for the door. As it did so, the powder that was still in the dish rose up and joined the rest of the powder heading for the door. "What's it doing?"

"I don't know," Robert said, regaining his speech before the others. "It seems to be leaving."

"I see that but how? Why?" I asked.

"You mean it's never done this before?" asked Max.

"No," Colonel Al had finally found his voice. "Nobody's ever poured the powder into the air before."

We followed the powder through the door and down the tunnel. It kept going as if it knew where it had to be. It went outside and picked up speed in the open air. It headed northeast away from the forest. We tried to run after it, but it was too fast; we lost it.

"Where did it go, go, go?" asked Marshal. "Nicky?"

"I don't know," I said but there was a theory forming in the back of my mind. What if the rock knew how to find the portal? What if that's what its purpose was? Maybe it could lead us there. We could be home by tomorrow! "I think we should get some more! We can carry it in a bowl and sprinkle more into the air when we lose track of where it's going."

"Yes, yes, yes," said Marshal. "Nicky, that's what we should do!" We headed back to the mine to crush up more rock.

"What if it gets windy out?" asked Billy. "Won't the wind take it away?"

"But it's not windy right now, Billy," I said, angered that the boy had brought this up. Of course, the wind would blow it away, but I didn't want to think about it. I was convinced that it would take us to the portal, and I didn't want any wind to delay it.

Twenty minutes later we had all managed to crush enough rock to fill a dish halfway. We headed out of the mine. Colonel Al carried the dish, remembering to put his hand over it so the powder couldn't fly out. When we got to where we had lost the first bit of powder, he reached into the bowl and took a pinch of it and sprinkled it into the air. Again, it took a turn and headed northeast.

"Let's go!" shouted Marshal. We followed as fast as we could, but we didn't get very far. This powder was going much faster than the first time. We must have looked ridiculous, seven adults, two kids and a dog, we left Cocoa back at the mine and tethered to a tree, chasing a small cloud of powdered rock. I giggled to myself at what the image must look like.

"What's so funny?" Max was walking right beside me.

"We are," I said. "Running through the woods, chasing rock powder. Who'd have ever thought that's how we would spend what's left of the afternoon."

"It is a peculiar sight," he laughed. "But, somehow, I can't seem to stop."

"Me neither," we both laughed and picked up our pace to keep up with the rock.

The powder led us out of the trees and into the fields that led to Marshal's. We were a bit further north but not a lot. It seemed to gain even more momentum over the fields, and it wasn't long before we lost it again. Kitten and Billy started throwing a stick for Barker to play fetch and he started barking as he waited for it to be thrown. Colonel Al reached into the dish and pinched more powder between his fingers. I watched him closely and then felt the air go still around me. A shiver ran up my spine and I looked over to the kids playing with Barker. The sound of a gunshot filled the air and I saw Kitten fall to the ground. What the…I started to run to the fallen girl.

"Kit? What's wrong?" Billy ran to his friend. Another gunshot and Billy went flying through the air as the bullet ripped into his back. He fell face first, dead before he hit the ground. I finally got to Kitten who was being vigorously licked by Barker. Her tiny face was still, here eyes open and empty. Blood covered her coat and I tried to hold back a scream as I reached down to her neck to look for a pulse. There was none. She was gone. I looked to find Billy and saw Emma Lee crying over him. What the hell just happened? Another gunshot and a patch of ground inches from me flew into the air.

"Come on!" Max grabbed me around the waist and lifted me into the air. "We have to hide!"

"But Kitten, Billy," I cried out.

"They're dead!" Max shouted. "Everyone let's go! They're here, Howling Wolf, the Demons. Let's go!"

We ran for the woods, hearing more gunshots behind us. I didn't see anyone else go down, but I didn't see everyone either. It was happening so fast and the things around me were a blur. I knew Max was beside me, holding my hand and I could see Barker running ahead of us. I couldn't see anything else. I guessed we were heading back to the mines to hide in the tunnels but, all of a sudden, I didn't know the way. Max pulled me along through the trees.

"Cocoa!" I suddenly remembered our horse tied to a tree with no hope of escape. "We have to get to Cocoa and turn her loose; make her run away through the forest!"

"We will," answered Max as if he had thought the very same thing. "We'll get to the mine, turn her loose, camouflage the entrance and hide inside but we have to hurry. They must have sent out a scouting group to find us and they're on horseback. It won't take them long to catch up."

"Where are the others?" I still couldn't see everyone. "Did anyone else get shot?"

"They're all heading to the mines. We're just a little quicker," he answered. He was watching Barker and following every step the dog took. "Hurry!"

"I am!" I shouted back. I heard Robert's panicked voice yelling from somewhere behind me.

"Pick him up!" He ordered. "Don't leave him!" Terror filled my mind. Someone was hurt but who? Not Robert; maybe the colonel or Marshal or Cornelius. I kept running, hoping we could get to the mine before they spotted us.

Chapter 20

We made it! We got back to the mine before any of the
Blood Demons spotted us. We even had a chance to untie
Cocoa and send her on her way. It was easier than I thought it
would be, too. It was if the horse knew that something bad
was happening and couldn't wait to be untethered. Once we
took her bridal off, she ran further into the woods away from
the direction of the demons. We also had time to cover the
entrance with tree branches and now, hopefully, we were
hidden enough that they wouldn't see us. We needed time to
figure out what to do. We also needed to save Marshal's life.

When I heard Robert give the command to 'pick him up',
I had no idea who got hurt or how badly they were hurt. Max
had a hold of my hand and was pulling me and urging me to
go faster and faster. I didn't find out that it was Marshal who
got hurt until after we cut Cocoa loose and started piling up

branches in front of the mine. By then, Colonel Al and Cornelius arrived carrying an unconscious Marshal. I felt my heart drop as I stared at my friend. The crazy redhead was the only reason I was still alive. He took me into his underground fortress when I would have surely died in the winds that followed the 360.

"Marshal?" I ran over to him and couldn't believe how pale he was. "What happened?"

"He was shot," said Robert. I looked at Marshal searching for the bullet wound. I noticed blood on the colonel's hands and realized the bullet must have hit Marshal in the back. "Come on, get him into the tunnels. Take him…"

"To my room," finished Colonel Al. "We can put him on my bed. I have some bandages and alcohol in my trunk."

That was fifteen minutes ago and now we all sat in the colonel's room keeping as quiet as possible and watching Marshal's chest rising and falling with each breath. As long as he kept breathing, we still had time to help him. How we were going to do that, I didn't exactly know. The bullet had entered near the bottom of his ribcage, just narrowly missing his spine. There was no exit wound, so, that meant the bullet was still inside somewhere. None of us had the knowledge nor the expertise to help him. What he really needed was a doctor or, at least, someone with medical training. Robert and Cornelius could think of no one. It didn't matter, though, because we couldn't risk leaving the mine and having the demons find us. So, now we were sitting in the colonel's room, looking at one another with no plan to get us out of this situation.

"Are you sure it was them?" I asked Max.

"Yes," he answered.

"How could you tell?" I asked.

"I could see Howling Wolf," he explained. "You can't miss the long, black hair. It was him alright."

"But I only saw about twenty men," said Colonel Al. "I thought he had an army of a hundred men?"

"He does, trust me," Max said, angry that they were doubting him. "I was in their camp; I saw them. But I was thinking…"

"What?" asked the colonel.

"Well, I was thinking that he and his best fighters rode ahead," Max said. "Maybe he actually believed some of the things I told him about there not being many people here. If he came here quickly and unexpectedly, he wouldn't need a lot of men to conquer us."

"And the rest of his men?" I asked.

"Will be coming in a few days," he said, "after the land has been taken. Then they'll come and set up their community."

"It's a bold move," said the colonel. "Taking the chance that we would not be ready for them. A sneak attack. It's what

I would have done. This Howling Wolf is smart; a good leader."

"Yeah, well, lot of good that does us," I said. I was getting sick of how these guys were in awe of this guy. He was a psychopath and only killed people because he liked it. Our biggest concern right now was helping Marshal and we weren't going to do that by sitting here waiting to be found. I had an idea and the more I thought about it, the more I liked it.

"Nicole?" Robert sensed my anger and he knew that when I was angry, I did crazy things. "What are you thinking?"

"I have an idea," I said.

"What?" asked Robert, leaning in closer to listen.

"Well, I think we should make a run for the portal," I said.

"What?"

"How?"

"That's crazy!"

"Give me a minute," I knew they would question my idea, but it might be the only way out of this. "I think we take the rock powder and sneak out in the dark. We can head north through the woods until we get to the edge of the forest. Once in the field, we'll start heading east. I have an idea where Calgary should be, and we'll go that way. When the sun comes up, we'll use the powder to lead us directly to the portal. If you're right Max, and most of his army is still days away, I think we have a chance."

"How?" Cornelius sounded doubtful of my plan.

"Let her finish," Max said, sticking up for me.

"Well, I think this Howling Wolf will stick by Marshal's," I explained. "He doesn't know that there's a portal. He'll be expecting us to fight our battle somewhere between Marshal's and the forest. He won't have any patrols north; what would be the point?"

"Nicky," Cornelius started, "we don't even know if there is a portal. We're going off of flying rock dust and a dream!"

"Well, I believe there's a portal," I said. "And we have to find it and go through it because there's no way we'll ever defeat one hundred men."

"What about the assassination plan?" asked Emma Lee.

"I think that went out the door when they killed the children," said Robert. "If they could kill Billy and Kitten so easily, they won't hesitate to kill Nicky if she even tried to approach them."

"I agree," said Colonel Al. "I think Nicky's right; we go for the portal. The private can help with that. He's been through it enough times; he can show us how."

"Barker?" asked Max.

"Yeah," I said. "It seems my dog knows a lot more than any of us. If he could talk, we probably would have been out of here a long time ago."

"What about Marshal?" asked Cornelius.

"We take him," said Emma Lee. Everyone looked at her as if she were insane. "Well, we can't leave him! Besides, when we go through the portal, we should be able to find a doctor right?"

"She's right," I said. "We have to take him."

"It will slow us down," said Cornelius.

"So, it slows us down," said Colonel Al. "You're a man, you can handle it. We should never leave a fallen comrade behind."

"I was only pointing out that carrying a wounded man was not going to be easy," Cornelius didn't like the way the colonel talked to him. "We need to find a way to stop the bleeding before we go because; first, moving him will make him bleed more, second, if he keeps losing blood, he'll bleed to death and third, the blood will leave a trail in the snow. Now, does anyone know how to sew?"

"Sew? I know how to sew," said Emma Lee.

"Good," said Cornelius, "you can stitch him up." Emma Lee's face grew pale and I could tell that sewing wounds wasn't what she had in mind.

301

"Duct tape," I said. "Colonel, do you have any duct tape?"

"I have tape, yes," he answered. "In the communication room. Why?"

"Because, we can put duct tape over the wound. It will stop the bleeding. I saw it on one of those emergency room shows," I said, then took off down the tunnel to the radio room.

I returned minutes later with the wide, silver tape. I went over to Marshal and turned him on his side so I could see the wound. The sheets and bed were covered in blood. I reached to the pile of towels Colonel Al had gathered and dipped one in a bowl of water that had also been brought when we first got here. I carefully wiped away all the blood on Marshal's back and then dried it as best I could. He felt cold to me. I would wrap him up in whatever clothes and blankets I could after I taped the wound. Colonel Al helped me with the tape and watched in fascination as the blood stopped seeping out of Marshal as soon as I taped it up.

"Amazing," he said, looking closer at the wound. "How long will this last?"

"Hopefully, until we can find a doctor," I said. "But we'll take the rest of the tape with us just in case."

"Ok, let's figure out what we're going to do," said Max. "I presume you dropped the powder when the gunfire started?"

"Yes, I did," said Colonel Al. "I was in the middle of getting more powder when the first shot rang out. I dropped it then. I'm sorry."

"It doesn't matter, now," said Max. I didn't like the accusatory way he said it. Anyone would have dropped the powder under those circumstances. "We have to make more. We should do that before anything else, but we have to do it quietly. We should grind them rather than smash them; it makes less noise. Did you hear that, Billy? No, loud…" We all stared at him as he realized his mistake. It was always so easy to tease the little boy for being over enthusiastic in tense situations. It was automatic to warn him before he did something without thinking. Max turned and headed for the tunnels to gather rocks for grinding.

"I hate this world," said Robert as he turned down the tunnels to follow Max.

A half an hour later, we had grinded enough rocks into powder to fill a cup three quarters full. It was more than we had before, and it would have to do. Cornelius and Max had just returned from the entrance and informed us that it was now dark. So far, no one had found us. I changed Marshal's shirt to one of the Colonel's. He would have to wear black; the colonel had no yellow. I could only imagine what Marshal would say when he discovered this horrible mistake when he woke up. If he woke up. I quickly flushed the thought from my mind and continued dressing Marshal as warmly as I could.

We had to figure out how we would carry the redhead and who would carry him. I volunteered but knew they wouldn't let me. I was strong but not strong enough to carry Marshal. He weighed about 140 pounds, thirty pounds more than I did. I could barely drag him let alone carry him through the trees and the snow. The men would take turns; Robert would go first. Max, Cornelius and the colonel were better at fighting and we may need to do just that as soon as we left the mine.

We packed a backpack with some water, a little bit of food and some extra matches. I put some extra rocks in my pockets and carried the backpack. At least, I could do something to help. We all had a gun now thanks to the well-prepared Colonel Al. He had a cache of guns hidden in the calendar room. We strapped Marshal to Robert piggyback style and headed for the mine entrance. It was now or never.

Chapter 21

The first few feet out of the mine were the scariest. If Howling Wolf had any idea where we were, he would most likely be waiting to attack us when we emerged. No one was there. Our hiding place was still hidden. Max tried to keep the entrance covered in case we needed to come back. We went slow, trying not to make any noise. It was a little easier with snow still covering all the dead branches and twigs that would have snapped under our feet. We had no light, agreeing that a lantern would surely give up our position to the Blood Demons. It all reminded me of when Robert and I left Madge behind in the out-of-towners' camp. We had been trying to find Marshal's hidden cave then. I never thought I'd be sneaking through the forest in the middle of the night again.

We let Barker take the lead simply because he was faster in the dark and more agile through the bushes and trees. Besides, he seemed to know exactly what path would take us out of the woods. I wondered if he could find the portal without the powder. It didn't even occur to me that he could probably lead us all the way. On the other hand, maybe he was just as lost as I was in the city or, rather, without the city and all the streets and avenues to navigate by. We made our way through the trees, crouched low to the ground, single file. Max led the way followed by Colonel Al, Cornelius, Robert, with Marshal on his back, Emma Lee and me. I kept turning and searching behind me, hoping no one was following us. So far, so good.

After about ten minutes everyone stopped. I could hear a small whimper come from Barker and wondered what was wrong. I tried to see what was going on but, being last in line, I couldn't see anything. As I got closer, I saw the men standing in front of something, their guns lowered. 'Did something happen to Barker?' I wondered. He whimpered again and I heard Colonel Al's voice.

"Shhh, Private," he whispered. "You'll give our position away!"

"What's wrong?" I tried to see what had stopped them, but they were blocking me.

"Nicky," said Max. He gently grabbed my arm and tried to lead me away. "You don't want to see this."

"See what?" I tried to break free of Max.

"No, Nicky," he said. "We'll go another way." Then I heard Emma Lee gasp and cover her mouth.

"What happened?" I asked thinking that if Emma Lee could see why couldn't I? I pulled away from Max and went over to see what they were looking at.

"Oh, my god," I felt my legs go numb as I looked at the mass in front of me. Cocoa lay on the ground, her neck twisted at an odd angle, her eyes wide open. Her chest had been cut open; her heart ripped out. Barker was lying on the ground beside her, licking her, trying to wake her up. I went numb and fell to the ground beside Barker. She must have thought it was safe to come back. She was so loyal to me, to us. I had saved her from her terrible life with Butcher and she trusted me. She must have thought it was safe to come back. I stared at her body and twisted my fingers into Barker's fur. He turned and looked at me. He tilted his head, cocked his ears and let out a quiet whimper. He wanted me to wake her up, but I couldn't; no one could.

"Come on, Nicky," Max had his hand around my arm once more, trying to pull me up but I couldn't move. I felt like I weighed a thousand pounds. "We have to go! If they killed Cocoa here, that can't be too far away. Come on!"

"I-I...," I couldn't form any words as I continued to stare at Barker. He looked at me and dropped his ears. He turned back to Cocoa, gave her one last lick and then stood up. He reached out his paw to me. I touched it and knew we had to go. If I could have dug her a grave, I would have but there was no time for that. Somewhere, out there were the Blood Demons and I hated them for what they had done. What cowards they were! Killing two children and a horse made them less than men and I hoped this world would be their eternal hell.

We kept low to the ground and made our way north, purposely staying in the trees as far as possible. The trees provided some kind of cover for us. Robert carried Marshal quite far before finally letting someone else take over. It was Max's turn now. He carried him effortlessly, still able to dart in and out of the trees. He said it was because he had travelled so long carrying a full backpack while searching for the Blood Demons. Still, he was a strong man.

"We have to stop," said Cornelius.

"Why?" I didn't want to stop. We should keep going, get to the portal as fast as we could.

"We've reached the edge and should rest," the Englishman said. "We should wait until daybreak so we can see the powder. It's too hard in the dark. Besides, we should be totally rested before we step into the open field. What if we have to run? We should be ready to run or fight if we have to."

"I guess you're right," I gave in, "but someone should stand guard. I'll do it. There's no way I can relax yet."

We tried to stay together around some bushes which would provide some kind of cover. Max lay Marshal down under a part of the bush where there was no snow. He tried to pour some water into his mouth, but it just dribbled down his cheek. He was deathly pale now, with dark patches forming under his eyes. We needed a doctor now. I hated that we had to stop. I wished we could just keep going but Cornelius was right. We'd just be guessing at which way to go if we went out now. I walked a few feet away from everyone and sat with my back against a tree, gun across my lap, watching for any sign of the Blood Demons. Barker stayed with me and was lying on his stomach while I stroked the fur on his back.

"Need company?" It was Max and I smiled at him. Not long ago we had been in an embrace that neither one of us wanted to break. Now, we were running for their lives. I reached up for his hand and pulled him down beside me.

"I would love to have company," I said, shifting over so he, too, could rest his back against the tree.

"Not the way I wanted our relationship to begin," he said as he reached for my hand to hold.

"No?" I replied sarcastically. "You mean running from a group of psychos doesn't turn you on? How else would you start a 'relationship'?"

"Well, I did have other plans," he gave me his half smile and I felt my heart race. "They didn't involve Blood Demons or running through the woods in the middle of the night unless, of course, we were naked, and the moon was a little brighter. No, I wanted you all to myself where I could seduce you properly."

"Is that so?" I could hardly get the words out through my halted breathing. He was good at rendering me speechless. "Well, all of that will have to wait. There're more important things to do first."

"Yeah, I know," he turned serious, no trace of the flirtatious smile on his lips. "Do you really think there's some kind of veil across the worlds?"

"You mean a portal?" He nodded his head. "I'm not a hundred percent certain. I do know that Barker must have come through it more than once."

"How can you be so sure?" Max looked at the shepherd-cross lying beside me.

"I know that Colonel Al's been with him for a few years," I explained. "I also know that he's wearing a dog tag on his collar from my time. Someone had to put it on him. I think he went back to our world and was rescued by one of those pet rescue people. He was probably adopted and given the collar by his new owners."

"They have pet rescue people?" he asked.

"Yeah."

"And they just pick up any dog they want to?" He seemed shocked by this.

"Well, not any dog," I said. "Just the ones that don't have a home. You know, the ones that live on the streets; strays."

"But if an animal lives on the street, they are looked after by everyone in the village," he said. "They're not captured and given to one family to raise. Dogs and cats on the streets look after things. They kill the vermin."

"No," I said, shaking my head. "Not now. Now, if a dog or cat is a stray, they're picked up and taken to the pound and if they're owner doesn't come to get them or they can't be adopted, they're put to sleep."

"Put to sleep?" he asked.

"Yeah, you know, euthanized," I said but he didn't get it. "They're given a needle with some kind of drug that kills them."

"They're killed?"

"Yeah," I said.

"Why?" He sounded so appalled.

"Because we have too many dogs and cats," I tried to tell him. "If they were all left alive, their population would get out of control. We wouldn't be able to feed them."

"That's why you leave them in the streets," he said. "They eat the vermin. Nobody has to feed them, even though some choose to. You see, that way, the rats and mice are taken care of and so are the cats and dogs. My way is much better and a lot kinder to the dogs."

"Anyway, if they have a license," I said, "they must have an owner."

"A license?" he asked.

"Yeah," I said. "Your dog has to have a license. So does your cat."

"Do you have to buy this license?"

"Yeah," I answered.

"Who do you buy it from?" he asked.

"The city," I answered.

"Ah ha," he laughed. "The real reason you need a license. It's no more than tax collection for the mayor. Does every city have this tax?"

"Yeah, I guess." He was making it sound like some kind of scam by the government.

"I admire the government of the people," he said. "Always coming up with new ways to bleed money from the people. Paying to keep an animal. Ingenious!"

"Bottom line," I said, trying hard not to be angry with him. "Barker's been through the portal more than once."

"What about us?" he asked.

"What about us?" I repeated his question.

"Well if there *is* a portal," he continued, "and it's only located in one spot, how did *we* get here? We didn't all fall through the same portal."

"I think," I started, "the veil between worlds becomes porous when the 360 hits, leaving little holes all over the world. We're just the unfortunate ones who unknowingly found them and fell through."

"Hmm," he said. "That makes sense."

"Thank you," I smiled at him. "Sometimes I come up with reasonable explanations for things."

"That you do," he lifted my hand and gently kissed the back of it. I blushed uncontrollably as he lowered our hands back down. He looked over at Marshal. "Do you think he'll make it?"

"I don't know, I hope so," I said. I didn't want to even consider the possibility that Marshal could die. He was my friend and I loved him too much.

"I hope so too," he said.

We sat there, holding hands and staring at the stars. We didn't want to talk too much, afraid that we would alert the Blood Demons to our presence. I was hoping that they, too, had stopped for the night. It was just as hard for them to see in the dark as it was for us. After a while, I rested my head on his shoulder and fell asleep. What seemed like only seconds later,

Max was shaking me awake. My eyes flew wide open when I remembered where I was and what we were doing.

"Is everything okay?" I asked. I was scared that we had both fallen asleep and that the Demons were closing in on us.

"Everything's good," he whispered. "The sun is rising, and we should get going. I've wakened the others and they're all ready to go."

"Why'd you let me sleep so long?" I was angry that I was the last one up. I didn't like that everyone was waiting for me.

"You were exhausted," he told me. "You needed the rest. It doesn't really matter anyway; we should get going. Robert's going to carry Marshal again. Emma Lee's going to sprinkle the powder."

"Oh," I felt a little left out. Max recognized my self-pity.

"We need all the fighters ready to take on Howling Wolf and his men should they be waiting for us," he said. "Robert can't really help; he's carrying Marshal and, I figured, you're a better fighter than Emma Lee so, I suggested she take charge of the powder."

"Oh, okay." I felt a little better.

We slowly left the coverage of the forest and tentatively started walking east. We kept alert for the possibility of an ambush, our guns raised, ready to fire. Emma Lee took some powder out of the cup and sprinkled it into the air. The tiny particles of dust gathered together forming a cloud and then floated quickly in the same direction we were going. This was good; we had been heading the right way.

The cloud of dust took its time today; we followed it for about half an hour before it decided to swoop and swirl and then take off. We stopped and looked to Emma Lee who had already reached into the cup for more rock powder. Max took Marshal from Robert and Emma Lee released the powder into the air. It was going in a new direction now. It was still heading east but now it floated a little more towards the north. That made sense; Calgary was a little northeast of where we were.

This time we were able to follow it longer. The sky was clear, not a cloud in sight, and the powder held a steady direction so, we were able to see it from far away. We had been out of the woods for over an hour now and, still, no Howling Wolf and no Blood Demons. Maybe I was right, and they were sticking close to Marshal's, believing that we would eventually go back there. I thought about the house we had all built together. I could still see Barker digging out the wooden planks and smiled at the memory. It was heartbreaking to think what those men were doing to it. I wondered if they had discovered the underground fortress as well. What did it matter, though? If we found the portal, we would be leaving this world anyway; away from this savage world, away from the Blood Demons, away from the homes we had worked so hard to build.

"Okay, mate, it's my turn to carry the lad," said Cornelius. Max had been carrying Marshal for almost an hour and the strain was starting to show on his face.

"No," said Max, "I can go a little further."

"Look," said Cornelius. "You can't wear yourself out and I haven't carried him yet. Come on don't be such a hero and give him to me."

"But the powder…" Max started.

"I can use more," said Emma Lee. "Besides, the sun is in my eyes. Maybe we can stop for a bit while it rises higher and out of our line of sight."

"That's a good idea," said Robert. "We should check on Marshal. I want to make sure the tape is holding."

So, we stopped, although I didn't want to. The sooner we got to where the city should be, the better. I didn't like the fact that we hadn't seen anybody. Where were the hundred men that Howling Wolf had? Surely, they were somewhere around. If he was smart, he would have had them positioned all around the forest waiting for us to come out. He did see us when he killed Billy and Kitten. They were obviously close to the mine when they slaughtered Cocoa. So, where were they now?

"Worried?" asked Max when he noticed that I hadn't sat down to rest.

"It doesn't make sense," I said. "Where are they?"

"You're right," it was Colonel Al who had walked over to join us while Robert and Emma Lee checked on Marshal. "Any good commander would have established posts to look for their enemy. But just because you can't see them, doesn't mean they're not there. We shouldn't stop for very long. The further away we get, the more at ease they will feel."

"Why would we want to make them feel at ease?" I asked.

"Because," said the colonel. "If they feel at ease, then we know that all they want is a piece of land. If they leave that piece of land and start hunting us, then we know their goal is to kill us. That's when we worry. That's when we run. There is no changing the mind of a determined hunter; the kill is their drug and a powerful one at that. There is no addiction worse than killing. I've seen a lot of these addicts and there's no stopping them."

"So, have I," whispered Max. I looked over to him and reached out to touch his arm.

Barker came over to our little group and pushed his nose into my hand then did the same to Colonel Al. He looked from one of us to the other and whined before looking out into the field with his ears cocked and his tail curled high up in the air. We followed his line of sight and I felt my heart stop. There were two men on horseback about the length of two football fields away. They were holding what looked like binoculars to their eyes, searching all around them. They had not discovered us yet.

"Get down!" Colonel Al whispered. We all fell flat to our stomachs without being told twice. The grass was tall out here in the field where it had time to grow without anyone mowing it or trampling it. Hopefully, it was tall enough to keep us hidden.

"If we're going to proceed without being seen," said Colonel Al to Max, "we're going to have eliminate those two. It won't be long before they discover us and signal the others."

"You're right," said Max. "I think we should sneak through the grass and attack them."

"Right," said the colonel. "You go to the left and I'll go to the right. We'll attack them from the side, preferably with knives so, the others won't hear the gunfire."

"Okay," said Max, crouched and ready to go. I didn't like this plan, but Max shot me a look that said, 'don't interfere' and I kept quiet. If anyone could do this, it would be Max and Colonel Al so, I shut up and let them.

"They'll be okay," Robert said, and I looked over to him and nodded.

We watched as Colonel Al and Max took off through the grass. They were fast despite the fact that they were practically crawling through the grass so they wouldn't be seen. I kept my eyes on the two men on horseback, hoping they wouldn't see them. They still had the binoculars to their eyes and were focused on something to the south of them. I couldn't see what they were looking at, but I didn't care at this point just as long as they didn't see Max or Colonel Al.

They both got to the men at the same time. Neither Blood Demon realized they were there until their horses started to fidget and move backwards, heads high in the air, ears turned back. The men dropped their binoculars and tried to steady their horses. They still didn't detect Max or Colonel Al. Then it happened. I saw Max reach up and pull his man off of his horse and down to the ground; the colonel did the same. I held my breath as the men struggled on the ground, rolling through the grass and wrestling back and forth. I saw Max raise his hand and come down fast. A couple more lunges and it was over. He looked over to the colonel who had already killed his man, his military training obvious. The colonel had broken the man's neck before his feet touched the ground after being pulled off of his horse. I saw them shake hands then turned and waved at us to show that they were okay.

They weren't okay, though, and neither were we. While they shook hands and waved at us, celebrating their victory, the horses had run off. Killing those men was pointless if they let the horses make their way back to Howling Wolf with their riders no longer on them. I gestured for them to come back as quick as possible.

"Emma Lee get more powder," I said. "Cornelius, pick up Marshal. We have to go!"

"But it's okay now," said Cornelius. "We have a bit more time."

"No, we don't," I urged. "The horses ran off. It won't be long before the others come to find the missing riders. We need to go, now! And we have to travel faster than before because if they come and discover the bodies of those men, they'll send their whole army after us."

"Nicole is right," said Robert. "As soon as they get back, Emma Lee, throw the powder."

Max and the colonel were back in less than five minutes. They, too, realized what it meant to let the horses escape. Emma Lee released the powder and we all followed the small cloud faster than we had before; we were practically jogging. It wasn't long before the fast pace and the weight of Marshal became too much for Cornelius and we stopped so he could transfer him over to Robert. As we increased our pace, carrying Marshal became harder and we had to stop and transfer him a few times.

The good thing about our increased speed, was the fact that we didn't have to use a lot of the powder in the cup that Emma Lee carried. We were able to keep up with it as it flew through the sky. I knew we were getting closer to where the city was supposed to be when I noticed Barker getting more and more excited. He kept running far out ahead of us and coming back, wagging his tail and letting out low barks. We had to be getting close. We were into the afternoon now and the increased pace was making me thirsty. We stopped again to catch our breath and have a sip of water from the bottles in the backpack.

"I don't think anyone has found the bodies, yet," said Max. But just the fact that Max even mentioned this, showed me that he was worried. "We shouldn't stop long, though. They have horses and could easily catch up to us even if they found them now."

We finished our sips and moved Marshal to Robert's back for the third time. Emma Lee threw the powder and we were off again. We must be in the city now, I thought to myself. It was weird to see all the land without houses or buildings of any kind; no people or cars cluttering the roads. No roads! It was just land for miles and miles around us. It felt so open and free.

"Private, are we done?" Colonel Al's voice broke my daydreaming. I hadn't noticed that Barker had stopped. He was lying on his stomach growling at something none of us could see.

"Barker, are you okay?" I asked as I knelt beside him and scratched behind his ears. He looked at me and barked. "What?"

"Is this it?" asked Emma Lee. "Is this the door that leads to the other world?"

"I don't know," I answered. I reached out to check but felt nothing. I don't know what I was expecting the portal to feel like. Maybe I would see part of my arm disappear if I reached into it. I stepped a couple of more steps farther and reached out again. Still, I felt nothing. Maybe this was the wrong place. I looked down at Barker and he stood and started barking louder at the empty space in front of him. I didn't understand.

Then, the sound of a gun being fired filled the air and I turned to look behind us. The Blood Demons were coming! There must have been about twenty of them, all on horses, galloping toward us. They had guns raised and were firing one bullet after another. I looked at my friends to see if anyone had been hit and saw them all flat on the ground trying to avoid the gunfire. I looked down at Barker again.

"How do we get through?" I pleaded with him. The portal was our only escape now. If we didn't get through now, we would die! "Please, Barker, show me!" He came to me and started pulling on my coat. I let out a frustrated sigh and felt tears come to my eyes. Why was he trying to pull me down? It wouldn't help. They would be here within minutes to kill us. He pulled on my jacket again, growling and barking. "No, I don't want to get down! I need you to show us how to get through!"

"What's in your pocket?" It was Max. He had been watching Barker pulling on my jacket. I reached into my pocket and felt the pile of rocks I had put in there in case we needed to make more powder. I pulled one out and Barker started wagging his tail and barking uncontrollably.

"Will this do it?" I turned to where I thought the portal was and threw the rock towards it.

A ripple of air appeared and then a hole opened. I couldn't see what was inside. It all looked blurry and full of swirling colours. I stared at it in disbelief. Here it is, I thought. This is my way back home. An arrow flew past my head, catching a bit of my hair. I looked at the others and locked eyes with Max.

"Let's go!" His decision was made for him. I knew he didn't want to go, that he wanted to stay in this more familiar world, but he had no choice now. The demons were getting closer and their bullets would become more accurate. I reached out my hand, but he didn't take it.

"Go!" he shouted to me. "I'll keep them away." He turned and started shooting at the approaching men. Oh, how he frustrated me!

I looked to the others who were already on their feet. Robert went first with Marshal on his back followed by

Cornelius and Emma Lee who were holding each other's hand. I looked at Max who was still firing at the men on their horses. He had been joined by the colonel.

"Come on, you guys, let's go!" I yelled. "The others are through. It's just us. Please, let's go!"

"Go, Colonel," Max told the man standing beside him.

"Not without you," said Colonel Al and I was thankful he was on my side.

"I'll be right behind you," urged Max. "Go! Take Nicky with you."

"No!" I yelled but it was too late. Colonel Al grabbed me and started to leap through the hole that seemed to be getting smaller. It needed another rock thrown into it to keep it open, but the rocks were in my pocket and I couldn't get to them. I stared desperately at Max, hoping he would stop shooting and come through the portal. I saw Barker run over to him and grab the end of his coat in his teeth and pull him towards us. I love that dog, I thought as I saw Max lower his gun and turn towards us. The portal was shrinking fast and I prayed they'd get through before it disappeared. Our eyes locked and I felt relief as he and Barker started towards us. My relief turned to horror as I saw an arrow flying through the air, aimed at Max's back.

"Max!" I cried out as Colonel Al and I collapsed on the other side of the portal. I looked at the hole we had come through and saw nothing. The door had closed; the portal was gone. Max and Barker were still on the other side and I didn't know if the arrow had hit its target. I stood up and reached into my pocket for another rock. I threw it at the air where the door had once been. Nothing. I tried again, still, nothing. Why wasn't it working? I felt a hand on my shoulder.

"Perhaps those rocks don't work from this side," said Robert.

"But he's still on the other side!" I sobbed. "We have to get him here!"

"We will," said Robert, "but not with these. We'll have to find what works from this side but, first, we have to find shelter. I don't think it's safe to be here."

"What?" This was my world, of course it was safe here. I turned and looked around, confused by what I was seeing.

The city looked like it had been bombed several times over. All around us were burnt out houses, smashed cars, cracked roads and crumbled buildings. Smoke filled the air making the sky dark and the air thick. I coughed to get a breath. I could hear distant gunfire and rumblings that sounded like explosives. I saw no people and wondered where everyone was. There was graffiti sprayed onto some of the destroyed vehicles and some of the walls that were still standing. I looked at the others and saw them covering their faces with the ends of their shirts to escape the smell that hung in the air. It was the smell of death, rotting over time.

"What the hell happened here?" I asked but no one could answer me.

www.ingramcontent.com/pod-product-compliance
Lightning Source LLC
Chambersburg PA
CBHW062026170626
46813CB00001B/306